# THE HOUSE OF SECOND CHANCES

LAUREN WESTWOOD

First published in 2016 as *Finding Home*. Second edition published in 2022. This edition published in Great Britain in 2025 by Boldwood Books Ltd.



Cover Design by Emma Graves Design

Cover Images: Shutterstock



A CIP catalogue record for this book is available from the British Library.

Paperback ISBN 978-1-83656-998-5

Large Print ISBN 978-1-83656-997-8

Hardback ISBN 978-1-83656-996-1

Ebook ISBN 978-1-83656-999-2

Kindle ISBN 978-1-83678-000-7

Audio CD ISBN 978-1-83656-991-6

MP3 CD ISBN 978-1-83656-992-3

Digital audio download ISBN 978-1-83656-995-4

This book is printed on certified sustainable paper. Boldwood Books is dedicated to putting sustainability at the heart of our business. For more information please visit https://www.boldwoodbooks.com/about-us/sustainability/

Boldwood Books Ltd, 23 Bowerdean Street, London, SW6 3TN

www.boldwoodbooks.com

*To Eve, Rose and Grace with love.*

# PART I

The cup of tea on arrival at a country house is a thing which, as a rule, I particularly enjoy. I like the crackling logs, the shaded lights, the scent of buttered toast, the general atmosphere of leisured cosiness.

*— PG WODEHOUSE – THE CODE OF THE WOOSTERS*

'Is Thornfield Hall a ruin? Am I severed from you by insuperable obstacles? Am I leaving you without a tear —without a kiss—without a word?'

*— CHARLOTTE BRONTË – JANE EYRE*

# PROLOGUE

## OCTOBER, LONDON, NW—

On paper, the flat looks perfect.

I rummage in my bag and uncrumple the printout of the particulars. The blurb describes it as a 'bolthole with lots of potential, in an up-and-coming area, close to transport'. However, in the short time I've been flat hunting, I've learned that 'estate-agent-speak' is a different language from the King's English. I'm pretty sure that 'bolthole' means tiny, and 'lots of potential' means bad plumbing, a grotty kitchen, and no central heating. An 'up-and-coming area' means no Starbucks for miles, and the blister on my heel is testament to the fact that 'close to transport' means that, in the wilds of Zone 3, the Tube is a twenty-minute walk, but you can park a car in the street without a permit.

I double check the map. Finally, I'm getting closer to the arrow that marks Thornton Gardens. The name reminds me of Thorn*field* – the house where Jane Eyre met Mr Rochester. The road sign is obscured by a flame-coloured Boston ivy on the corner house. Leaving behind the squeal of bus brakes and the smell of fried chips, I enter what feels like another world.

Thornton Gardens is lined with London plane trees, and as I crunch through the yellow leaves on the pavement, I spot not one, but two blue plaques on the houses of the slightly down-at-heel Victorian terrace. I've never heard of either the composer or the Crimean War journalist that apparently lived there, but I love the strong current of history flowing like an underground river – a good omen for my new job teaching English literature at the college.

At the end of the terrace, a for sale sign shaped like a giant lollipop overhangs the pavement. I make my way towards the house; the flat I'm viewing is on the top floor. Outside, the paint on the windowsills is chipped and the brickwork needs repointing, but something flickers inside my chest as I crane my neck and look upwards to the top of the tall, red-brick edifice. From the frieze of cherubs over the door to the pigeons swirling in the sky high above the Dutch gable, I have a strange feeling that I've been here before; that I'm meant to be here now.

While I wait for the estate agent, I mentally rehearse how I'm going to convince Simon, my boyfriend, to come for a viewing. Whilst I'm content to find a place that 'just feels right', the flat is over our budget, and Simon will want to crunch the numbers. I can say that between cycling to work and climbing all those stairs, I won't need a gym membership to keep fit. And we can do loads of the renovation work ourselves – it will be fun to strip wallpaper, sand floorboards, and choose paint colours together, not to mention scouring little antique shops for period furniture. Maybe I can take a weekend course in upholstery and make the curtains and cushions myself...

The fragile sun goes behind a cloud, and the chill jars me back to reality. The estate agent is late. To be honest, I'm a little nervous to meet him. When we spoke on the phone, he didn't sound overly impressed with my budget or the seven years I spent doing my PhD. In the end, I exaggerated ever so slightly about my salary and Simon's promotion prospects. Surely finding the perfect home is about more than just facts and figures; noughts of a bank balance. It's about finding the place you've been looking for all your life without even knowing it; a safe little nest, an island in a turbulent sea. Mum always says that 'every pot has a lid'. I want to believe she's right.

A dark green Mini with a racing stripe down the bonnet turns into the road and nips into a tiny spot on a double yellow. A man with spiky gelled hair and wearing a pin-striped suit jumps out. His eyes flick past me, and I wish I'd worn a smart suit and heels rather than a vintage skirt from Camden Market and ballet flats.

'Hello?' I say.

Realising that I must be the client, he breezes over to me. 'Sorry I'm late,' he says. I recognise his drawled vowels and nasal intonation from the phone. 'I'm Marcus Hyde-Smythe. And you must be...?'

'Amy Wood.' As we shake hands, I'm annoyed with myself for forgetting the *Doctor* Amy Wood part.

'Are we waiting for anyone else, or are you on your own?' He gives me a little wink.

'Just me today. When I find the right place, I'll bring my boyfriend round. We've been renting for a few years, but now we're ready to buy.'

*Or, I am*, I don't say. Because when I told Simon that I'd registered with a few estate agents, 'just in case something comes up', he didn't actually sound too keen. He was even less keen when he started receiving a daily barrage of emails with particulars of every available flat in a five-mile radius. Sometimes I worry that, to him, our rented ex-council flat in Docklands feels a little *too* much like home.

'Good, good.' Marcus Hyde-Smythe's lips curve into a smile. 'Now remind me again, are you looking for modern or a fixer-upper?'

'Oh, nothing too modern. I'd love a place with lots of character and original features.' I look again at the front of the house, picturing the women who might once have lived here: their long silk skirts rustling as they come out the front door; hailing a hansom cab, rushing off to attend a fitting for a new hat on Regent Street, followed by tea at Fortnum and Mason... 'In fact,' I say dreamily, 'this house seems perfect.'

'Original features.' His nostrils flare at the words like there's a foul smell. 'Good, good.' He checks the gold watch on his wrist. 'Well, let's go up. The other viewing should be finishing.'

'Other viewing?'

'This flat is listed with a few agents. Another couple is viewing it before you.'

'Oh.' Worry clumps in my chest. Unfortunately, my perfect flat might be someone else's perfect flat too – lots of people's, in fact. People with more noughts on paper than Simon and me. But I can't think about that now. 'Great,' I say briskly. 'Let's go up.'

He fishes out a bundle of keys and opens the door. I step inside reverently. The foyer is littered with junk mail, but I love the original tiled floor. At the rear, a staircase with a railing painted in layers of white gloss rises upward below a cracked moulding of plaster fruit. I breathe in the smell of Mr Sheen, old house, and a slight undernote of wet dog. An unfamiliar smell, but one I could definitely get used to.

A clip-clop of heels sounds from above. A fake-tanned, ginger-haired woman in a red trouser suit appears on the stairs.

'Hello, Florence,' my estate agent smarms. 'Good viewing?'

The woman rolls her eyes. 'Give them a few more minutes,' she says. 'They can't keep their hands off each other. They love the flat – I think they might try out the bedroom before the offer's even gone in.'

The breath freezes in my lungs. Have I lost the flat before I've even seen it? 'Um, I'd still like to view it, if that's OK.'

My estate agent looks like he's a bit sorry for me. But I'm determined not to be put off by the competition. Before anyone can suggest otherwise, I march up the stairs past the first and second-floor flats. The final flight of stairs that goes up to the attic flat is narrow and rickety. From behind the shiny black door, high-pitched laughter devolves into a passionate squeal. I'm reminded of the scene where Jane Eyre discovers Mr Rochester's nasty little secret locked away in the attic and her ill-fate is sealed. My resolve begins to waiver; maybe I should come another day...

'Do you want me to go first?' My estate agent comes up beside me. 'Make sure they're decent?' He gives me another irritating wink.

I steer him back to business. 'So can you tell me how this works?' I say. 'If I love the flat can we put in an offer today, or what?' I'm counting on the *or what* option since I'll need to get Simon on board. As we reach the top of the stairs, I take out my phone and draft him a one-line text. If he can meet me after work to view the flat, we might have a better chance of getting in before there's a bidding war.

'One step at a time,' Marcus Hyde-Smythe says. 'Let's make sure you love it first, OK?'

'OK.' My thumb hovers over the send button.

I turn the brass knob and push open the door. One glance and I just *know*. It's the right home for Simon and me: the perfect canvas for our new life together. My heart curls up inside me like a contented cat in front of a fire. I step inside a lovely little reception room with a polished wooden floor. On one wall there's a cosy cast-iron fireplace with blue and white tiles. Under the eaves I spot a perfect corner for me to set up my desk – just below the row of sash windows that flood the flat with autumn light. I can picture us here: me holding little soirees for my book group; Simon having a dinner party for his workmates. Standing together at the window, clinking our wine glasses and watching the sky grow dark and hazy over the chimney pots of London.

The sound of footsteps and cooing voices coming from the kitchen shatters my daydreams. Hopefully the lovey-dovey couple will get a room for a few hours so I can get the ball rolling. I hit 'send' on the text I've drafted.

'Let's look at the bedroom again!' the woman says. I glimpse a flash of blonde hair at the kitchen door. Inside, a phone beeps with a text message.

'Oh bugger.' A male voice. 'Just a second.'

The man comes to the kitchen door.

Our eyes meet.

The moment freezes into slow motion.

'Simon?' I gasp.

'Amy?'

Everything speeds up again as the terrible truth registers. The rising nausea in my stomach, and the guilty look on Simon's face. The weight of the phone in my hand; the lightness as I swing back my arm and let go. The phone flies through the air, bridging the gap between us. There's a horrible little thud as the throw goes wide and my iPhone makes impact with the woman's pert little nose. And she screams, and I scream. And I turn and run out the door as the walls of my life come crumbling down around me.

# 1

*Rosemont Hall*
*10 April 1952*

*Dear Henry,*

*I trust that you are studying hard in your last few weeks at university. Soon you will return home to Rosemont Hall. I fear you will find it changed for the worse.*

*Yesterday I sold the Gainsborough that hung in the green salon. It was like losing your mother all over again. The house is diminished: the walls stark and empty, the room devoid of the life and laughter it once held. It is little consolation that the beams in the attic may now be replaced, the boiler fixed, and the rose bedroom repapered. I know what you would say if you were here – 'The house is just a house, a painting just a painting.' We would argue about it and agree to disagree.*

*But now, my indulgence has ended. It is time for you to make something of yourself. I have a plan that will end this sorry plight and restore the fortunes of our family and our proud heritage. By the time you return, the arrangements will be in place. Until then, I remain...*

*Your father*

# 2

## NOVEMBER

*Nailsea, Somerset*

The car sputters as I pull into the driveway of the bungalow, as if it doesn't want to be seen here. I find third gear instead of first, and everything clunks to a halt. Mrs Harvey, the neighbour, twitches the curtains at her kitchen window and peers out. I force myself to smile and wave until she disappears again, no doubt off to phone her friends at the Scrabble club to tell them that not only is Amy Wood back at home living with her parents, but she can't drive properly either.

I can't quite muster the will to get out of the car. Everything that happened on that horrible afternoon (was it really a month ago?) comes rushing back. The horror, the crushing panic, the jealous disbelief at seeing my long-time boyfriend standing there in that quaint little flat, canoodling with another woman. Afterwards, I realised that I knew her – Ashley, the PE teacher at the sixth-form college where I taught – a petite, blonde, American thing who's also some kind of Olympic athlete. Now with a wonky nose, thanks to me and my poor aim.

But worst of all was the aftermath... the head of department's voice: 'I'm sorry, Ms Wood, but the board of governors cannot condone a staff-on-staff assault, no matter what the circumstances.' My tears and protestations, and his further reply: 'Yes, I'm sure the flat did have the most wonderful original features...'

'You OK, princess?'

I blink back to reality. Dad is standing on a ladder at the front of the bungalow, tussling with a drooping wisteria vine. I get out of the car and go over to him. The 1970s bungalow is all red-brick and pebbledash, identical to the others on the road. When I was growing up, we lived in a quaint, half-timbered cottage. When eventually they sold it, I felt like a little plant uprooted from my plot of earth and plopped into a plastic pot. I hated the bungalow; everything – from the orange-pile carpet to the avocado bathroom suite – felt *wrong*.

To be fair, Dad's worked hard on the place over the years. The bungalow has a fresh coat of white paint around the door, and the garden looks lush in the pale November sun. To them, *home* is being walking distance from the church, the shops, and the pub where they play Scrabble and bridge every week. It's a comfortable, friendly place for their retirement, and I really can't argue with that.

Dad sets the ball of twine on the top rung, and it promptly rolls off and unwinds.

'Yes, Dad, I'm fine.' I accept the coddling that my parents have inflicted on me ever since the night I turned up on their doorstep, tearful and incredulous at having lost my boyfriend, my perfect flat, and my dream job all in less than twenty-four hours. I pick up the ball of twine. 'Do you need a hand?'

'Sure.'

Dutifully, I snip a piece of twine; he ties the recalcitrant tendril to the trellis. It's the first time I've felt useful all day. I cut two more pieces and hand them to him.

'Have you been out shopping or something?' Dad asks.

'No, I went to see about a job.'

'A job!' He comes down the ladder and shakes my hand like he's amazed I would do something so grown up. 'What is it? Let's see… Badminton Girls' School? Teaching impressionable young ladies about the dangers of corsets?'

'Actually, it was a comprehensive in Bridgwater. And unfortunately, they're not hiring.' *Me* – they're not hiring me. Nor are any of the other schools I've tried over the last month.

'Well.' He scratches his receding hair. 'Chin up. You'll find something.'

'Thanks.' I smile bravely. 'I will.' *But what?* Everything in the local area involves cleaning toilets at a pub or stocking groceries at Tesco. And just like Victorian times, even they probably wouldn't hire a mobile-phone-throwing troublemaker who's been sacked without a reference.

'That should do it.' Dad balls up the remaining twine. 'I'll take it from here.'

'Sure, Dad. I'm going to get changed.'

The screen door slams as I enter the house and peek inside the kitchen. Mum's at the stove cooking a huge pan of sausages. The grease sizzles and spits in the pan as she painstakingly adds the onions and leeks. My stomach roils – I've always hated sausages. But I wouldn't want to hurt Mum's feelings by actually saying so.

'Smells good, Mum.'

She glances at me and frowns. 'The top button on your

jacket is hanging by a thread. Do you want me to sew it back on?'

I wish I could blame my failure at the interview on looking bedraggled, but that's wishful thinking. 'That's OK, Mum. I'll do it later.' I walk off towards my bedroom.

'How was the interview?' Mum says.

I stop and turn back. 'It wasn't exactly an interview – it was more of an enquiry.'

'Oh.' She rolls the sausages with a fork. 'So you didn't get the job.'

'No.'

She turns the heat down on the hob and covers the foul-smelling concoction. 'Well, if you're really keen, Mrs Harvey from next door might be able to help. Her niece is pregnant and her office is looking for a temp.'

'A temp?'

'Until you get back on your feet.'

'A temp what?' I practically choke. 'In an office?'

'It's in Bath – that's all I know. I can get the details.' Mum dishes out the sausages, heaping spoonfuls of congealed grease onto three plates.

'I don't really think that's quite what I'm looking for. I've got a first and a doctorate...' The words dissolve. I may be great at writing clever little essays – I wrote a thesis on *Houses as Characters in 19th Century Fiction* that won a prize. As a teacher, I prided myself on bringing to life the great literary classics for my students. Together we explored every nuance of Mr Darcy's behaviour through the eyes of Elizabeth Bennet in *Pride and Prejudice*; studied Jane's every fluttering heartbeat in *Jane Eyre*; jumped at sinister shadows at Manderley with the second Mrs de Winter in *Rebecca*. But let's face it – those aren't exactly real-world skills.

'Suit yourself,' Mum says.

I hang my head. 'I guess it couldn't hurt to have the details.'

'That's my girl.' Mum nods smugly. 'When the going gets tough, the tough get going...'

'Yeah.' I give her a half-hearted high five. 'Stiff upper lip and all that.'

Mum gleefully phones Mrs Harvey next door and gets the details, which consist only of a name and address in Bath: Tetherington Bowen-Knowles. The name gives me heart: it sounds like an ultra-respectable firm of solicitors, or maybe an accountancy office. I picture comfortable sofas, brass lamps, leather-bound books and yellowing papers. My parents have terrible internet access, so I can't find out for sure.

'She says to go there tomorrow,' Mum says. 'Apparently her niece is "about to pop".'

I grimace at the image. 'OK, I will.'

* * *

At dinner, I douse the sausages with mustard and pick at them, half-listening to Mum and Dad gossiping about their neighbours, the church-roof fundraiser and the merits of Aldi vs Lidl. Afterwards, we spend a quiet evening in front of the television watching *Celebrity Antiques Road Trip* and *Mastermind*. When Dad puts on a recording of *Autumnwatch*, I excuse myself on the grounds that I want to 'see about the temp job' first thing the next morning. 'OK, princess,' Dad says. 'We'll be cheering for you.'

'Great,' I say. 'That's nice to know.'

'And make sure you sew on that button,' Mum adds.

Leaving the room, I go to the bathroom to rub on a facial mud mask and stick cucumber slices over my eyes. The more I try not to think about the past, the clearer it is in my mind. Simon in vivid colour – sitting two rows behind me in the lecture hall and sharing the same night bus home. Great love stories are built on less, I suppose. One thing led to another, and soon, Simon concluded that it was 'mad to throw away money renting two flats'. Not, admittedly, the most romantic reason for moving in together. Dutifully, however, I moved my books, my clothing and myself into his bachelor pad in Docklands – already complete with free weights, Xbox, nose-hair trimmer, and trouser press. It never felt like my space, and I was fond of imagining the day when we could afford our first 'together home'.

In many ways, Simon was a model boyfriend. In the early days, he often bought me tokens of affection: half-price supermarket flowers, day-old sushi, M&S lingerie. When the tokens dwindled and the lean years began – me working round the clock on my thesis, and him working round the clock at the investment bank – at least we still had weekends together, curled up in front of the TV on the crushed velvet sofa found in a skip in Wapping. We ate a lot of takeaways, drank a lot of wine, watched a fair few films, and when we weren't too tired, had sex in the bed decorated with the crocheted duvet cover I bought at Petticoat Lane market. Perhaps it was a nice existence rather than a great love story, but it was comfortable and familiar. And in the last few months, things had been looking up. I had a new job teaching English literature at the college, and the bank promoted Simon to vice-president of emerging markets. My life, signed, sealed and delivered. My life...

I pick off a cucumber slice and eat it. The sight of wall-to-wall Artex and avocado bathroom suite turns my stomach. Why am I here instead of presiding over a room of clever and interested students, engaging in intelligent debate about 'the myth of feminist identity in Jane Austen'? What happened to the future involving a romantic restaurant, wine and candles; Simon taking something from his pocket, down on one knee, everyone else stopping their conversations and turning to watch? I imagine the ring: a gold Victorian setting with seed pearls and tiny diamonds. I imagine joining the sisterhood of women who, after going through toil and hardship, finally get a happy ending.

*A happy ending*. Was I so wrong to want one?

I wash the mud off my face. The woman staring back at me in the mirror is a little thinner than a month ago, with what a novelist might glibly describe as a heart-shaped face and porcelain skin. Her shoulder-length hair is thick and dark, and cut in a long bob. Only her eyes have lost some of their sparkle. While the sting of being usurped by Ashley ('I'm really sorry, Amy, but when I met her at that little "do" for new teachers, I just knew it was destiny') has begun to numb, the ache of what the hell I'm going to do next lingers on. A temp job is not what I had in mind. But I must try something – anything – to get back on my feet. I do a few facial exercises in the mirror and practise my best interview smile. Applying for a job is nerve-wracking, but really, how bad can it be?

I brush my teeth, don my fuzzy slippers, and poke my head into the hallway to check the coast is clear. A light is on under my parents' door. I hurry past to my own bedroom and pop in a pair of earplugs I bought following a nocturnal emergency – noises coming from my parents' room in the middle of the night. Crawling under the duvet, I pull the pillow over my head and cross my fingers that I'll get a job quickly, earn some money, and be able to afford 'a room of my own'.

# 3

Two little words.

My heart plummets as I stand outside the golden Bathstone office of Tetherington Bowen-Knowles. This isn't an ultra-respectable firm of solicitors or an accountancy office. The office where, if I'm lucky, I might be able to get a temp job, is none other than an...

*An estate agency.*

Estate agents – the profession that everyone loves to hate. I associate them with my ultimate humiliation. The shock-horrified and ever so slightly amused look on my estate agent's face after I threw the mobile phone at Ashley is permanently etched onto my brain. The unfurling of a spotty silk handkerchief, coming to the rescue of the damsel with the bloody nose. His parting words to me as I ran out of the flat, my dreams in tatters: 'Miss Wood, does this mean you won't be putting in an offer?'

I take a deep breath, the button on my jacket straining across my chest. The bottom line is, I need a job – any job. It's the only way I'll be able to afford a flat that I can make my own.

A bell tinkles as I go in the door. The office is open plan with a number of people at desks. As I enter, everyone springs to life, creating a buzz of energy and activity. A spiky-haired man in an impeccable suit gives me a wave as he laughs into a phone cradled on his shoulder. An older woman wearing tweed flashes me a coral-lipped smile as she sips her coffee, and even the pregnant woman at the reception desk – Mrs Harvey's niece, I presume – grins at me like a Cheshire cat. I seem to be the only one who can't make my lips curve upwards.

I approach the niece. Everyone leans in like plants growing towards the sunlight.

'Hi, uhh… I'm Amy Wood. Your aunt was going to ring this morning. About the job for maternity cover?'

Instantly, the buzz in the room fizzles out. Everyone falls back into their various tasks like marionettes with broken strings. The niece looks at me with disdain.

'Take a seat. Mr Bowen-Knowles is on the phone.'

I skulk my way over to the waiting area that's, in a word, *beige.* No leather-bound books or cheery brass lamps here. I sit at the edge of a beige sofa and gaze at the pile of property particulars. I recognise some of the mysterious lexicon: 'top-quality fixtures and fittings'; 'good transport links'; 'heaps of potential'. The 'newly reduced' price of a flat in Bristol deflates me even further. How will I ever be able to afford even a small flat on my—?

'Amy Wood?'

'Yes, that's me.' I stand up; the button on my jacket heralds my grand entrance by popping off onto the floor and bouncing like a flat rock skimming the surface of a placid lake. And unfortunately, the man standing at the door of a beige inner office is *not* smiling. His eyes follow the progress of the button until it comes to rest under the reception desk.

He looks down at the tiny wrinkle of black lace that is now peeking out of my blouse. I wait – for his eyes to reach my face just as my cheeks flush bright red.

'Come into my office. I'm Alistair Bowen-Knowles.'

The large desk that takes up most of the office is unnaturally tidy. On the walls are architects' drawings of modern houses and six framed 'Salesman of the Year' certificates, all arranged to the millimetre. Mr Bowen-Knowles is wearing a starched pink shirt with cufflinks, pin-striped trousers and a purple and silver tie. His eyes are close-set, his nose long and wolf-like.

'So, Miss Wood.' He sits behind the desk steepling his fingers. 'What can I do for you?'

Smiling, I launch into my prepared answer. 'I understand you might have a job opening. I thought I'd make a good... uhh... fit.' I hand him my CV, which he scans in disdain.

'Are you sure you're in the right place? The bookstore's down the street.'

I shift in my chair, ready to make a dignified exit. Things are hard enough without adding Mr Salesman-of-the-Year to my woes. But then I spot his business cards, neatly displayed in a Links of London holder. Beneath the name of the firm is a line of small print that I hadn't noticed before: *Specialists in unique and historic properties.*

Two little words...

*Unique. Historic.*

Just like that, the noxious mist clears from my mind.

'You may think I'm overqualified,' I say, pointing to my CV.

His right eyebrow twitches like he'd had no such notion.

'But the truth is, academia was a bit stodgy. I've read a lot of classic books that feature "unique and historic properties". And I'm the perfect person to sell them. Your agency's speciality is right "up my street" – so to speak.' I smile, warming to the theme. 'In fact, I've loved old properties ever since I was a girl and my dad did up our cottage. It was full of character and quirks, just like a person. I adored it, and I was gutted when they moved.' I lean forward. 'I'm sure I'll be able to sell lots of unique and historic properties and maybe be... uhh... salesman of the year – like you.' I laugh nervously. 'Saleswoman, I mean.'

Mr Bowen-Knowles fiddles with his right cufflink. 'Are you finished?' he says curtly.

'Yes.' I shrink in the chair.

'Good.'

He picks up his phone and frowns at the screen.

'How old are you?' he says, without looking up.

'I just turned thirty... one.'

'And where did you go to school?'

'I did my PhD in history and literature at UCL.'

'Before that?'

'Willowdale Comprehensive. In Wookey Hole.'

'It shows.'

'Sorry?'

Mr Bowen-Knowles sets down his phone with an irritated sigh. 'Ms Wood, Tetherington Bowen-Knowles has a very exclusive clientele. Our buyers demand taste, refinement, and discretion.' He looks down his nose at me. 'I'm sure it's impressive that you've read books about historic houses, and that your father "did up" an old cottage. But frankly, this is a business – it's about numbers and commissions, not some kind of pie-in-the-sky matchmaking service. We expect the refinement and gravitas of Cheltenham Ladies' College. Not Wookey Hole.'

In truth, I'm not sure whether to laugh in his face or storm out. Maybe I've been blathering, and maybe I don't have any sales experience. Maybe he's testing me, or maybe he's just rude. But now that he's telling me I'm not worthy to be an estate agent – even a temporary one – I'm determined to prove him wrong.

'Mr Bowen-Knowles...' I lift my chin. 'I understand your concerns. But if you hire me today, you won't regret it. I'm smart and I learn quickly. Plus, I know the local area like the back of my hand. Give me a chance...'

*Give me a chance* – I said that to Simon just before he officially broke up with me. Give me a chance to learn to cook and to organise my books and clutter. Give me a chance to watch Sky Sports instead of *Antiques Roadshow*. Give me a chance... please.

Did I really say those things?

How pathetic.

Mr Bowen-Knowles doesn't bother to respond. I stand up, sighing inwardly. No point in sticking around to be humiliated further. I can leave with my head held high and forget I ever set foot—

Just then, a commotion kicks off. 'Shit, Sally!' someone yells.

'It's not shit, it's my waters breaking!'

'Shit!' Mr Bowen-Knowles echoes.

I fling open the office door. The pregnant niece – Sally – is standing at her desk, with gooey fluid running down her leg and puddling at her feet. The spiky-haired man looks disgusted and horrified.

Rushing forward, I strip off my jacket, pushing up the sleeves of my ivory silk blouse. Sally's body tenses and she begins to moan. The sound crescendos into a deep groan and rises in pitch, climaxing into a shriek.

'Oh God, it hurts!'

I put one hand on her back to steady her. She leans over the back of her chair and knocks my jacket into the pool of fluid. Kicking it aside, I pick up the desk phone. I may not be worthy to work in this office, but even I can dial 999.

'I think it's coming,' Sally gasps.

'What? Now?'

'I've had pains since last night. Oh... God!' She doubles over again.

With forced calm, I speak to the operator: pains since last night, waters oozing over my jacket and the posh parquet floor of Tetherington Bowen-Knowles. I give them the address. No, I'm not her friend or her doula. No, I'm not a colleague. I'm just an interviewee who was about to be shown the door when—

'Oooohhh!'

'Can you type?'

Putting down the phone, I wheel around. Mr Bowen-Knowles's eyes skim to my chest; I'm suddenly aware how sheer my blouse is.

'Sorry?'

'Type, Ms Wood – as in, on a computer.' His eyes return to my face and he mimes a keyboard.

'Yes, of course. One hundred words a minute.'

'Help me!' Sally cries.

Mr Bowen-Knowles gives Sally an irritated shake of the head. 'Obviously I'm not going to have time to do any more interviews. So you can cover for her as temporary admin support.'

'Admin?'

'Sally's the receptionist.' He looks at me like I'm an idiot. 'You don't think we'd trust her with anything else, do you?'

'I don't really know...' He must have thought I was a complete moron spouting off about selling historic properties.

'I'll tell you what. Since you're so – keen—' He grins

wolfishly, glancing at my chest again. 'If you earn your spurs, I might let you do the odd viewing. We've got more rich Londoners down here at the weekend than we can handle.'

'Viewings?' I say. 'That sounds interesting.' Certainly, my one and only viewing was all that and more. At least this time, I'd be on the other side of the fence.

'Oh God, it's coming!'

Outside, a siren wails.

Sally leans over the desk and hikes up her skirt. I'm vaguely aware of the two men standing behind me, their faces paralysed in horror. I grab her hand and squeeze it. 'Just hang in there,' I yell. 'You're doing great!'

The door bursts open, and two paramedics arrive. They lift my predecessor onto a stretcher, ply her with tubes and monitors, and give her a gas mask to breathe into.

'I want an epidural!' Sally yells.

'Too late for that.'

'No!'

I hold the door open as the paramedics wheel her out. Sweaty and rumpled, I turn to face my new employer.

Mr Bowen-Knowles's frown is deep enough to germinate seeds in his brow. 'Well, do you want the job?'

'Yes, but—'

'So don't just stand there.' He points to the mess on the floor. 'Take some initiative.'

'Yes, Mr Bowen-Knowles,' I say through my teeth. Picking up my soggy jacket, I head to the back of the office to look for a bucket and mop.

# 4

By mid-morning, I feel like a veteran of foreign wars. In the span of a few short hours, I've got a job, played maternity nurse, mopped the floor, taken my jacket to the cleaners, and find that I've become the 'face' of Tetherington Bowen-Knowles – the other estate agents leave for viewings and Mr Bowen-Knowles is closeted in his office – so I'm on my own. I use the time to explore the office. In the back there's a disabled loo with a Salesman of the Month chart tacked to the door (someone has crossed out 'man' and written 'person' instead), a stationery cupboard, and a coffee machine that hisses and wheezes, percolating a heavy black sludge. I settle for a cup of freezing water from the cooler.

My new desk is covered in pink objects of all description: stickies, toy bunny rabbits, nail polish, a clock shaped like Cinderella's glass slipper, and a pink mug. I whisk most of it into a desk drawer that's overflowing with chocolate, baby magazines, and used tissues. A clean desk equals a clean slate. I keep the Cinderella clock – somehow, it seems appropriate.

Next, I look over the stickies and find a number for IT.

They issue me a new work email address: amy.wood@tbk.com. For the first time in weeks, I feel almost confident. I have a desk, a computer, and an email address. I have a new job, and soon I'll have my first pay cheque. Things are definitely looking up—

My confidence fades as I notice a couple lurking outside the window. Having a desk and an email address is one thing – having actual clients is quite another! I hold my breath... They're at the door... They're coming inside.

The man guides the woman through the door with a hand on her back.

'Hello!' I spring to my feet with a welcoming smile, channelling Kirstie Allsopp. I've watched every episode of her vintage home show, and she's great with people.

'I'm Amy Wood. May I help you?'

'Uhh...' The man looks at the woman; she twiddles with the faded paisley scarf around her neck. Both of them look as nervous as I feel. 'We're looking for a new house.'

'Great, we've got lots of lovely properties that I can show you, or...' I hesitate, remembering that I'm only supposed to be doing admin. 'Or maybe you want to take a seat and wait for my colleagues – or... I can I take your details?'

Looking confused, they sit down on the beige sofa. I scribble my pen in the notebook to get the ink flowing.

'Your names, please?'

'Mary Blundell,' the woman says. 'And this is Fred.'

'Pleased to meet you,' I say. 'And your budget?'

'Three million.'

I sit back and look at her, stunned. Three million? Pounds? Sterling? I'd had them pegged as first-time buyers who'd be after a higgledy-piggledy little cottage in Pucklechurch – or something. My instincts as an estate agent are rubbish!

'Well...' Mr Blundell seems worried by my reaction. 'I guess we can stretch to 3.2 for the right place, you know?'

'Absolutely.' I stand up. 'Let me get you some brochures and—'

A door slams in the back. The spiky-haired man has returned. If I'm Kirstie, then maybe he can be Phil Spencer. But when he catches sight of me with the clients, he glares in the spitting image of Mr Bowen-Knowles. My fantasy of happy colleagues fizzles like a dud firework.

'What do you think you're doing?' His accent is like cut glass.

I glance towards the couple. Counting them and the newcomer, three people are looking at me like I have two heads.

'The Blundells are looking for a new home,' I say.

When Spiky-Hair turns to the prospective clients, his demeanour changes, his face erupting into an obsequious grin. Pushing past me, he approaches them.

'Sorry for the confusion – she's new. I'm Jonathan Park-Spencer. Please come into my office and I'll help you right away.'

The couple stand up, looking bewildered.

'It's fine,' I say, secretly seething. 'Jonathan can take it from here.'

The three of them disappear into an inner office.

I sit at my desk, deflated. Obviously, it was right for Jonathan to take charge of the clients, but I was hoping to learn the ropes for when I'm called upon to do viewings. To make myself more useful for next time – if there is a next time – I flip through a stack of particulars. New-builds, modern flats, development sites, office space, semis... My eyes glaze over. Where are the 'unique and historic' properties that this place is supposed to specialise in? If I had a budget of three million (three million!) pounds like Fred and Mary Blundell, I wouldn't come to Tetherington Bowen-Knowles to see properties like these. Surely they could buy themselves a Thornfield, a Pemberley, a Manderley. A notable house – grand, quirky, sometimes even a little bit sinister – all unique and special. My heart flutters with excitement. I would love to find a buyer for a historic home: a kindred spirit. I could help them source antiques, find qualified craftspeople for restoration work, do historical research or—

The back door slams again. An attractive Asian woman with shiny bobbed hair comes in, looking daring in a teal satin suit and matching heels. She sets her handbag on the desk opposite mine and actually smiles at me.

'Hi, I'm Amy Wood – new here today.' I proffer my hand.

'Claire Kumar.' She shakes my hand firmly. 'Is he back?' She nods at Jonathan's desk.

'Some clients came in. He took them to the spare office.'

'Typical. The one day I'm late, Uriah Heep gets all the action.'

The literary reference makes me warm to her instantly. Before I can muster up my own Dickensian reply, Mr Bowen-Knowles bursts forth from his office.

'Wood,' he yells, 'where's my coffee? I always have it at half eleven. And Kumar' – he makes a show of checking his gold watch – 'nice of you to join us. There's a viewing today for that dump in Chipping Sodbury. You know the drill. It's a "character property brimming with potential, in need of a little TLC".' He wrinkles his nose. 'Make sure you whisper in their ears that the vendor's desperate to sell and will probably pay some poor sod to take it off his hands. Just don't mention the subsidence, or the roof, or the new chicken-shit plant, or the frackers or... anything really. I want that place under offer in a fortnight.'

'But Alistair' – Claire sounds incensed – 'Jonathan's supposed to be handling it—'

'Save the arguments for your barrister course – if you get there. And at this rate, your hair will be grey and you won't have to bother with a wig.'

He returns to his office and slams the door.

'Ugh,' Claire says. 'He's so insufferable.'

'Are you studying to be a barrister?'

'Yes. And as soon as I can get a pupillage, I'm out of here.'

A less-than-ringing endorsement of my new place of employ, but I'm hardly surprised. Mr Bowen-Knowles's outburst has shaken the chat out of her. I clear my throat. 'Um, I was wondering if you could show me how to use the coffee machine?'

'Sure.' With a sigh, she stands up and we go to the kitchen. She disembowels the machine, puts in a filter, empties the sludge from the pot, fills it with water, and presses a series of buttons. At my teaching job, all the coffee was instant. Even the memory of the chalky, acidic taste triggers a pang of loss.

'The boss takes it black with two sugars,' Claire says as the machine hisses and gurgles. 'And you'll need his special mug.' From a cupboard she takes out a huge white and green mug with the words 'I'd rather be... GOLFING!' scrawled in black across it. Instantly, I recoil. Simon loved golf, whereas I always secretly agreed with Mark Twain that golf is 'a good walk spoiled'. When Simon and I were together, I always found an excuse never to go golfing, even to watch. One of my many mistakes. I imagine Ashley in a short skirt and polo shirt, giving Simon a bee-stung smile as he tees off with his prized three wood. My hand trembles a little and I almost drop the mug.

'Black, two sugars,' I repeat lamely.

Claire returns to her desk, and I bring Mr Bowen-Knowles his mug of coffee. Luckily he's on the phone, and other than a frown that lingers a good eight inches below my chin, I escape unscathed. As I close the door, Jonathan emerges from the spare office in all his pin-striped glory. The Blundells trail after him, looking positively downtrodden.

'Goodbye,' I say as they walk past me. 'I hope you find your perfect home.'

'Oh, we will,' Mary Blundell says with a twinkle in her eye. I get the impression that she's neither impressed nor intimidated by Jonathan's posh personage. Nor should she be – not with a budget of three million (three million!) pounds.

As the Blundells are leaving, the older woman from earlier returns. Apparently she's called Patricia, and when she opens her mouth to greet the others, I peg her as the Cheltenham Ladies' College ringer: tweed suit, horsey laugh, calls people 'dahling'. Everyone but me, that is. When I introduce myself, she gives me a pained wince and turns to Jonathan to talk cricket.

* * *

The hours tick by on Cinderella's glass slipper. Claire leaves for her viewing and returns looking sour. No other clients come in, and except for the odd moment of everyone perking up whenever someone hovers on the pavement outside, the atmosphere is one of boredom.

'Can I help out with anything?' I ask each of them in turn. No one takes up my offer. I lament the many books I could be reading, the young people I could be teaching. In this environment, I feel like a nameless woman whom history has forgotten, lacking meaningful status or occupation.

The office phone rings; everyone sits up. Patricia answers, and we all listen in: 'Yes, we do… you've come to the right place.'

'New instruction!' she whispers animatedly.

Excited glances are exchanged. Jonathan leaps to his feet.

Slowly, however, Patricia's smile begins to melt. 'Please hold,' she says, covering the phone with her hand. 'It's a probate,' she announces grimly. 'Some old woman who popped her clogs. I did the Harris estate – it's someone else's turn.'

'No can do.' Jonathan plunks down, elbows spread behind his head. 'I'm shooting off now to do a valuation. You do it, Claire. Working with a solicitor will be good practice for you.'

'I'd love to, but the childminder just texted.' Claire gives an unapologetic shrug. 'I've got to get Atul early today.'

Silence ensues. Patricia taps her fingers on the desk, her horsey face resembling a stubborn mule.

'I'll do it,' I say in a small voice, wondering what I'm agreeing to; vainly hoping someone will fill me in.

'Line two,' Patricia says. 'Mr Kendall.'

I fumble with the headset and get my pen and paper ready. Everyone is watching me… judging. I take a breath and press the button.

'Amy Wood speaking. How may I help you?'

The solicitor on the other end speaks quickly and with purpose. He represents the deceased woman's estate, and the heirs want to sell the house immediately. But it's not just any house. My heart thrums with excitement as I scribble down the details:

*Rosemont Hall, a Palladian-style Georgian manor house with 120 acres.*

*A historical gem that's been in the family for 200 years.*

*Partially derelict and needs total modernisation.*

*Exclusive listing.*

'Miss Wood? Are you there? Can you send someone round to do the valuation?'

'Absolutely,' I say. 'How about tomorrow?'

'Tomorrow's Saturday. Can you come round on Monday, three o'clock?'

'Monday sounds great.' My hand quavers as I write down the address. 'I'll definitely see you then.'

# 5

*Rosemont Hall.*

By the time I arrive home, my mind is overflowing with possibilities. I have a strange feeling – a premonition, even – that everything is about to change. A house from the books I love has jumped off the page and landed in my lap. Surely it's fate that no one else could be bothered. Now I just have to convince my new boss to let me stay involved.

In the kitchen, Mum and Dad are eating chicken casserole for supper; suddenly, I'm ravenous. 'Guess what!' I gush. 'I got the job.'

'Well done, princess.' Dad devours a Brussels sprout and gives me a proud smile.

Mum looks up and frowns. 'That blouse is practically see-through. Your bra is showing. What happened to your jacket?'

'Long story.' I pull the edges of my blouse together. Not that it helps.

'And what exactly is the job?' Mum says.

'It's at an estate agent's,' I say. 'Tetherington Bowen-Knowles.'

'An estate agent's!' Dad's next bite seems to go down the wrong way. 'I thought it was a solicitor's.' He looks at Mum.

'No wonder Mrs Harvey never said.' Mum pours gravy over her potatoes.

I look from one to the other, alarmed. 'What's the matter? You said I should go for it.'

'Well,' Mum tsks. 'You sounded desperate.'

'I wouldn't go that far. And besides, there's nothing wrong with it. Just think of Kirstie and Phil, Sarah Beeny – or Kevin on *Grand Designs.* I know you watch their shows.'

'Well, maybe once or twice.' Dad scratches his mop of hair. 'Becca, what was the name of that estate agent who sold us our house?'

'Frank Knightly. He told us the boiler was new and then, "bang" – within six months it needed a total replacement.'

'Two thousand quid!' Dad chimes in.

'And then there's the school extension practically in the back garden,' Mum says. 'Literally, not a mention. And now the kids are so close they can practically see into our loo.'

'I guess everyone has their horror stories,' I say through gritted teeth. 'But it's a good job – I'll help out at the office and do some weekend viewings. Country retreats for rich Londoners.'

'Londoners are pricing local people out of the market.' Dad pushes away his plate. 'I'm not sure we should be supporting that—'

I throw up my hands. 'Look, I'm sorry my new job does not involve developing a cure for cancer or teaching teenagers about the plight of wronged literary heroines through the centuries. Never mind that I spent the morning practically delivering a baby, and later on I took a call about an amazing Georgian house – a "historical gem" with "bags of potential".'

'Sure, princess,' Dad says. 'We're very proud of you.'

I turn away so he can't see the tear beading in my eye. I'm grateful that he's bothered to lie – and sorry that he has to.

'Worse things happen at sea.' Mum recites her go-to response in adversity. I nod silently as she peers at my empty plate. 'You haven't eaten a thing. If you don't like the casserole, there are some leftover sausages.'

'Thanks, Mum, but I'm not hungry.' I stand up from the table. 'And just so you know – I hate sausages.'

Leaving them in shock, I exit to my bedroom and remove my world-weary blouse. My parents may be unimpressed with my new job, but I can't let that defeat me. I focus on the positives: I'll get to meet new people, learn new skills, and maybe I can even help someone find their perfect home. That's worthwhile and exciting, surely.

As I get ready for bed, thoughts of Simon creep out of the shadows beyond the circle of lamplight. His features are beginning to blur in my mind, but I can still picture every detail of the darling little flat. Did he and Ashley buy it together? Are they together now, limbs coiled in an ornately scrolled brass bed? I force the images from my mind. For me, that future wasn't meant to be – I'll have to forge a new way myself. Getting a job is the first step to eventually buying my own flat. When I do, I know Mum will help me scour charity shops for old furniture to upcycle, and Dad will help with the decorating. I'll have wall-to-wall bookshelves, a comfy sofa, and maybe a little fireplace... And with my new job, maybe I'll get an inside track on new properties coming to market. When the next perfect home for me comes along, I want to be ready.

Before getting into bed, I take a well-thumbed copy of *Jane Eyre* off the shelf. It's been my favourite book ever since I was a girl, when Jane was like the sister I didn't have. To me, the book was so much more than words on a page – I breathed Jane's every breath, lived her every moment. And some of her moments – as her romance with Rochester unfolded – were the closest I've ever come to finding love.

I open the book to the passage where Jane meets Mr Rochester on the moor:

*Pointing to Thornfield Hall, on which the moon cast a hoary gleam, bringing it out distinct and pale from the woods that, by contrast with the western sky, now seemed one mass of shadow.*

I read a few pages, then close the book and turn off the light. 'Rosemont Hall,' I whisper into the darkness. *Rosemont Hall.*

# 6

*Rosemont Hall*
*8 May 1952*

*Dearest A,*

*My exams have finished and I arrived home last night. When can I see you? Will you meet me tomorrow night in our old place?*

*I'm sorry to say that my father is much changed for the worse. He has taken to wandering through the halls, staring at the blank spaces on the walls; mumbling to absent ghosts. At first, I thought he hadn't seen me. But then he spoke. 'I've put things in motion. It's time you made something of yourself.' I recognised that cold gleam in his eye. Whatever he's planning, I want no part in it.*

*The truth is, if I am to 'make something of myself', I need you by my side. We must plan for our future, my love. My fondest dream is for our children to chase each other through the corridors of this old house, to slide down the banisters, and play hide-and-seek in the secret rooms behind the panelling. And even if the roof leaks, and the plaster cracks, and the paint peels, we will be happy here. Together we will fill this sad place with laughter once again.*

# 7

On Monday morning I get up early and drive to Bath. I'm armed for my day at the office with a packed lunch (chicken sandwich and Mum's home-baked banana bread), my favourite 'Reader, I married him' mug, a new lipstick, and just in case any more babies need birthing, an extra jacket with reinforced buttons. I'm wearing the main staples of my office wardrobe: a black pencil skirt, pink twinset, black patent courts, and a rose-coloured pashmina.

The office is located in a Georgian parade not far from the Pump Rooms. The car park is mostly empty (secretly, I was hoping to be issued a Mini Cooper with a racing stripe like the estate agents drive in London), and the back door is locked. A narrow alleyway leads to the main street, and I walk along admiring the golden Bath stone bathed in autumn sunlight, and enter the office through the front door.

The other three estate agents are already at their desks. Everyone sparks to life – and fizzles when they see that it's only me. Mr Bowen-Knowles's door is shut. I need to tell him about the call I took on Friday afternoon, but I'm hoping to galvanise myself with a coffee first.

Feigning a confidence I don't feel, I go to my desk and greet Claire sitting opposite with a warm, 'Hi, how was your weekend?'

She seems puzzled by my friendly manner. 'It was good,' she says. 'It was my son's birthday.'

'Lovely,' I say. 'How old is he?'

'Twelve.'

*Twelve!* It amazes me when someone about my age has a child that old.

'Great,' I manage. 'And is there any word about Sally and the baby?'

Claire shrugs. 'Fine as far as I know—'

Mr Bowen-Knowles comes out of his office and yells for some coffee. Or – that might have been his original reason, but when he sees me, his face morphs into something reptilian. 'Into my office,' he gestures curtly. I stand up and march to the gallows. He sits down at his desk and steeples his fingers, and I know I'm in trouble because his eyes don't leave my face.

'I understand you took a phone call on Friday,' he says.

'Yes, that's right,' I say brightly. 'About a Georgian mansion – it sounds really special. The solicitor wants a valuation this afternoon. I wrote the appointment in the diary.'

He fiddles with the clasp on his cufflink and glares at me. 'Were you going to tell someone about this? Or did you plan to go on your own and pull a valuation out of your pert little arse?'

I bite my tongue. Hard. 'I was about to come and tell you.' I force myself to remain pleasant. 'It's like you read my mind.'

He takes out his phone and looks at the screen.

'Be ready to go at half two,' he says.

'You mean...? Yes, of course.' I leave the office before he can change his mind.

Back at my desk, I can't stop beaming.

'What's up?' Claire looks concerned.

'It's about that probate call,' I say. 'Mr Bowen-Knowles is doing the valuation today, and he's agreed to let me tag along for the experience.'

Patricia and Claire exchange knowing glances. Jonathan smirks, looking like a guilty public-school boy who's made a mess of the toilet on Parents' Day. Ignoring him, I focus on Claire. 'Did I say something wrong?'

'No, but are you married, Amy?' she asks.

'No. Why?'

'No reason.'

It's obvious there *is* a reason, but no one wants to tell me. So that's how they want to play it – fine. I grab my mug, go off to the kitchen, and lean against the sink with my fists clenched. 'Temporary,' I mouth to myself. 'This is only temporary.'

A moment later, Claire joins me, putting a finger to her lips.

'The walls have ears,' she whispers. 'Not to mention gaping gobs. But some night after work, let's grab a drink. I'll fill you in on the gory details.'

'OK.' My anger ebbs. 'Thanks.'

We seal our pact by clinking mugs of lukewarm, bitter coffee. I'm glad to have a potential ally, and even better, when I log into my computer, I've received a few emails (a system-generated welcome message and some spam). I still have no work, but that seems, at most, a technicality. Instead, I google Rosemont Hall.

The first entry is on a website about 'England's Heritage at Risk'. Apparently, hundreds of country houses fell to ruin after the war and were demolished prior to the 1970s. Even today, thousands are at risk of becoming derelict or are already in ruins. One of them is Rosemont Hall. I read through the article on the site, noting down the salient points.

The house was originally built in 1765 and is considered one of the finest examples of Georgian Palladian-style architecture in the South West. The original owner, a sugar merchant, lost the house in a game of whist to a small-time gambler called William Windham. Windham became a lord and commissioned his own family crest – a dog and unicorn – symbolising fidelity and virtue.

The house was passed down in the Windham family for generations. In the twentieth century, the most illustrious owner was Sir George Windham, a war hero who made a name for himself as an art dealer and collector. The house fell into disrepair after World War Two, and Sir George was forced to sell off his art collection to pay for repairs. The east wing of the house burned down in the early 1950s and Sir George died soon afterwards. The house was passed to his son, Henry Windham. The family fortunes diminished, the east wing was never rebuilt, and the house slid into further decline.

As I read, images of the house and its past take shape in my mind. Lords, gamblers, war heroes – it's straight from the pages of a romantic novel. And what of the unmentioned women who lived and worked at Rosemont Hall? The walls of the house will know their secrets. The final line of the article gives me goosebumps: 'Now in a perilous state, this important house has an uncertain future.'

Sitting back, I consider things with new clarity. Last week, getting this job was only about earning money to afford my own flat. But now, an important and imperilled piece of history is about to be placed in my care. I can influence its fate – maybe even its continued existence. *If* I can convince my boss to keep me involved.

I continue my research, concentrating so hard that I fail to notice the long shadow of Mr Bowen-Knowles frowning over my desk.

'Time to go – you coming?'

'Now?' I close my notebook. 'I mean, yes, I'm ready.' Grabbing my things, I mouth a quick goodbye to Claire and follow my boss to the car park. He beeps the locks on a gunmetal-grey BMW. 'Should I follow behind you?' I say.

'Where's your car?' he asks coldly. I point out my battered Vauxhall Corsa from Car Giant.

Mr Bowen-Knowles snorts. 'I don't want that thing within two miles of any of our clients – we're selling a lifestyle, do you understand?'

Hanging my head, I get into the passenger seat of his car. Another tick against me: wrong accent, wrong car, wrong everything. But I *will* persevere.

We pull out of the car park with *Talk Sport* blaring on the radio – Premiere League news; a new signing by Arsenal...

*Arsenal.* Simon's team. A cloud of sadness engulfs me.

He switches off the radio. 'Check under the seat, will you?' he says. 'I've got some printouts of local prices.'

'Sure.' I dig under the seat and pull out some papers, hoping he'll explain all the tricks of the trade.

*Tricks of the trade.*

Silly me.

At the top of the pile is a men's magazine folded open to a page featuring the assets of Amanda, age twenty-one from Huddersfield (enjoys diving, candlelit dinners, and netball) who is gracing the page in a pair of lacy knickers, and see out of the corner of my eye that Mr Bowen-Knowles is looking right at me. He meant for me to find it!

He grins wolfishly and switches the radio back on. 'Never mind, it must be in the boot. By the way, when we get to the house, I'll do the talking. You just stand there and look pretty.'

# 8

'You have reached your destination,' the satnav drones. I forget all about my irritating boss as we turn off the main road and head through a pair of ancient stone pillars each with a weathered urn on top. Twisted wrought-iron gates sag under their own weight, half-hidden by twining ivy and brambles.

Anticipation tingles in my chest as we make our way up the long drive, flanked by a thick woodland of beech, silver birch, and giant rhododendron. Flame-coloured leaves swirl in the air and settle on the windscreen. Eventually, the trees give way to acres of rolling parkland.

The car tops a little hill and suddenly, it's there before us – Rosemont Hall. Standing four storeys tall, the house consists of a main section of red brick and cream stone, graced by Palladian-style pilasters, and two lower symmetrical wings on either side. At the pinnacle of the roof, a huge round window stares out at the countryside like an ever-vigilant eye.

The moment I see it, I experience a powerful sensation almost like déjà vu. I am meant to be right here, at this glorious house, right now.

'What a dump,' my boss says, pointing to one of the side wings. 'Looks like it's about to collapse.'

I bite back a retort. Part of the right-hand wing does seem derelict. Huge burned timbers cut across the sky and weeds sprout from the remnants of the wall. The bricks are smoke-stained around the empty window frames, and streaks of damp darken the wall like tears. It looks so sad, but also hopelessly Romantic, standing silent and stalwart against the ravages of time, neglect, and the English climate.

The drive ends in front of the house where a sweeping set of stone stairs leads to the front door. We park next to a decrepit stone fountain where algae-covered nymphs stand frozen in a trickle of green water. I get out of the car and crane my neck to take in the full height of the house. Stone lintels and window cornices are cracked and decayed, and mortar crumbles between the quoins and bricks. I take a few photographs on my phone, as visions creep into my mind about how it must have looked in its heyday: armies of servants lining up to greet the master on his return home from a hunt; ladies sweeping out of carriages in dresses of silk, taffeta and velvet. The hedges trimmed in fantastical shapes, the fountain clear and bubbling, the imposing front door black and glossy with fresh paint.

A drop of water falls on my nose from a cracked stone pediment above the door. I can just make out the family crest of a dog and a unicorn. It's so weathered that I fear it might topple down on us.

I may be new to the job, but even I can tell that Rosemont Hall is in peril.

The weak sun disappears behind a cloud, leaving the house in shadow. Another car – a blue BMW – comes up the drive and parks next to its grey twin. My boss, phone in hand, stands at the ready.

'Must be Mr Kendall,' I say, stating the obvious.

'Remember what I said.' He gives me a disturbing grin that I ignore. The newcomer gets out of the car: mid-fifties, smartly dressed, greying hair and a kindly, grandfatherly face.

'Mr Kendall, I presume?' Mr Bowen-Knowles smarms all over him. 'I'm Alistair Bowen-Knowles – please call me Alistair.' He holds out his hand sheepishly, like they should be greeting each other with a Bullingdon Club secret handshake instead of meeting like complete strangers. 'Such an amazing place. Such history! Such a pleasure to work with you on this, err... project.' He twists his right cufflink.

'Yes... uhh... Alistair, pleased to meet you. Ian Kendall.' He looks awkwardly at me as they shake hands.

'Hello.' I step forward. 'I'm Amy Wood. We spoke on the phone.'

'Nice to meet you.' He shakes my hand firmly. 'Shall we go inside?'

We follow him to the door. Mr Kendall takes out an ancient bundle of keys that look like they might unlock the Bastille. It takes several tries before one turns in the corroded lock.

Inside, a vestibule opens onto an enormous main hall. My boss makes appropriate noises of appreciation – whereas I'm genuinely awestruck. The double-height hall is gracefully oval-shaped, with a chequerboard floor of grey and white marble. Ionic columns and statuary niches adorn the cool, white-marble walls. The decorative ceiling is painted with *in flagrante* Greek gods and goddesses. At the back, a staircase sweeps upwards and divides into two symmetrical galleries overlooking the main hall. Huge windows trap the sunlight.

The house is magnificent, to be sure, but neglect and decay

have taken residence. Spots of damp mottle the ceiling; wide cracks gape in the walls and floor. The cavernous room is freezing, and silently devoid of life. The beating heart of the house has grown still.

'The house has been in the Windham family for six generations,' Mr Kendall explains as we walk through the ground floor rooms. 'The last of the Windhams – Henry and his wife Arabella – were married for almost forty years. Henry died over a decade ago; Arabella passed on two weeks ago.'

'That explains it.' Mr Bowen-Knowles smirks, gesturing at the mounds of clutter, lattice of cobwebs and threadbare furniture. 'We see it a lot. A lifetime's worth of stuff that no one wants and no one knows what to do with.'

'It's like a time warp,' I say, rapt with fascination. The rooms are faded but elegant: the green salon, the library, the yellow dining room. The flotsam and jetsam of decades of married life is visible everywhere: dusty books and old magazines, vases filled with dead flowers, worn sofas, and time-darkened photographs. 'The Windhams must have been very happy here.'

'Perhaps,' Mr Kendall says. 'Though, it's a big house for a couple with no children. The heirs – Mr Jack and Ms Flora – are distant relatives. They're American.'

'How amazing to inherit a spectacular English country house!' I say.

Mr Kendall shakes his head. 'Neither of them has visited the house, nor are they planning to. They're keen to sell as quickly as possible.'

'Oh.' I don't know what else to say. The indifference of the heirs astounds and angers me. Why wouldn't they want to see the house that someone left to them? To be handed Rosemont

Hall on a silver platter would be a dream come true for me – and lots of other people, I'm sure.

As we continue on, I spot a few gems scattered among the clutter: a set of lovely antique tables, a collection of China vases and glassware, gilded mirrors in all shapes and sizes. But something is missing, and I can't put my finger on it.

'Do the heirs want anything,' my boss asks, 'or should we get a removal van to clear out all this rubbish?'

Mr Kendall raises an eyebrow. 'The Windhams' *belongings* need to stay for now,' he says. 'There's an elderly housekeeper – Mrs Maryanne Bradford – who was devoted to the house and nursed Mrs Windham through her last illness. She has a room upstairs, and some of the things may be hers.'

'Fine.' Mr Bowen-Knowles shrugs. 'A developer won't be bothered by a little clutter.'

'What will happen to Mrs Bradford?' I say. 'Where will she go?'

'She'll need to move out, of course,' Mr Kendall says.

'What a shame.' I feel sad for the old woman – having to leave one's home is a major cause of stress and premature death in the elderly.

'Her sister has a cottage in the village,' Mr Kendall says. 'She won't be homeless.'

He leads the way up the grand staircase. I feel like Scarlett O'Hara as I trail my hand over the cool marble banister. At the top landing where the staircase divides, I stop. In the centre of the wall is an exquisite, life-sized oil painting of a young woman. The background is a blend of murky blacks and greys, and her form emerges like an apparition. Her dark blonde hair is elaborately swept up and tied with ribbons, a few curls cascading around her neck. The boned bodice of her Victorian-style gown is pale-pink silk with a hint of lace at the neckline.

The fabric sweeps out from her waist in shadowy folds, catching the light and fading back into the blackness. But the most striking thing is the woman herself. Her eyes are bold and arresting, painted the delicate blue colour of forget-me-nots. Her features are soft, with high cheekbones and a delicately shaped nose. Her bow-shaped mouth is drawn up in a half smile, like she has a secret.

'What a lovely woman,' I say as Mr Kendall stands next to me. 'Do you know who she is?'

'No,' Mr Kendall says. 'Though I've often wondered.'

The painting is set in a heavily gilded frame that protrudes from the wall a good six inches. A brass plaque at the bottom is etched with a date: 1899. But there's no name or artist's signature.

My boss taps his foot impatiently, and I have to move on. We proceed through more rooms: bedrooms, bathrooms, dressing rooms, sitting rooms. Everywhere smells of damp, and some of the windows are literally rotting out of their frames. The walls are covered with mildew-spotted wallpaper in garish colours and patterns – and I realise what's missing. Other than the portrait of the woman in the pink dress, there's no artwork on the walls. No smoke-darkened portraits of scowling ancestors, views of Venice or caricatures of favourite horses or hunting dogs. It seems strange that a house of this age would have such bare walls.

We climb another staircase to the servants' quarters. Instead of damp and must, I smell baking. 'That's Mrs Bradford's room.' Mr Kendall points to one of the doors. 'She has a little kitchenette where she does her baking.'

Cinnamon, ginger... My stomach rumbles. It's sad that a nice little old lady who bakes nice things will be turfed out. It may well be part of my job to see it done.

'Whatever she's baking smells delicious,' I say.

'Yes, but let's not disturb her,' Mr Kendall says.

'Oh, of course not.'

Finally, we go up again to the very top of the house – a huge attic with an oak-beamed ceiling. It's full of old boxes and furniture, but just below the round window is an area that looks like an artist's studio. Two easels are set up near a rack of canvases covered with cobwebs. There's a wooden box of well-used paint tubes, a dried palate of oils, and a wine glass with a dusty residue in the bottom. I can almost smell the ghostly vapours of turpentine, feel the presence of an unknown artist who might return at any second to resume his work.

'The father, Sir George, was an art collector, was he not?' As I ask the question, I run my finger over a stack of old gilded frames, sending up a shimmering shower of dust motes.

'Yes,' Mr Kendall says. 'He was.'

'But there's no art here except the portrait on the stairs.'

Mr Kendall stares out the oriel window. 'After the war, most of Sir George's collection was sold off to pay for repairs. A few paintings were kept, including a Rembrandt. But that was destroyed when the East Wing caught fire.'

'A Rembrandt was destroyed?' I say. 'How tragic.'

Mr Bowen-Knowles flashes me a look like a rook threatening a pawn. I realise that contrary to instructions, I've been talking too much. 'So, Ian,' my boss says, 'there's clearly a lot of potential here – for the right developer, at the right price.'

'And what, in your professional opinion, would that be?' Mr Kendall leads us down a servant's staircase.

'Well, the heirs could auction it. But that's unlikely to get them "top dollar", so to speak.'

'And what will?'

'Finding the *right* buyer.' Mr Bowen-Knowles looks smug.

'Someone with the cash and wherewithal to jump through the hoops to develop it.' He rubs his chin. 'I'm thinking, gut the building and turn it into top-end luxury flats. Swimming pool complex, spa, the works.'

'But that would be awful!' I blurt out.

Mr Bowen-Knowles glares; this time, I ignore him.

'Surely it should be a family home,' I say, 'with people to love it. Or, failing that, restore it for the public.'

'Amy...' my boss warns.

'It just seems a shame,' I say. 'There's so much history here that ought to be preserved.'

Mr Kendall gives me a kindly smile. 'You're right,' he says. 'In an ideal world, Henry Windham would have wanted the house to be preserved in its original state. But unfortunately, there's no money in the estate for that. My job is to realise the most value for Mr Jack and Ms Flora. And flats might be a good result – better than the alternative.'

'How's that?' I challenge.

'A big American developer called Hexagon is buying up land for a golf course and recreation complex. "Golf Heritage", they call it – there's another one near Minehead.'

'Ah, of course.' Mr Bowen-Knowles sounds like he's sorry he didn't think of that.

'There's lots of local support around here for recreation facilities,' Mr Kendall adds.

I try to blot out the vision of this amazing, special house with checked-trouser-clad golfers clomping through it, a pro-shop just off the main hall. Sprinklers watering the lawn and golf buggies zipping over hill and dale. A huge car park out front, a floodlit driving range at the side. Simon and Ashley coming here for a long weekend of Pimm's on the terrace, canoodles on the eighteenth green, 'his and her' massages in the spa. 'Golf Heritage': a historical tragedy.

'What about the National Trust or English Heritage?' I say. 'Have you tried them?'

'There are lots of derelict old piles around and nowhere near enough money to fix them all. It's a listed building, so Hexagon can't demolish the place.' Mr Kendall sighs. 'Though, I'm afraid they don't have the best reputation for conservation.'

'Has Hexagon made an offer?' my boss says.

'Not officially. They threw out a figure, but frankly, it was a joke. I told them as much.'

Mr Bowen-Knowles laughs. 'It's an old trick. Force them to auction it and Hexagon will pick it up for a song. Unless *we* can find you a buyer.'

'And can you?'

'Having come here today,' my boss says, 'I'm confident that Tetherington Bowen-Knowles can achieve the best possible price for the property. I've got a list of developers who might be interested.' He grins smugly. 'At the very least, I'm sure I can get Hexagon to up their offer.'

'That's good news,' Mr Kendall says, his voice flat. 'For the heirs at least.'

I walk over to one of the tall French windows at the back of the house. In the distance, an ornamental lake shimmers in the fading light and a small summerhouse in the style of a Grecian temple glows like a jewel. The gardens are overgrown, but I'm sure they must have been magical in their day. Just like everything else here – everything that will be lost for good.

We return to the main hall. Mr Kendall points out a door that leads to the east wing. 'There isn't much there,' he says. 'It was gutted by the fire.'

'How did the fire start?' I ask.

Mr Kendall shifts on his feet. 'There was an investigation at the time involving a servant, but nothing was ever proved conclusively.'

'But it was an accident?'

'I believe in the end it was an open verdict.'

'Oh.' The English literature teacher in me claws her way to the surface. In *Jane Eyre*, the fire at Thornfield was started by the 'mad woman in the attic' – the first Mrs Rochester. She ended up being killed in the fire, and Mr Rochester lost his eyesight. And then there's the sinister house called Manderley in *Rebecca*. The psychotic housekeeper, Mrs Danvers, burned the place down after she learnt how Rebecca had really died. And now, a fire at Rosemont Hall – I naturally feel intrigued. 'Can we see the east wing?' I say.

Mr Bowen-Knowles steps in front of me like he's hiding a divan under a dust sheet. 'We've seen enough,' he says through his teeth. 'We need to start marketing the development potential. I'd like to thank you once again, Mr Kendall, for thinking of Tetherington Bowen-Knowles.'

'Fine.' Mr Kendall avoids meeting my eyes. 'Provided your commission arrangements are satisfactory, let's consider it settled. You can be sole agents for three months. After that, it will go either to Hexagon, or to auction.'

*Three months.* Cinderella's clock ticks inside my head. Three months to find a buyer to preserve and restore Rosemont Hall. Three months to save it. Can I do it?

I have to try.

As the men discuss the details, I have another look at the portrait of the girl in the pink dress. From her vantage point over her ruined domain, she looks lonely. Was she happy in life? Was she thinking of someone special when the painter captured that secret smile? Did she live at Rosemont Hall; find love here? In her hands she's clutching something – indicated with thick yellowish brushstrokes. Some kind of paper or letters? In the early days, Simon used to send me funny little texts to let me know he was thinking of me. If we'd been born in a different era, would things between us have worked out? Even now, my chest aches with hurt and humiliation. Was the girl in the pink dress luckier in love than me?

'Amy.' Mr Bowen-Knowles's voice jars me back to reality.

'Goodbye,' I mutter to the portrait and rush down the stairs.

I join the two men. 'Hi,' I say. 'I was just familiarising myself for the viewings—'

Mr Bowen-Knowles holds up his hand. 'As I was saying, Ian, my most senior agent, Jonathan Park-Spencer, will handle the marketing *and* the viewings.'

The air goes flat in my lungs. Jonathan! How can he do justice to this place? I speak in a small voice: 'Sorry, but I was hoping that... maybe... I could do it.'

Mr Kendall's eyes meet mine; he turns to my boss. 'I'm happy to keep dealing with Ms Wood. She seems very competent and enthusiastic about the house.'

There's a long moment as Mr Bowen-Knowles looks like he's hoping the earth will swallow me up. I stand up straighter, trying to look 'competent and enthusiastic'. My boss lets out a long sigh, his brow withered like a prune. 'Of course,' he says to Mr Kendall. 'You're the client.'

My heart leaps. For a second I imagine the house shifting, rekindling a tiny flicker of life. 'Thank you, Mr Kendall,' I say. 'I won't let you down.'

A satisfied warmth creeps across my cheeks as Mr Kendall locks up and hands me the keys. I've succeeded – for now.

I'll be coming back again.

# 9

*2 June 1952*

*H,*

*I am delighted that you are home at last, and I am counting the hours until tonight when I will see you again! The months we've been apart have seemed endless. How I long to see your face and feel your fingers on my skin. Because as much as I cherish your letters, when I lie awake alone at night, my mind is full of whispers and doubts. Until you have told your father about us, as you say you will, how can I allow myself to hope?*

# 10

Rosemont Hall lingers in my mind over the next few days as I settle into life at the office. Mr Bowen-Knowles seems to have accepted that my presence is required, and I develop a rhythm of answering phones, responding to enquiries, and springing to life like a puppet whenever prospective clients come in. I find a box of Christmas baubles (in an antique gold colour that looks remarkably like beige) and trim a little fake tree in the waiting area. The lights twinkle on and off, bringing a tiny bit of cheer to the shortening days.

But I'm aware that the clock is ticking on my three months to find a buyer for Rosemont Hall, and I'm worried that my boss has made no further efforts to involve me in the process. In my free time, I do more research, hoping to find some real historical flavour to add to the particulars.

I can't find any information on the sugar merchant or the gambler, but I have more luck with the modern generation. Arabella Windham's recent obituary was published in the local paper, and her husband Henry's obituary from a decade earlier is in the archives. They seem like a typical couple of privilege and family wealth, involved with the church and the gardening club. Was theirs a great love story? Only the house knows for sure.

More interesting, however, is Henry's father, Sir George Windham. Born in 1900, he attended Eton and Oxford and began collecting art in his twenties. By the time he was thirty, he had amassed a number of valuable paintings. Like many idealistic (and wealthy) young Englishmen, he joined the International Brigades to fight the fascists in the Spanish Civil War. During World War Two, the house was requisitioned by the RAF and left in a miserable state. A series of bad investments decimated the family fortunes, and Sir George died in 1955.

I find a few photos of Sir George, but more interesting is a black and white photo of the inside of Rosemont Hall, dated 1939. The elegant walls are covered with paintings, and the caption describes Sir George's collection as including several Gainsboroughs, a Caravaggio, and most notably, a Rembrandt called *Orientale*. I look for the painting of the girl in the pink dress, but I don't see her. How did she alone escape the fate of the others – the auctioneer's gavel, or the fire in the east wing that destroyed the Rembrandt? I wish I knew who she was.

It's exciting to play historical detective, and as I recall my first glimpse of Rosemont Hall – its grand silhouette stark and lonely against a grey sky – I feel a strong sense of responsibility. The house is an important piece of English history that's kept its identity for hundreds of years. It doesn't take a card-carrying member of the National Trust to believe such things are worth preserving.

Eventually, Mr Bowen-Knowles instructs me to prepare the listing for Rosemont Hall. I spend an entire day drafting the text under the headline 'Historic family home in need of TLC', and include highlights of the fascinating history. When I email him the draft, I feel proud of my work. But ten minutes later, he storms out of his office with a printout of my text, struck out in red pen. He's written a new headline: 'Outstanding green-belt development opportunity for flexible accommodation and commercial recreation facilities'.

'Flexible accommodation?' I say, with a strong sense of dread.

'Flats.' He sniffs. 'We're marketing the future potential here, not some crumbling wreck. I want to see a bullet-point list – the 120 acres, the outbuildings that could be developed, the number of en suite bedrooms that could be converted into apartments. Dimensions and numbers, not fluff. And what about the photographs? We've got a tight deadline here. You need to upload the information onto all the property websites ASAP. And what about the quantity surveyor – has he been round yet?'

I stare at him with dismay. Maybe it was obvious, but I didn't realise he wanted me to do all those things. I've wasted almost a week of my three months. Tick tock.

'I'm sorry.' My voice catches. Desperate to avoid the sack, I hand him my phone with the pictures I took of the house. 'Will any of these work?'

The silence lasts a lifetime. He flicks back and forth between the photos with his thumb.

'That one will do.' He hands me back the phone. 'No point printing photos of the inside. The place is a tip.'

When he finally returns to his office, I let out a long breath.

'Don't worry,' Claire says from across the desk. 'I'll show you how to upload the particulars.'

'Thanks.'

'Let's see the photographs, then.'

I hand her the phone. 'Wow,' she says. 'Impressive pile. Haven't seen one of these on the market for a while.'

Jonathan meanders over to see the photo. I'm petrified that he'll gazump the project from under my nose. 'Hmm,' he says with a condescending grin. 'Hope you're not planning your retirement. Looks like a "sticker".'

'A "sticker"?'

'As in, a property that sticks. Your tits will sag to your waist before you sell it.' He laughs at his own vile joke and returns to his desk.

'Don't mind him.' Claire hands me back my phone. 'Even if it doesn't sell, it'll be good experience. Fancy a trip to the pub after work? I'll give you some survival tips.'

'Yes, please,' I say. 'I'd appreciate that.'

* * *

When the day ends, I rinse out my mug and put it in the cupboard (moving it far away from the one that says 'I'd rather be... GOLFING'). Jonathan breezes by me on his way out the door without so much as a nod or a wave, and Patricia does the same. When I return to my desk, Claire has her make-up bag out.

'You ready?' She puckers her lips at the compact mirror.

'Yes, just give me two secs to—'

Mr Bowen-Knowles's door bangs open. 'Where's Jonathan?' He checks his watch.

'I think he's gone for the day,' I say.

'Gone for the...? Bloody hell.' He glares at me. 'A couple just called – the Blundells. They want to see that new penthouse apartment in Bristol Docks tomorrow. Jonathan was dealing with them.'

I look at Claire, expecting her to jump at the chance to usurp Jonathan's clients. Instead, she shrugs. 'I can't do it – Atul's got football.'

'Bloody hell!' He pulls out his phone; I'm sure he'll ring Jonathan.

'I'll do it,' I say quickly.

Mr Bowen-Knowles looks at me like I have three heads. 'You?'

'Why not?' I challenge. 'You said I could do weekend viewings. I'm happy to do it.'

'You?'

I wait.

'Great idea,' Claire says.

'Well...'

He checks his watch again like he's hoping something miraculous will happen so he can deny my request to help him out. Nothing does, so he ducks back into his office and returns with a torn piece of note paper with the address and a set of keys attached to a souvenir wine opener. Reluctantly, he hands everything to me. 'Just remember,' he says, 'talk the place up. It's a "stunning, ultra-modern penthouse apartment in a top-quality development".' He glares pointedly. 'Don't say anything – anything at all – that might put them off.'

Claire puts away her make-up bag. 'Hmm, the Bristol Docks penthouse. Bit toppy, that one. Haven't there been some break-ins? A local gang or something?'

'Well, obviously she shouldn't mention that,' my boss snaps, 'or the fact that the residents are suing the developer for faulty wiring and safety concerns with the lift.'

'Or the old lady downstairs who got an ASBO against the previous owners for watching *Newsnight* too loud?' Claire is obviously enjoying this. 'Or—'

'—the ambulance dispatch next door,' Mr Bowen-Knowles beats her to the punch. 'In fact' – he turns to me – 'don't volunteer any information at all. Just let them inside and look professional.'

'Sure,' I say. 'No problem.'

At least I no longer have to 'look pretty'.

* * *

Outside, I punch the air. I've managed to secure a real viewing with real clients! Claire, however, has a different interpretation of my success. 'That was a lucky escape,' she says. 'The way he's taken to you, I'm surprised he didn't invite himself along to the pub.'

I laugh, certain that she's joking. 'He really hates me, doesn't he? And I thought all that Cheltenham Ladies' College stuff was just for show.'

'Oh no, I'm serious. When I started, he didn't speak to me for two months. It was three months before he trusted me with showing a property.'

'He must be desperate.' I force a laugh, recalling the newspaper under the seat.

'Oh, he is,' she says. 'Though he used to be OK, believe it or not. A regular bloke's bloke, good for the odd laugh and a round down the pub. But two years ago, his wife walked out. She found him with Sally in the loo at the Christmas party. Since then, he's been your garden-variety bastard.'

We arrive at All Bar One and find an empty table. 'We all thought he'd go crawling back to his wife,' Claire continues. 'Instead, he bought a Porsche and a swish flat with home cinema, sauna and gym – the works. To hear him talk, he's probably got a round vinyl bed with a fur coverlet and a harem of models popping out from underneath.'

I shake my head. Alistair must be ten years older than Simon, but the mid-life-crisis mentality is the same.

'The only one who's got any time for AB-K is Patricia,' Claire says. 'She's fancied him for years now. And naturally, she's the only one he's never looked twice at. Anything else female has to put up with the odd roving glance here and there, not to mention the sexist digs.'

'Yes, I've noticed.'

'It's a living,' she says. We sigh in unison.

Claire buys the first round (Diet Cokes for both of us), and we settle easily into conversation. She regales me with more stories of AB-K, Jonathan, and the Ghost of Christmas Parties Past. I end up telling her about my own ghosts – Simon, Ashley, and the perfect flat, found and lost.

'And did they end up buying it?' she says.

'I don't know. But when I saw Simon for the last time, he said the only reason he'd even thought about looking for flats was because of the estate agent alerts I'd signed him up for.'

Claire laughs with unrestrained delight. 'That's a brilliant story! You're so lucky.'

'Lucky?'

'To be shot of that arsehole. And you get a new start. A new home, a new job...'

'I haven't really thought of it that way.' Maybe it's time I did.

Claire tells me of her own woes: her husband who wants to move the family to Birmingham and live in a three-bedroom semi with his relatives from Goa, and her dad who thinks she should be a stay-at-home mum. In some ways, her situation seems bleaker than mine. We finish our drinks and leave the bar. Suddenly I remember why we came out in the first place.

'Is there any trick to these viewings?' I say. 'Am I really supposed to lie like Mr Bowen-Knowles... uhh... AB-K said?'

'Ninety-nine per cent of viewings are a waste of time,' she says. 'The property will sell itself – or not. Just be yourself.'

As I get in the car and drive home, I find that I'm smiling. Tomorrow, at the viewing, I will be myself – Amy Wood – who has just made her first new friend in her new life.

Amy Wood: *Estate Agent.*

# 11

When I drive to Bristol the next morning, I'm wishing I was the Amy Wood who'd had one less cup of coffee this morning and is now desperate for the loo. To distract myself, I think again of Rosemont Hall and how this viewing will be great practice for all the ones to come. I practise my spiel aloud. '*I'm confident that I can find you the* perfect *home.*' With a budget of three million (three million!) pounds, maybe I can persuade them that it's not the penthouse lifestyle they're after, but lord and lady of the manor.

Bristol city centre is vibrant and trendy; the waterfront is bustling with people. Cascades of coloured lights are strung in the trees along the esplanade, ready for the big switch-on. I park the car a few blocks from the flat. A group of teenage hoodies is loitering across the street from the pay-and-display machine. As the machine spits out my ticket, they cross over to my side of the street and lean against a wooden construction fence. I'm careful not to make eye contact as I walk past, but even so, one of them whistles and a glob of spittle lands on the pavement in front of me. I'm relieved I'm only showing a flat here, not buying one.

My spirits revive as I walk along the embankment, the water shimmering in the sunlight. Many old warehouses have been converted into expensive apartments with shiny glass atria and hothouse flowers in the lobbies. In between are trendy restaurants and chain coffee shops. The quayside is abuzz with people: families with prams going towards the tall ship museums; couples laughing and drinking coffee; elderly people sitting on benches watching the gulls. I find the building: a converted warehouse in yellow brick with a glass atrium. There's a Costa Coffee in the lobby, and a tall Christmas tree that smells fresh and piney.

I pace back and forth. The Blundells are late. The new situation is making me nervous, and part of me hopes they won't show. But when they walk through the door fifteen minutes later, my pulse jolts with excitement. I have actual *clients*. The moment has arrived.

'Hi.' I wave in their direction. They both look startled as I walk over.

'I'm Amy Wood. We met before at my office. I'll be showing you around today.'

'I'm glad it's you, Amy,' Mary Blundell says. 'Not that... toff.'

'Mary!' Her husband nudges her with his elbow.

I like them already, and their sentiments on Jonathan seal the deal. I want to find them their forever home. But will it really be here?

'Shall we go up to the penthouse?' I suggest.

'Yes please,' Mary says.

We walk over to the lift (which fortunately seems to be working) and rumble up to the top floor. The door opens onto a stark white marble foyer. There's a vase on a marble pedestal full of purple and pink orchids. Natural light floods in from a cantilevered skylight. It's all very chic and minimalist. Mary Blundell admires the orchids while I stand in front of the solid walnut door and rifle through my handbag for the keys. I find them at the bottom of the bag, slightly damp and sticky from a leaking hand sanitiser.

Only – they don't fit. I try all three keys. Nothing. Embarrassed, I turn to Fred Blundell. 'Slight hiccup,' I say. 'As you can see, the security is state of the art.' I give a little laugh as my hand quavers. The keys are wrong – they must be.

I try again, but they still don't work. 'I'm really sorry,' I say. 'Maybe I can get a key from the concierge?'

'Do you mind if I have a go?' Fred says.

'OK, sure.' I hold out the keys, but he waves them away. Bending down, he examines the lock, then takes out his wallet and removes a flimsy plastic card with a notch cut in it.

'State of the art,' he says. 'No problem.' He wriggles the card into the door jamb. There's a click; the door swings open.

Fred grins at me. 'Amazing, eh? Just like in the films.'

'Yes...' I resist the urge to tell him that it's less like a film and more like breaking and entering. I follow them inside, hoping they don't try any other 'special effects'.

Inside, the penthouse *is* impressive – and they love it so much that I give up any hope of them viewing Rosemont Hall. The enormous main room is all white with a double-height ceiling and a wall of windows looking out over the docks and the city.

'It's perfect!' Mary Blundell rushes to look at the view. 'Just what I imagined. We've come a long way from Hull, haven't we, Freddie?'

Fred Blundell puts his arm around her waist and kisses her fondly. 'It's great,' he says. 'It really feels right.'

'I'll leave you two to explore on your own,' I say. 'When you're ready, just shout and we'll go up to the roof terrace.' They go off to explore the space-age kitchen, and I look around on my own until I find the well-appointed downstairs loo. By the time I join them again, to my chagrin, Fred has discovered the surround-sound system, and suddenly, a Beethoven symphony floods the flat at concert-hall volume.

'Wow! Fantastic!' he yells above the booming din.

'Uhh, maybe you should turn that down just a little,' I say. 'The neighbours, you know.'

'What's that, Amy?'

He presses a button and the room goes quiet.

'Nothing.' I purse my lips.

'Quite the acoustics, eh? Hope the neighbours are deaf.'

I open my mouth to agree with him, but I just can't do it. The deceit is painful – they love the place too much. I, of all people, know that there's nothing worse than finding a seemingly perfect home, only to have it end in disillusion. 'Mr Blundell, Mrs Blundell,' I say solemnly. 'There are a few things you need to know about this property. It may not be *quite* perfect.'

I tell them about the elevator, the downstairs neighbour, and the local street gang, complete with a personal anecdote about the hoodies I'd encountered earlier.

I'm expecting some well-deserved recriminations – Mr Bowen-Knowles could have told them all these things over the phone and saved them a wasted journey. But Mary's excited smile hasn't budged. Fred wanders back over to look at the view. The noonday sun glimmers on the white tower tops of the Clifton Suspension Bridge, just visible in the distance.

'I'm sorry if you were misled,' I say. 'I guess every property has its problems, but I think it's only fair that you should know upfront. It's a shame really – otherwise it really is a lovely flat.'

'The particulars mention four bedrooms and a roof terrace,' Mary says. 'I'm dying to see it all. Can we go upstairs?'

'Of course – if you still want to.'

Without further ado, they head upstairs. I follow behind at a safe distance, continuing to let the flat 'sell itself'. I catch up with them in the master bedroom; Fred is admiring the gigantic fireplace wall.

'That will be a great space for the big Picasso, won't it, Mary? We may as well enjoy it before we've got to flip it.'

'It sure will.' She grabs his arm affectionately. 'Though let's not count our chickens until it's through customs.'

'Ha!' Fred laughs. 'Piece of cake. He's changed the frame – old wine in new bottles and all that. It will fool the best of them.'

Mary chuckles. 'It's pure genius—'

She spots me and cuts herself off. 'Yes,' she adds, 'it will look great.'

I retreat awkwardly to the staircase landing. My head is starting to hurt. The Blundells seem so ordinary. But door jimmying, Picassos, old wine in new bottles, customs? Who exactly are my clients?

After the bedrooms, we climb the stairs to the roof terrace. The wind is bracing, but the view is astounding.

Fred turns to me. 'So, Amy, anything else we should know about before we make an offer?'

'An offer? Really?'

'We both agree it's just what we're looking for, eh, Mary? And fifty grand under budget.' He winks at me. 'You only live once.'

'Oh yes, Amy.' Mary grabs my arm like they've won the lottery (or successfully managed a heist of the lottery funds). 'It's perfect.'

I hardly know what to say. Didn't Claire and the others say that most viewings are a waste of time? Is this beginner's luck – or are they pulling my leg?

'I can phone the vendors on Monday,' I say. 'What would you like to offer?'

'Why, full asking price.' Fred looks surprised. 'We wouldn't want to lose it.'

'Isn't that what's normally done in these situations?' Mary says.

'I'm sure the vendor will be thrilled,' I say.

'Great, then, it's settled.'

As we head back down the spiral stairs, I can't help but ask, 'And those things I mentioned earlier about the neighbours, and the lift – they don't bother you?'

'Oh no,' Fred assures me. 'Not a problem – I doubt that the grand piano and artwork will fit in the lift anyway. And as for the little old lady downstairs' – he gives what can only be described as a villainous laugh – 'she's unlikely to be a factor for long.'

The door to the flat clicks shut, locking automatically when we leave. We ride down the elevator. Instead of shaking my hand, they both engulf me in a three-way hug. 'Thank you so much, Amy,' Mary says. 'You're a lifesaver.'

'You're welcome.'

I mean, some questions are better left unasked.

# 12

On Monday morning I arrive at the office still aglow after my success (the only downside was returning to a smashed beer bottle on the bonnet of my car) and determined to build upon it. The others are already at their desks, and hellos are grumbled.

'Guess what?' I say to Claire. 'The Blundells loved the penthouse flat.'

'That's nice.' Claire smiles without warmth.

'Just don't get your hopes up, dahling,' Patricia butts in. It's only about the second time she's spoken to me, and her tone is saccharine with pity. 'Most of them say that. They don't want to hurt your feelings.'

'No – they really loved it,' I say. 'Mrs Blundell said it was perfect. It's just what they've been looking for *and* under budget. They want to put in an offer.'

'An offer?' Patricia looks at Jonathan.

'Blundell?' Jonathan's voice is pure ice.

'Well, yes...' I take a breath. 'They phoned after you left on Friday. Mr Bowen-Knowles asked me to do the viewing—'

'The Bristol penthouse?' Jonathan stands up and moves menacingly towards my desk. 'You know, don't you, that the Blundells are *my* clients?'

I stifle a laugh, recalling Mary Blundell's words: *I'm glad it's you – not that... toff.*

Just before he gets to me, Jonathan swerves and bulldozes straight into Mr Bowen-Knowles's office. The door slams shut.

'Coffee?' Claire nods her head towards the back of the office.

'OK.' I'm a little miffed by her lack of enthusiasm, but I grab my mug and follow.

In the kitchen, I pour myself a coffee.

'Great job,' she whispers. 'But don't get your hopes up yet.'

'Fine, I won't. But the place was *right* for them – the proverbial match made in heaven. Surely you get those sometimes?'

'Sometimes.' Claire sounds like it's been a while. 'But lots of things can go wrong.' She takes a sip of her coffee and grimaces. 'My first viewing was a cute little cottage in Bradford-on-Avon. The clients walked in and it was love at first sight. For them it was a new start; a new lease of life. I was so excited for them, and for myself.' She smiles faintly. 'I booked an expensive holiday to Disneyland Paris for the whole family. But on the day they were supposed to exchange, the husband called. They'd decided on a different "new lease of life" – getting a divorce. The whole thing went down like the *Titanic*.'

'Oh, that's a shame.'

'We still took the trip – thank God for credit cards. The cottage sold through another agent. But enough doom and gloom.' She clinks her mug against mine. 'If you do sell the Bristol flat, it'll be a real coup. The Blundells must be super rich. How did they make their money?'

'I don't know.' My bubble threatens to burst. Claire is right:

so many things can go wrong. What if they 'can't get the "Picasso" through customs'? What if they can't 'flip it'? What about Jonathan—?

Mr Bowen-Knowles's door whooshes open, banging against the wall. Jonathan blusters out, glares at me, and goes back to his desk. He rakes his fingers through his spiky hair and begins furiously stabbing at his keyboard.

'Amy.' My boss beckons.

I square my shoulders and brandish my coffee mug.

'Good morning,' I say as I enter the office.

'We've got a situation,' he says.

'So I gather.' I'm determined to stand firm and stick up for myself. The Blundells are my clients now, and I'm not about to let two old boys—

'We've got three months to shift this place, right?'

'Sorry?'

'Rosemont Hall.'

'Oh... yes.'

He frowns like I'm completely thick. Did I not just witness Jonathan's tirade? Is my boss going to sweep the Blundell debacle under the carpet? I don't know, but I decide to play along. 'I've put the details up on the websites,' I say. 'I'm happy to help in any way I can.'

'I got an email from Kendall,' he says. 'Apparently his client – Mr Jack? – has his knickers in a twist. He's been in direct contact with Hexagon already.'

'What?' My stomach drops.

'He sounds like one of those American tightwads who's trying to screw us out of our commission. But we're not going to let that happen. Are we?'

'No, sir.' I feel like I ought to salute.

He hands me a sheet of paper. 'This is a list of all the people who are registered as looking for a country property.'

I flip through the list. Over two hundred names!

'Ring round to all of them and send out the details. It'll be a complete waste of time, but we need to look like we've got our skates on.'

'What about Mrs Bradford?' I say.

'Who?'

'The elderly housekeeper who lives there.'

His glare sends a chill through the office. 'What about her?'

'Should I speak to her about moving out?'

'That's Kendall's job,' he snaps. 'We just assume we're selling with vacant possession.'

'Of course.' I feel sad for the old woman whose life at Rosemont Hall is nothing more than 'vacant possession'.

'What about the price?' I say. 'If they ask.'

He fiddles with his right cufflink. 'Excess of two million plus renovation costs. Which reminds me, I phoned the quantity surveyor – he's going round tomorrow morning. He'll estimate the costs needed to gut the interior.'

I grimace; he smirks. 'You need to be there to let him in. You've got the keys, right?'

'Yes.'

His eyes stray down to my (high) neckline, and he frowns. 'That's all.' He waves his hand like he's dismissing a servant.

'What about the Blundells?' I say.

'Oh, that.' He swats away my question like a pesky fly. 'It will almost certainly come to nothing.'

'But—'

His phone rings; I walk to the door.

'Oh, hello, Mr Blundell,' he says. I stop and turn. Mr

Bowen-Knowles covers the receiver with his hand. 'That's *all*,' he says. 'Shut the door.'

Resistance is futile. I leave his office.

* * *

My boss stays closeted away all morning. Jonathan refuses to look at me, and I'm relieved when he finally leaves for a viewing. Meanwhile, I begin the task of cold-calling the list of potential buyers for Rosemont Hall. I leave a few messages, and when I do finally reach a person, I find he's been sacked from his hedge-fund job. The next three have already bought their dream country piles. The one after that – an American – listens to my entire pitch, and then informs me that his country 'fought a revolution to get rid of the Georges', but to let him know 'if you've got any nice English Tudors on the books'.

I cross each name off the list; already, it's a thankless task. Taking a break, I google Hexagon to see what I'm up against. I find photos on their website of emerald-green lawns, modern glass clubhouses, smiling weekend golfers. But as I scroll down, I find a few articles that paint a less rosy picture. Hexagon bullying old age pensioners; Hexagon finding loopholes in conservation regulations. I find an article about a historic home they purchased to build an adjacent water park, which is now up and running, the house left roofless and crumbling. The more I read, the more I'm determined not to let Rosemont Hall become a pawn in their chess game. Closing down the websites, I pick up the phone. A dozen more calls and nothing.

At lunchtime, I eat my sandwich on a bench near the Roman Baths. Tourists are flocking in and out of the Pump Rooms and in front of Bath Abbey the Bavarian Christmas market is in full swing. I lose myself among the little chalets strung with icicle-shaped lights that are selling local products, jewellery and knitwear. I buy Mum a bag of chocolate-dipped gingerbread and end up eating it as I walk. Everything is busy and festive, but time is passing quickly. Three months – I'm supposed to have three months to sell Rosemont Hall. How dare this Mr Jack get involved already?

As I return to the office, I consider this faraway scourge on the future of Rosemont Hall. I bet Mr Jack has a nice life. I picture him: middle-aged with a beer belly, wearing a baseball cap over his balding head as he mows the lawn at his house in a dusty American subdivision full of huge houses on tiny plots of land, all identical to each other. He'll drive some kind of fancy 'mid-life-crisis' car – maybe a Porsche – no, a vintage Mustang. In candy-apple red. Roaring off to work while his wife piles the kids into a huge SUV to drop them off at school on the way to yoga class. And at the weekends – of course! – golf at the local country club.

Meanwhile, back in Blighty, a house that he's never seen will continue to crumble. A hollow shell where once there was laughter, warmth and life. The memories it holds will crack and fade like old paint, and its Palladian grandeur will end up as little more than a paragraph on a website about England's lost country houses.

Unless I do something.

I hurry back to the office, determined to 'keep calm and carry on' with my task. All the agents are there, and as I enter, a silence descends.

'What?' My cheeks flush in the dry office air.

Mr Bowen-Knowles clears his throat. 'The Blundells were impressed with the flat Jonathan found for them.'

'Jonathan...?'

'Their offer of the asking price has been accepted.'

Instead of the joy such a proclamation should merit, a noxious cloud descends over my mood. 'Fantastic!' is what I ought to say. 'I told you so,' is what comes out of my mouth.

My boss gives Jonathan a high five. I feel sick to my stomach as Mr Bowen-Knowles turns to me. 'So this one goes to Jonathan,' he says, 'but the good news is – I've decided you can stay on permanently.'

Claire gives me a thumbs up. I mumble a 'Thank you.' I should be happy – I've got a permanent job.

Here.

I stifle the urge to punch Jonathan in the fake-tanned nose, sit down at my desk, and spend the rest of the afternoon cold-calling. All I can do is keep at it, and surely, success is the best revenge. When out of the fifty-three people I phone, four ask me to send them the details on Rosemont Hall, I somehow *know* I'm destined to get to the top of the sales chart on the door of the disabled loo. I *can* do this – and eventually I *will*.

After all, Rome wasn't built in a day.

# PART II

'And of this place,' thought she, 'I might have been mistress! With these rooms I might now have been familiarly acquainted! Instead of viewing them as a stranger, I might have rejoiced in them as my own, and welcomed to them as visitors my uncle and aunt. But no,'—recollecting herself—'that could never be; my uncle and aunt would have been lost to me...'

This was a lucky recollection—it saved her from something very like regret.

— *JANE AUSTEN – PRIDE AND PREJUDICE*

# 13

*Rosemont Hall*
*5 June 1952*

*A,*

*Seeing you again was like a glimpse of the sun after a never-ending winter. I will tell my father about us as soon as I can find the right moment. I want to do this properly so he will realise that I know my own mind.*

*Yesterday, he surprised me – he's planning a ball for my coming of age – would you believe it? At first I laughed at the very idea. But on reflection, it is a nice gesture and one designed to bridge the gap between us. It will be a fitting start to my new life back at Rosemont Hall. I want to do him – and you – proud.*

*In fact, the preparations have already begun. This morning he stood in the great hall and oversaw every delivery – flowers in crystal vases, wine glasses and champagne flutes, musicians' instrument cases, crates of taper candles, mountains of food and drink. And in his face I caught a glimpse of the father I remember: strong and proud and a patron of the arts. Seeing him like that, I too caught the sense of excitement. It has been so many years since the chandeliers sparkled and the floors smelled of wax and polish. So many years since there was a sense of life about the old place. He's even hired an artist to paint my portrait.*

*I'll tell you more when I see you. Can you meet me tonight in our usual place?*

*All my love, H*

# 14

The next day, I scrape a layer of ice from the windscreen and drive to Rosemont Hall to meet the quantity surveyor. As I approach the house, I'm transported to another era. I'm Jane Eyre glimpsing the stark silhouette of Thornfield, contemplating her life as a governess; Elizabeth Bennet touring Pemberley, wondering if she's been a tad hasty in rejecting Mr Darcy's advances. The scene is dreamlike – familiar and real, but just out of reach. Silhouetted against the winter sky, the house is a thing of beauty – a true work of art.

Outside the car, everything is quiet except for the mournful cooing of a pigeon and the grinding of the key in the lock. Inside, the house is even more vast and stunning than I remember – it's like walking through a jewel box. It's also absolutely freezing, and I pull my scarf over my chin. The great hall smells of 'old house': thick layers of varnish, dust settled over antique furniture, the sour odour of mice and rising damp. Despite the decay, I appreciate the artistry and detail that went into every carved moulding and mantelpiece, the handiwork of every inlaid floor and plastered ceiling.

What would it take to bring the house back to life? To restart its heart so it can breathe again. The answer seems obvious: people. I picture children roller-skating on the marble floors and sliding down banisters; a man making coffee in the kitchen; a woman baking scones. Gardening on a summer day, a book group meeting in the library, Father Christmas leaving toys under a candlelit tree. Births and weddings, deaths and holidays. Arguments, goodnight kisses, homework, DIY, bad jokes, lazy afternoons on the terrace. People resonating with the house. People like me.

If the house were mine (and even *I'm* not such a romantic as to delude myself that that could ever happen), I'd be a hands-on owner – one who's not afraid to go up a ladder to strip wallpaper or repaint a cracked window frame, bleed a radiator, or oil the hinge on a door. I walk through the hall to the library. Every surface is cluttered with papers, mildewed books, and trinkets. Hopefully Mrs Bradford was a better companion to Mrs Windham than she is a housekeeper.

I leave footprints in the dust as I walk to the window. The frame is rotting but the latch is intact. Carefully, I push it open; cold air stings my face. At the back of the house is a weedy terrace flanked with stone urns. Beyond, untidy lawns sweep down to a yew avenue, a tangled jungle of a rose garden and eventually the Grecian folly by the lake. The frost on the grass shimmers in the morning light. I fall in love with Rosemont Hall all over again.

I straighten a pile of yellowing papers here, wipe the dust off a fireplace mantel there. All the while, I imagine the place as it might have been. A lady doing embroidery in front of the fireplace; a girl practising Chopin on the pianoforte; a man in riding clothes writing letters; servants tiptoeing in and out with tea trays, ostrich-feather dusters and the daily post on a silver tray. I can hear the whisper of silk and crinolines through the doorway and smell the linseed oil and rosewater perfume. The walls close in around me, leaning closer to whisper in my ears.

Eventually, I climb the grand staircase and stand before the painting of the woman in the pink dress. Her bold eyes stare back at me, her lips keeping their secrets. The shadowy folds of her dress are so real that I can imagine the sheen of silk beneath my fingertips. Was hers a great love story, or a romantic tragedy? The house knows.

A chime echoes through the hall. I run down the stairs to the main door; the hinges creak when I open it. Standing outside is an attractive, sandy-haired man with green eyes and freckles. His face sprouts a grin when he sees me. 'Hi, I'm David Waters, the surveyor. You must be the lady of the manor.'

'I wish,' I say as we shake hands. 'I'm Amy Wood, the estate agent.'

'And here I was expecting the honourable Mr Bowen-Knowles.' He puts on a fake posh accent. 'A nice surprise, I must say.'

He's flirting with me – which is a surprise. I feel a little bit flattered, and a lot rusty. I'm grateful, however, that he's not uptight and stuffy, which was what I'd been expecting. As he looks around the main hall, his eyes skim over me; I wish I'd taken a little more time over my hair and make-up and worn a skirt less tight across the hips.

I offer to show him around, pretending that it's a viewing and he's a prospective buyer. As we move through the house, he forensically examines each room for defects – many of which I hadn't noticed until he points them out. Structural cracks, woodworm, damp, sagging ceilings, and rotten floors. He makes notes in a little notebook with yellow graph paper.

In the main bedroom, he points to a cracked area of the

painted panelling that marks the outline of a door. Intrigued, I walk over to it. 'Is it a secret room?' I say.

'Maybe.' He takes a quick look inside and slams the door shut. 'Closet.' He fans the air in front of his nose. 'Pheew, something died in there, that's for sure.'

'Oh.' I move on, slightly disappointed.

We go up to the next floor where Mrs Bradford has her room. This time there's no smell of baking, and when I knock on the door, no one answers. We move on down the back stairs to the subterranean level, where we find a warren of damp, cold rooms: the unmodernised kitchen, pantries and larders with crumbling wooden shelves, and the enormous boiler. David Waters regales me with doom and gloom about probable burst pipes and water leakages. When I spot the electric box, he takes my arm. 'Stay back – it could be a death trap!' My enthusiasm ebbs; David Waters scribbles fast and furiously on his yellow paper.

'What are you writing down?' I ask as we head back to the main hall.

'I'm noting down the structural issues so we can consider some options. Mr Bowen-Knowles thought a conversion to flats might be possible.'

'What about the costs to reinstate it as a family home?'

He laughs like I've made a joke.

'What?' Hands on hips, I stare him down.

'I doubt that will happen,' he says. 'I don't need a calculator to tell you that the restoration costs will be a lot more than it's worth as a family home – even if you did manage to find some rich nutter.'

'Oh.' Visions of 'Golf Heritage' dance in my head.

'Plus, there's a big push to develop recreational facilities and low-cost housing. With all the land here, Hexagon could make a lot of money.'

'You know about Hexagon?' The name seems synonymous with the incarnation of evil in the universe.

'It's my job to keep on top of things.'

'And is it your job to note that turning this place into Disneyland for rich golfers would be a crime? This house is an important piece of history. It should be restored.'

Without realising it, I've walked towards him, standing closer than a polite distance. He gives me a disarming grin.

'That's not *strictly* in the job description.' He touches my arm. 'But I'll tell you what – if you come out with me for a drink tonight, I'll add your comment to my report.'

'What?' I step back, stunned.

'Or another time?'

'No... uhh... tonight is... fine. It's fine.'

'Great.' His eyes linger on my face. My cheeks glow, and not just with the cold.

'I'm going to look at the east wing now,' he says. 'It may be unsafe, so will you wait here?'

'OK.' Although I want to see the east wing, I'm too flustered to go with David Waters.

He goes out the main door; I pace the floor and take stock. It's over two months since I split with Simon. Occasionally, I've begun to wonder why I thought our relationship was the 'be-all and end-all'. Now, other possibilities creep into my mind. I've got a new job and a new project – this house – to occupy my imagination. Could there be someone out there – someone like David Waters – to make it a hat trick?

While I wait for him to finish, I return to the library to do some tidying up. All the property shows advise you to reduce the clutter before the viewings begin. I go over to the huge mahogany desk that's piled high with papers, books, and old bills. As I shuffle the top layer, I deduce that Arabella Windham was a hoarder who saved every bill and scrap of paper.

Underneath the bills I find a stack of newspaper clippings – obituaries, recipes, crossword puzzles. There's also a ledger of household accounts, filled with careful entries for light bulbs, floor wax, petrol, and sundries. In addition to being a hoarder, Arabella – or whoever kept it – must have been quite the penny pincher.

At the back of the book I find something interesting: a page labelled 'artwork' written in a tighter, bolder hand. The page lists artwork purchased as early as the 1920s. I read through the names: Gainsborough, John Singer Sargent, Van Dyck, Matisse, Rembrandt, with a new respect for Sir George. It must have been wonderful to buy beautiful paintings to hang on the graceful walls of Rosemont Hall!

But his dream came to a bitter end. Stapled to the page is an auction receipt from Sotheby's for a fine art sale in London in 1951. The paper lists a number of illustrious works placed in the sale by Sir George, including their condition and price estimate. All but one, a John Singer Sargent, were in their original frames. The prices look ridiculously cheap in today's money. After the war, the appetite for buying art must have dwindled. How sad that Sir George was forced to sell off his collection, and even more tragic is the fate of the Rembrandt. The painting, *Orientale*, is listed as having been withdrawn from the sale. Sir George managed to retain his greatest treasure, only to have it destroyed in the fire.

As I close the ledger and move it to the side, I accidentally knock a pile of *Telegraph* gardening sections off the desk. I pick them up, almost slicing my hand on a piece of glass. Underneath the papers I find a broken picture frame with a black and white wedding photo. From the bride's waved hairstyle, fit and flare dress, and pillbox hat, I deduce the photo is from the fifties. I turn it over. Written on the back in faded black ink is *Henry and Arabella, 1952.* The couple is holding hands, but neither one is smiling.

As I replace the photo, something else catches my eye. Wedged between the desk and the wall is a bundle of folded-up, yellowing papers wrapped in a dusty, faded ribbon. Using a pen, I ease it out from behind the desk.

The ribbon comes apart in my hands, and I unfold the paper on top. It's an old letter, dated 1952, addressed to 'A' and signed 'H'. Arabella and Henry. I skim the text – it's a quaint, heartfelt love letter saying how much 'H' is looking forward to seeing 'A' after being away at university. He expresses some worries about his father's health, and waxes poetic about life at Rosemont Hall.

I refold the letter. It's all so romantic. I'd love to find out more about Henry and Arabella's life here. But do I dare take the letters? I doubt anyone would miss them, especially since the correspondents are both dead. Surely no one will mind if I 'borrow' them?

Behind me, footsteps creak over the parquet floor. Decision made, I shove the letters into my handbag and turn around.

'Hi.' David Waters rakes a hand through his sandy hair. 'The good news is, the east wing isn't about to come down on anyone's head anytime soon.'

'Great,' I say. 'And the bad news?'

'It's causing strain on the main house. I found some huge diagonal cracks which are sure signs of major subsidence.'

*Subsidence* – the dreaded word.

'Unfortunately, it's going to raise the costs considerably, and if it's not dealt with, the whole house might pull apart. The bottom line is, you'd need to find buried treasure to save this place.'

'Buried treasure? As in – actual buried treasure?'

'Or divide it into a whole lot of flats.'

'Oh.'

'So, Amy,' he says, 'I think I've got everything I need – except your number.'

He flips open his notebook to a blank page. Our fingers brush as I take his pencil and write down my details. We agree to meet at the White Swan in Clevedon. Back in the main hall, he leans in and gives me a kiss on the cheek.

'See you tonight, Amy. Eight o'clock.'

'Eight o'clock.'

# 15

I retreat to the staircase landing and stand before the portrait of the lady in the pink dress. I stare at her lovely face, her mysterious smile. The letters I found – for a second I wonder if they were hers, before realising it's impossible. The letters are from the 1950s; she was painted in 1899.

'What did you think of David Waters?' I say aloud to her. 'Should I have agreed to go on a date with him?' My words echo in the cavernous space, and I feel a pang of longing for my imagined life with Simon: weekend breaks to country B&Bs, browsing second-hand bookshops, having dinner parties and book groups at our lovely little attic flat in Thornton Gardens. We had so much history together – but history doesn't always create a solid foundation for the future. The memories can't begin to make up for all that wasted time.

Downstairs, there's a creaking noise, followed by tapping. Mice? Hopefully it's not the sound of something about to collapse. I go down to investigate.

The hall is empty and silent. A draught of chill air sweeps the room. I walk towards the corridor.

An enormous furry beast leaps at me. I scream, raising my hands to my face. Wet and sticky; I scream again – and I'm pinned down and—

'Captain!' a voice yells.

The giant pauses in my murder – I'm being licked within an inch of my life by a huge Saint Bernard with glassy blue eyes.

'Down, boy!'

With a gruff bark, the dog bounds away down the corridor. An ancient woman appears in the doorway of the east wing, standing hunched and unsteady on swollen ankles, stockings rumpled beneath a floral-patterned dress. With a gnarled hand she brandishes a stick – at me.

'And you are...?' Her blue-grey eyes are sharp and lucid as she peers at me over the top of half-moon glasses.

'I'm Amy Wood, the estate agent.' I use my sleeve to wipe off the dog slobber.

She stands silent for a moment, assessing me. Finally, she speaks: 'Maryanne Bradford. Mrs.' The lines in her brow furrow. 'Estate agent. Hmmpff. Vultures, more like. I know why you're here. You want to tear this place apart brick by brick.'

I give her the kindliest smile I can muster. 'That's not why *I'm* here, Mrs Bradford. I'd like to find a buyer who will restore this magnificent house to its former glory. My agency specialises in unique and historic properties. I want to find it a good home, so to speak.' I laugh nervously. 'That's what the Windhams would have wanted... surely?'

'Oh, so you knew them, did you?'

'No. But—'

'Then don't assume anything.' She whistles to the dog. 'Captain!' From the darkness of the corridor, the dog bounds back, his mouth dripping drool like the Hound of the

Baskervilles. He growls at me, then sinks to the old woman's feet. His eyes stare past me – I realise he's blind.

'Of course,' I say, taken aback. 'I didn't mean to imply anything.'

In truth, I was expecting a nice, grandmotherly, scone-baking old lady, not someone quite so sharp-tongued. On the other hand, why should she be polite? If I was in her orthopaedic platform shoes – devoted to the house and nursing Mrs Windham through her last illness – I'd be upset too. It's natural that she sees me as the enemy.

Mrs Bradford rubs the dog's tummy with her cane, her mouth pressed in a line.

'It's a shame, isn't it, that the heirs haven't come to see the house?' I make another attempt to charm her. 'If I'd inherited a place like this, I'd jump at the chance, wouldn't you?'

'The *heirs*,' she snaps, clacking her dentures for effect. 'Jack and Flora are good-for-nothing... peasants. They called in *your lot*, didn't they? They'll never understand – never! It took all these years to put things right. They don't deserve a teaspoon of soil from this place.'

'I agree.' I gulp. 'Though it's a big project for someone to take on. It will take a lot of money and wherewithal.'

She hobbles towards me, the dog slinking along at her feet. 'The house is fine as it is,' she says. 'Oh, I know all you young people have your property makeover shows, with your white walls, beige carpets and whatnots. But that's not what matters, is it?'

'You're right,' I say. 'It's the people who matter. I want to find the right person who will fall in love with the house. Someone who will appreciate its history and care about its future.'

'You've been reading too many novels,' she says, her frown deepening. 'But I'll tell you this for free: none of the *people* cared about this house when they lived here. Arabella hated the place – she thought it was too big and draughty. And Henry was Henry. Even Sir George...' She closes her eyes, her mind wandering corridors I can only imagine. 'All those promises, and then... poof! Everything was gone. Up in smoke. Without another word or a how d'ya do.' She snaps her fingers; her eyes pop open.

'You were here in Sir George's time?' I quickly do the maths. If she was here back then, she must be well into her eighties now.

'My mother was the housekeeper. I practically grew up at Rosemont Hall.'

'How fascinating,' I say. 'You must know so much about the house and the family. I'd love to learn more. I've read about Sir George – he sounds very dashing and illustrious.'

'Oh, so you've read about him, have you?' Her face curdles like there's a sudden bad smell. 'And do you think your history books tell the truth?'

'It was the internet actually—'

'You want to know about Sir George? Well, I could tell you a thing or two – not that it's any of your business.' She sucks in a breath. 'He was no hero, that's for sure. He was a devil.' She bangs her cane for emphasis.

'Oh,' I say, startled. 'Really?'

'And Henry – he was weak. No match for his father. And Arabella was a pawn in their chess game.' She turns away in clear disgust.

What can I possibly say to that? My hand goes reflexively to the letters in my pocket. The private life of Henry and Arabella is none of my business and I shouldn't have taken them – I'll put them back. Later.

Mrs Bradford hobbles off; I follow at a discreet distance. I can't make her like me, but hopefully I can keep her talking. 'I was wondering, Mrs Bradford, about the woman in the portrait. The one on the stairs? Who is she?'

'Her?' She wheels around, her sunken eyes flaring. 'Why do you want to know? You ask a lot of questions.'

'Sorry – I'm just curious. The picture is so lovely. The frame says 1899. I was wondering if she was Sir George's wife. Or his mother?'

'No!' She waves her stick at me. 'Not his wife or mother. *She* was nobody. No one at all.'

She pivots again and begins hobbling down the corridor to the east wing, the huge dog plodding beside her. Once more, I follow, anxious to see for myself what remains after the devastating fire. The door at the end of the corridor opens with an unsettling creak, and she goes through. Half-turning towards me, she speaks again. 'The truth was, Sir George needed money,' she says. 'The house was requisitioned, and the soldiers left it a wreck. Sir George sold off his art piece by piece, but it wasn't enough. And Henry was never going to make a fortune by working. So Sir George found another way. He planned the whole thing right from the start. And look what happened.' She hisses through her teeth. 'He was a demon. Those black eyes – they could pierce through your flesh, devour your soul.'

'Planned what, Mrs Bradford?' I'm equally intrigued and unsettled. 'What happened?'

'Lives were ruined, that's what.' She purses her lips like a silent fortress.

I step through the door and stop, aghast at what's before me. The remains of the east wing are a cross between a bomb site and a tip. A narrow path meanders amid heaps of charred wood, soggy plaster, broken glass, and scraps of furniture that went up in the blaze. Charred rafters bisect the sky, and a whole colony of birds has taken up residence in the half-collapsed chimney. Tufts of grass and weeds grow among the detritus. The rain has long ago washed away the smell of smoke, but not the sense of desolation.

'I come here when I want peace and quiet,' Mrs Bradford says. 'And to remember things as they were.'

I nod without speaking.

'This was once the grand ballroom.' She gestures with her cane. 'It had a ceiling of glass that let in the starlight. The walls had cornices of plaster flowers and mirrors that reflected the candles a thousand times over. There was a stage for the musicians over there.' She points to a corner of the ruin. 'And the tables of food were set up there.' She indicates with her head. 'It was Henry's twenty-first birthday. Everything was perfect – the flowers, the champagne, the music. And the guests...'

She picks her way through the rubble, losing herself in the past. 'Arabella was such a pale slip of a girl – a waif in a green dress. All eyes and hollow cheeks. And the way Henry looked at her... like she was some kind of rare China doll...' She sniffs. 'When the flames began to rise, the sky turned a queer shade of red. Angry, like hell had risen up from the ground and swallowed the moon and stars. All those cars with their headlights and not one of them stopping. And then the rain began to fall, black and thick like coal dust.' Her eyes glisten with the memory of towering flames. 'The ash from the fire.'

I watch her as she speaks, imagining every word.

'And after the fire, Sir George was like a ghost, they say. Walking through the rubble, day and night. Tapping his stick, tap, tap. Muttering to himself and staring at the empty walls where his precious paintings once hung. Luckily, he had the courtesy to die soon afterwards. It's the only good thing he ever did.'

'It sounds awful,' I say. 'How did the fire start?'

Her blue eyes turn hostile as she looks in my direction. 'What do your history books say?'

'Well – nothing. I haven't found any mention of that.'

She stops abruptly, looking at the ground. In front of her is a tight ball of twigs and dried grass – a bird's nest, fallen down from the smoke-blackened beam above.

She pokes at the nest with her cane. Something glints gold in the sunlight.

'It's a magpie's nest,' I say, picking it up. 'Look – it's stolen something.' I unwind the tangle of twigs and remove a small gold object.

'What is it?' She peers over her glasses.

I take out a tissue and wipe it off. 'It's a cigarette lighter,' I say. 'There's an engraving on it. "To H, love A. Happy Birthday".'

Mrs Bradford lets out a strangled cry.

'Here.' I hold it out. 'Do you want it?'

'No!' She recoils with a hiss. The dog suddenly barks and leaps to her side. 'Why is that here? Is this some kind of trick?' Her aged body begins to tremble.

'No – it was in the nest.' I tuck it in my pocket out of sight. 'I didn't mean to upset you. Can I make you a cup of tea or something?'

'I want you to leave,' she says. 'You don't belong here.'

'As I said, I'm the estate agent, so—'

'Go!'

She brandishes the stick like a cudgel and herds me towards a gaping hole in the collapsed front wall. I scramble over bricks and rubble, desperately trying to stay on my feet. Captain streaks back and circles me, barking and baring his teeth. Mrs Bradford yells again: 'Go!'

# 16

I go. The tyres spit gravel as I drive off, covered with dust and dog slobber. I'm as perplexed as Jane Eyre hearing maniacal laughter in the night; as panicked as the second Mrs de Winter when Mrs Danvers finds her holding Rebecca's nightdress. What did I say? What did I do wrong? The cigarette lighter must have been a gift to Henry from Arabella that got lost many years ago. Why did it upset her so much? I take a deep breath, but my heart is still racing. As far as Rosemont Hall is concerned, the woman is a living skeleton in the closet.

As I put some miles between me and the house, I try to put things in perspective. Mrs Bradford seemed genuinely upset that the past denizens of the house – Sir George and Henry Windham – didn't appreciate what they had. And now the house will go to two distant heirs who not only don't appreciate it, but have called in 'my lot' to get rid of it. Add Arabella's passing into the mix and the fact that Mrs Bradford has to move out of her room at Rosemont Hall – it's enough to make anyone a little irrational. If the incident with the lighter is any indicator, she's not going to take kindly to any more change.

In the aftermath of the incident, I've totally forgotten about the day's other unsettling occurrence: agreeing to a date with David Waters. I pass a sign for Clevedon and it all comes rushing back. While the strain of being chased off the premises by Mrs Bradford might be a reason to cancel, sadly, I failed to get his mobile number.

When I get home, I put the bundle of letters and the lighter in my knicker drawer and prepare for my night out. I have to unpack a number of boxes looking for an elusive handbag to go with an outfit that I ultimately reject. When I finally emerge from my bedroom wearing jeans, a V-neck jumper and Ugg boots, Mum asks me where I'm going. Sheepishly, I admit that I'm going out for a drink with a man.

'You don't look like you're making much of an effort,' she says, eyeing me askance. We argue about it for a few minutes; I change into a vintage red dress I bought at Camden Market. Now I'm worried that it *looks* like I made an effort.

When I reach the car park of the White Swan, my heart is thrumming...

I'm officially on the rebound.

The night is freezing, but at least the pub is warm and inviting. A cosy wood fire burns in the inglenook and there's a homely smell of gravy and spicy mulled wine. The bar is draped with a garland of holly and evergreens hung with reindeer lights. It's an unwelcome reminder that Christmas is less than a month away. Almost three weeks have gone by since the phone call came in about Rosemont Hall. Tick tock.

I take a cursory walk through the pub, but there's no sign of David Waters. Detouring to the bar, I order a glass of mulled wine. The bartender hands me an overflowing glass at the same time a hand touches my arm. I jump, and the wine sloshes down the front of my coat. 'Oh!' I blurt out.

'Amy, hi.' My date looks horrified. 'Sorry, I didn't mean to startle you.'

The bartender hands me a towel, and I dab at the wet spot. 'No problem.' I force a smile. 'Let me buy you a new one,' David says with a grin. 'Do you want to find a table?'

'Sure.'

Grateful for the excuse to get my bearings, I go off to find somewhere to sit. All that's available is a loveseat next to the fire that a canoodling couple are in the process of vacating. It seems too cosy and romantic for the occasion, but there's no alternative, so I hover until they giggle off into the sunset. David returns with our drinks and a plate of sticky toffee pudding with two spoons. He gazes appreciatively at the low neckline of my dress and sits down next to me, our hips touching.

'I took the liberty of ordering the house speciality,' he says, indicating the pudding. 'That is, if you want to try it.'

'Sure.'

Despite the fact that I've already eaten supper, the spongy cake and oozy syrup makes my mouth water, and eating it is a welcome reprieve from making small talk. He watches me take the first bite.

'You look fantastic,' he says. 'Even with a garnish of mulled wine.'

As we (mostly I) eat, he tells me about his job (he used to be in construction and worked his way up to quantity surveying), his flat (two streets away from the Grand Pier in Weston-super-Mare), and his dog (a yellow Labrador puppy called Stevie). He asks me a few yes or no questions that I grunt an answer to in between bites (Q: Did you just move here? A: Uh-huh; Q: And you're enjoying your job at Tetherington Bowen-Knowles? A: Yuh-huh). Before I know it, only a few streaks of syrup remain on the plate. I set down my spoon, embarrassed.

'Would you like another?' he says.

'No. In fact, I ate earlier. My mum cooked—' Too late, I catch myself.

'So, you're living at home then?'

'Just until I get settled.' I take a long sip of mulled wine. 'My job in London didn't work out, and here I am.'

He looks at me intently. 'What happened?'

'I thought it was time to try something different,' I say, foregoing a recount of ancient history. 'As for the job at Tetherington Bowen-Knowles, it was the right place at the right time.'

'I'll drink to that.'

We clink glasses, and when he goes to the bar for another round, I give him a surreptitious once-over. He's attractive in a boy-next-door way: tousled hair, athletic build, smartly dressed in jeans and a leather jacket. I doubt we'll be having a deep intellectual conversation about metaphysical poets or houses as characters in fiction anytime soon, but maybe that isn't a bad thing. As the wine takes hold, I wonder vaguely what he has in mind for the evening, and why I'm more intrigued than put off by the prospect.

When he returns with our drinks, I take one sip and set down the glass. 'How did you get on with your estimating this afternoon?' I ask.

He looks a little disappointed that I'm 'talking shop'. 'My PA will type up my notes,' he says. 'I've got pages and pages.'

'I'm sure. After you left, I got a look at the east wing. The housekeeper, Mrs Bradford, showed me around.'

'Quite the wreck, isn't it?' he says. 'Best thing would be to bulldoze it and start again.'

'I don't agree,' I say. 'Mrs Bradford remembers glittering occasions held in the grand ballroom. Maybe someone will want to rebuild it someday.'

He starts to laugh, then sees my face and stops. 'Maybe,' he says, like he's lying to a child.

I tell him briefly about the magpie's nest and the ruckus over the gold cigarette lighter. 'Mrs Bradford seems a little unbalanced by what's happening,' I say. 'I suppose she was hit hard by Arabella's death and now has to move out. She's pretty old – I feel bad for her.' I stare down at the dark liquid in my glass. 'I was hoping she'd tell me more about the house and its history, but the fact that I'm an estate agent seems to have put us on the wrong foot.'

'Why are you so interested?' David looks genuinely puzzled. 'It's just a house – and somebody else's family history.'

'The house is special. I knew that from the very first moment I saw it. I felt like I'd stepped into the pages of a novel. I believe that there can be a strong connection between people and properties: a person can belong to a house just like a house belongs to a person.' I smile dreamily. 'That's how I feel about Rosemont Hall. It's my responsibility to help save it.'

'What do you mean, save it?' He frowns like I'm a few sandwiches short of a picnic.

'I want to find a buyer who will restore it to its original glory and bring it back to life – not convert it into something else.' I lean against him. 'That's why I need your help. Your report can demonstrate to a sympathetic buyer that it's possible.'

He raises an eyebrow.

'I'm not asking you to lie...' I add quickly. 'It's just that Hexagon doesn't have the best track record for dealing with old properties.'

'Well, restoring old properties is expensive and time consuming. It's easier to build from scratch.'

'Then let them do it – somewhere else,' I say. 'But since encountering Rosemont Hall, I've learned that there are lots of old properties at risk – historic gems that are worth preserving. It might sound preachy and sentimental, but I want to make a difference.' I put my hand on his arm. '*We* can make a difference.'

If David Waters is impressed by my poetic activism, he doesn't let on. 'I hope that's not the only reason you're here.' He puts his hand over mine.

'Of course not.' I take another sip of wine. While he hasn't actually agreed to help me with Rosemont Hall, right now, he's my best ally. Plus, I'm enjoying the long-forgotten feeling of having a man fancy me. And he *is* attractive...

I finish the wine and things become pleasantly vague. I stop him before he can order another round. 'I'm a lightweight when it comes to alcohol,' I hear myself saying. 'As Dorothy Parker says: "One martini, two at the most, after three I'm under the table, after four I'm under the host."'

'Dorothy who?'

'Never mind.'

He leans in and kisses me. At first I'm startled, and his mouth tastes like beer. Then I worry that I'm rusty at it. Finally, I stop thinking and allow myself to relax. Just like riding a bike, you never really forget how. The room swims when we finally come up for air. 'I don't think I can drive home,' I say.

'Do you want to go home?'

'With you?'

He laughs. 'You said it, I didn't.'

'I guess I did.'

We leave the pub and he drives me to his flat, where a little yellow dog is sleeping in a basket just inside. Gulping down a glass of water, I decide to dispense with all the 'will I, won't I?' arguments with myself and cut to the chase. In the bathroom, I take off my dress and leave it on the hook behind the door.

When I return to the main room, David's eyes pop when he sees me. I think he says something quaint like: 'Wow, you look amazing.' My hands wander over an unfamiliar body, and his skin smells different than I'm used to. Part of me wants to go and another part of me wants to stay, and a little voice keeps repeating over and over like a ticker tape: *Rebound Man. Rebound Man...*

* * *

Late in the night, I open my eyes in a panic, until I remember where I am. I stare into the darkness and listen to the snores coming from the pillow next to me. *Isn't it exciting?* – I try to convince myself. After all, it isn't every day that I have sex for the first time with someone who is not my boyfriend of seven years. *Ex*-boyfriend. Failing that, I try to muster up some guilt, but I don't feel that either.

I gingerly remove the duvet and swing out of bed. In the hallway, I fumble for a light switch. The brightness hits me like a physical force. The hall is mainly a repository for sporting equipment. I squeeze past a surfboard, a cricket bat and a set of dumbbells, and gaze with detached interest at his photos on the wall: David Waters with a group of mates on skis; David Waters kitted out in diving gear holding up a dead shark; David Waters playing five-a-side football. He's obviously a sports fanatic – a passion we don't share. I put my dress back on, feeling a pair of eyes upon me from another photo hung above the towel rack: David Waters and a short red-haired man with glasses. They're both wearing white collared shirts and hideous checked trousers. Between them, they're hefting a golf trophy.

*Golf.* I lean over the sink and splash water on my face. I don't know why it never occurred to me that David Waters might be an avid golfer – after all, a lot of people are. Normally, that would be fine, but not in this case. Not when I need him onside for Rosemont Hall.

I return to the bedroom, failing to spot the yellow dog stretched across the floor. 'Oh!' I cry as I trip over him, setting off a cacophony of yelps. A light switches on.

'Amy?' David mumbles groggily.

'I'm fine.' The dog growls when I try to pat him. I jerk my hand away. I do a quick check under the bed for my tights, but I can't locate them.

'Do you have to leave so soon, babe?'

I cringe inwardly at the generic term of endearment – something I imagine Simon might say to Ashley. 'Yes, sorry.' I hope he doesn't notice that according to the clock, it's only 5 a.m. 'You sleep,' I say. 'I'll get a taxi.'

'OK – there's a number by the phone in the kitchen.'

I lean over and give him a quick kiss and leave the room, relieved. In the kitchen, I find the number of the minicab written on a yellow sticky. (I note with indifference that there are two other yellow stickies by the phone with the numbers of 'Susanna' and 'Valerie' written on them with x's and o's.)

I slip out of the flat and ring the taxi. The wind gusts in my face and I can smell the seafront. Walking to the estuary, I sit on a bench and stare out at the leaden grey water. I feel surprisingly serene – like I've been in a train wreck and walked away a different person. David Waters may or may not be the proverbial 'one', but I've fulfilled another leg in my post-Simon trinity: new job, new home, new man.

When the taxi arrives and I get inside, I take out my phone and scroll through my contacts. I find 'Simon Work' and 'Simon Mobile' and hit delete. I know the numbers by heart, of course, but eventually I'll forget them. For once, I'm almost glad that there's no going back.

# 17

I'm still reeling from the night before when I arrive at the office later that morning. Everyone is standing around eating soggy mince pies, grumbling about low Christmas bonuses and who should have got the commission on the sale of two condos in Minehead. When I turn on my computer, I see a new email inviting me to the company Christmas party.

'Who wants a party when there's so little to celebrate?' Claire is saying to Jonathan.

I don't hear his reply because I'm reading the details closely. Specifically, the line that says 'Dear colleague + 1'. The dreaded plus-one! Should I ask David Waters, or some as yet unidentified Rebound Man Two, or just go it alone?

As I'm ruminating over it, my mobile rings. I dare to hope it might be someone ringing me back in response to my cold calls about Rosemont Hall. It is about Rosemont Hall, but not a prospective buyer. It's Ian Kendall, the solicitor. I make breathless small talk, trying to mask my disappointment.

'I understand there was an incident at Rosemont Hall yesterday,' he says.

'Incident?'

'Mrs Bradford was apparently quite upset. Her exact words were, "Some chit of a girl came round poking her nose where it doesn't belong".'

'I went round with the surveyor,' I say. 'I'd describe the "incident" as her humongous dog jumping on me and nearly giving me a heart attack.' The cheek of the old woman ringing the solicitor!

'I understand,' Mr Kendall says. 'But please keep in mind that Mrs Bradford is an important beneficiary under the Windham will. She's inherited the artwork and many of the personal effects.'

'Did she inherit the painting on the stairs?'

'Yes,' he says. 'But that doesn't concern the sale, Ms Wood. And that's what I'm ringing about. One of the American heirs, Mr Jack, is keen to get things moving faster.'

'We all want that, surely...'

'He's been negotiating with Hexagon directly. They are definitely interested in the land for their golf course development, though their numbers are on the low side.'

'But you said I had three months,' I protest. My internal Cinderella clock races forward in double time.

'Things have changed. Mr Jack and Ms Flora will go with Hexagon unless someone makes a better offer. That's why I need a status update. Is there anything else on the table?'

'Oh yes, definitely.' The lie escapes my lips in effortless Tetherington Bowen-Knowles style. 'You can tell your "Mr Jack"' – I practically spit out the name of this blight on Rosemont Hall – 'that I've spoken to several interested buyers looking for the exact thing: a "historic gem with lots of potential for flexible, family accommodation". It's practically selling itself.'

There's a moment of silence at the other end of the phone. Have I gone too far?

'Fine,' Mr Kendall says. 'Keep going with that, then. Hexagon wants to meet with the planners before they finalise the offer. See what kind of hoops they'll have to jump through. They've got a meeting scheduled for next week.'

'Next week? But how can Mr Jack allow that? The probate isn't final, is it? And Hexagon doesn't own the site. And' – I crawl out onto a narrow limb – 'they won't ever own the site. Please tell your clients that I'll get them a better offer from someone who will restore the house. Or I can email him directly.'

'I'll talk to him,' Mr Kendall says. 'And I do admire your determination. I hope you get lucky.' I detect a strong note of doubt in his voice.

'I'd better get to it then.'

'Fine. Oh, and one more thing. The other heir, Ms Flora, is coming to the house to look over Mrs Windham's personal effects...'

'Good.' I dare to hope that one of the heirs has an ounce of sentiment after all.

'...to see if there's anything valuable enough to auction.'

So much for that.

'Anyway,' Mr Kendall says, 'I just wanted to let you know in case you run into her.'

'Thanks,' I say. 'But what about Mrs Bradford?'

'I'll make sure she knows you'll be about the place doing your viewings.'

'Fine,' I say. 'Maybe she just needs some time to adjust. I certainly didn't mean to upset her. I was just curious about the house and the Windhams. I didn't realise she was there when

Sir George was alive. She must have seen some fascinating things—'

He clears his throat. 'It's kind of you to take an interest, but it really doesn't have anything to do with you selling the house.'

'Of course – sorry.' I accept the rebuke. It's not my job to learn the truth about the Windhams and Rosemont Hall. It's not my job to spend time there, soak in its atmosphere, or uncover its history. It's not my job to placate displaced old ladies, play tour guide to an appreciative audience, or find someone who will take on the house as a labour of love. It's my job to sell the house to the highest bidder. Thus, while I've mentally cast Mrs Bradford as the unstable housekeeper Mrs Danvers, in reality, I'm the one acting irrationally. If the two American heirs, the solicitor, my boss, and the eighty-four people I've phoned don't care about the fate of Rosemont Hall, then I've got no business doing so.

Except, I do.

'Mr Kendall,' I say stoically, 'I understand completely. It's my job to sell the house quickly. And I will. We've got some lovely particulars printed up, and the quantity surveyor is providing an estimate for the renovation. I've got a lot more people to ring, and I will find someone. Just give me a chance. Please.'

He sighs. Fundamentally, I have him pegged as a nice man who doesn't want to see the house gutted any more than I do. But he has a job to do – and so do I.

'I can keep the wolves from the door for now,' he says. 'But not too long. I'll ring you again when I hear from Ms Flora.'

'Thank you, Mr Kendall, for giving me this opportunity.'

'Goodbye Miss Wood.'

The line clicks off.

* * *

As I return to my desk, I turn the force of my fear over the fate of Rosemont Hall to thinking evil thoughts about Mr Jack. I reimagine him as a shrewd businessman. Maybe he's a hotshot investment banker in New York living in an ultra-modern penthouse apartment on Park Avenue, with a doorman in a red coat who tips his hat and calls him 'sir'. He'll have a driver who takes him to work each morning on Wall Street, wearing his thousand-dollar Armani suit, Bill Blass tie, and Ferragamo loafers. Then, dinner and theatre in the evening with his underwear-model girlfriend. And on the weekends? A drive to Long Island or the Hamptons for a little sun and a round of golf. Golf – it always comes back to that.

And meanwhile, back in Blighty, the last of his family history is slowly slipping away towards the unforgiving oblivion of time. The house will be 'modernised' into something unrecognisable. The girl in the portrait will be dispossessed of her rightful place above the staircase landing, ending up in some newbuild banker's mansion in Surrey.

It just seems so *wrong.*

I turn the glass slipper clock face down, put on my telephone headset with a flourish, and continue my cold calls. I leave more messages, talk to a host of people who, despite my hyperbole, are not interested, and two people who ask me to email them the details. No one schedules a viewing. The lie I told Mr Kendall seems to have poisoned my efforts. I take off my headset, my shoulders drooping.

'Fancy a quick sandwich?'

I look up. Claire's face is sympathetic across the low wall that separates our desks.

'I don't know... I doubt I'll be much company.'

'All the more reason to get out of here.'

'You're right,' I say.

Outside the office, the town is buzzing with Christmas shoppers, carollers, and tourists traipsing in and out of the Pump Rooms. We buy sandwiches at Pret, find an empty bench and sit down.

'Do you want to talk about it?' Claire coaxes, like I'm a reluctant witness.

I sigh. 'It's stupid, I know. It's just... I lost a lot before getting this job. I didn't get my happy ending, but I wanted one for Rosemont Hall. But obviously, that was ridiculous. If no one else cares about the house, then I have no business doing so.'

'Except, you do.'

'Yes.'

Claire takes a thoughtful sip of her coffee. 'Do you want some advice, Amy?'

'Please.'

'You've got two options. One is to forget about Rosemont Hall. Do your job, make your calls, and let the heirs sell it for a golf course. Focus on reality, move on.' Her smile is brittle. 'Because let me tell you, in this job, your dream is not going to happen.'

'But—'

'We sell houses, not happy endings. Semis, flats, newbuilds, terraces – bricks and mortar. To people who want normal lives with a mortgage, a minivan, kitchen diners, and bifold doors onto the garden. We deal with our lousy boss and make our lowly commissions. Most of us dream of doing something else. That's what you need to focus on.'

'Hmm.' I take a bite of my sandwich. 'You mentioned a second option?'

She laughs. 'Well, Amy, in my professional capacity, I really can't advise it. But' – she lowers her voice – 'you could get creative. You're into books, right?'

I nod.

'Then stop thinking Brontë and start thinking Jilly Cooper. There must be loads of country busybodies out there looking for something to do. Start a "Save Rosemont Hall" campaign. Get the nutty housekeeper to rally the troops of local grandmothers. Ring English Heritage and tell them about the nefarious plot to turn it into a golf course. Write an article about the house for *Country Life*. There's loads you can do. In your spare time, of course.'

'Yes – you're right.' I hear the excitement in my own voice. Claire's words are magic – suddenly the air seems alive with possibilities.

'And if all else fails, you can lay naked in the path of the bulldozers.'

I sputter with laugher. 'But I'm supposed to be—'

'Selling the house for the highest price? Then it seems you have a conflict of interest.'

'Yes, it does.' Smiling, I crumple up my rubbish. I can't wait to get back to the office and get started. The job is just a job, but Rosemont Hall needs me. 'Thanks, Claire,' I say. 'I'll take it all under advisement.'

# 18

*My dear H,*

*I have a birthday present for you that I think – I hope! – will make you happy. I came to see you but you weren't at home. I managed a peek into the ballroom, and you are right about the change that has come over the place! It is as sparkly and shiny as a jewel; I have never seen anything so magnificent!*

*When I turned around, a shadow fell – your father was standing there, watching me. The look he gave me – I felt like my heart might freeze mid-beat. 'You?' he hissed, like he'd guessed our secret. I'm ashamed to say that I turned and fled.*

*A*

# 19

My new determination fuels me to take action. I research charities and historical societies in the area who might want to sponsor a Save Rosemont Hall campaign and phone a few of the relevant busybodies. There's some polite interest, but none of them are optimistic that they can raise the money. I ring the head offices of the National Trust and English Heritage, but all I get is a few hard truths. There are hundreds of 'buildings at risk' all over the country and neither organisation has the budget to fund their restoration.

It's not the silver bullet I'd been hoping for, but I can't afford to stop now. And when one of my cold calls – to a couple who are looking to move from Wolverhampton to Bristol and have a whopping budget – finally pays off, I'm over the moon. I schedule the first Rosemont Hall viewing for the coming Saturday!

As I'm about to phone Mr Kendall to tell him the good news, my mobile rings: David Waters. My stomach flips, and I leave my desk to take the call in the privacy of the disabled loo. I'm glad he enjoyed our evening and wants to see me again (and has sent me several texts to that effect that I haven't replied to). I'm just not sure what I want.

'Hi, David,' I say, locking the door. 'You well?'

'You haven't responded to my texts.'

'I'm really sorry, but I've been in a flurry over Rosemont Hall. Someone wants to view it on Saturday. This is my chance to find someone who'll fall in love with the house.'

'Am I going to see you again?'

'Oh, yes.' A list of 'buts' flashes across my mind: *but* I'm not ready for a relationship; *but* I've developed an allergy to dogs; *but* you're into golf... But – then I remember why I can't voice any of those doubts...

'In fact, I was about to ring you,' I say breezily. 'It's our office Christmas party – also on Saturday, in fact. Do you want to be my plus-one?'

There's silence for a moment. 'Well... I guess so.'

'Good.' I ignore the fact that he sounds like he'd rather be having a root canal. 'I'll text you the details.'

'Okey dokey.'

I cringe. 'Great.'

'And Amy...'

'Yes?'

'I'm looking forward to seeing you again.'

'Me too.' I take a breath. 'And sorry to talk shop, but I was wondering about your report on Rosemont Hall. Is it ready yet?'

'I'll email it over later.'

His tone tells the whole story – he's annoyed; probably with good reason. We exchange awkward goodbyes, and when the call is ended I stare at myself in the mirror. My eyes have dark circles under them from the stress of this job, and my skin seems paler than usual. I'm not getting any younger, that's for sure. I ought to give David Waters a chance. He's a perfectly nice man, and we had a perfectly nice time. What more can I ask for?

A hard knock on the loo startles me. 'Hurry up, will you?'

'Sorry,' I mutter to a desperate-looking Patricia, and head back to my desk.

* * *

That night, I plan my strategy for the Rosemont Hall viewing. I'll get there early and tidy up, but I also want to have a good look at some of the old photographs. Before bed, I take out the bundle of letters I found. I've read through them several times, and they've given me a better understanding of the Windhams and their life at Rosemont Hall. But there are still some missing pieces and unanswered questions too.

The first few letters are between Henry and his father, mostly discussing Henry's time at university, and his career plans (or lack thereof). In Sir George's final letter to his son, I detect a distinct undercurrent of disappointment. He writes of his distress at having to sell off his art collection, and about how he's put some plans in place for Henry. It reminds me how Mum called up the neighbour when I was looking for a job. Presumably Sir George had similar (if more illustrious) strings to pull.

There are also letters between 'H' and 'A'. They all seem to be written in the lead-up to the ball that was held for Henry's twenty-first birthday – the night of the fire, according to Mrs Bradford. The writing is sentimental and old-fashioned – two people expressing undying love for each other and worrying that Henry's father might disapprove of their union.

Given the fragile relationship between Henry and his

father, it seems somewhat odd that Sir George would organise a ball on his behalf, especially given their reduced financial circumstances. Henry surmises that it's down to his father wanting to 'bridge the gap' between them. Apparently, Sir George was even arranging for Henry's portrait to be painted. But if it was ever finished, I haven't seen it in the house.

The letters between 'H' and 'A' end abruptly. Their engagement was announced; their happy ending signed, sealed and delivered.

Or was it? I flip to the last letter, which I've placed in a plastic wallet to preserve. It's a fragment of paper, half burned away.

*Darling A,*

*God forgive me, but I have been such a fool. He means to ruin our plans – but I won't let him. We must play along with this little charade for tonight, but tomorrow—*

The rest of the letter is lost, with only a thin brown edge of ash remaining. What did Henry mean? It must have been the last letter between them before the ball went out in a blaze – literally. What happened between this letter and Henry and Arabella's subsequent engagement and marriage? I surmise that Henry must have spoken to his father, stood up to him, and somehow talked him around. Perhaps Henry burned the letter himself so Arabella wouldn't learn about his father's strong objection to their plans and get upset. But if Henry or someone else meant to burn it, then why is it part of the bundle at all?

And what about the fire? Was it just an unfortunate coincidence that occurred as Henry and Arabella were able to reveal their love to the world? I put the letters back in my drawer, trying to imagine myself at the ball, as described by Mrs Bradford. The mirrors reflecting the candlelight, the stars visible through the glass ceiling. The scent of roses, the interwoven melodies of a string quartet, liveried waiters serving champagne. A couple dancing together, eyes only for each other. But what of the aftermath? The rising flames blacken my fantasy to a cinder. Whatever the truth is, I can only find it by returning to Rosemont Hall.

# 20

As I'm about to leave the office on Friday afternoon, I double check that I've got the keys to Rosemont Hall for the Saturday viewing. I've rehearsed my sales pitch over and over in my head, and I know I'm ready. This is my big chance to find a sympathetic buyer, and instead of being nervous, I'm quite excited – especially about going to the house early for a nose around.

But as I'm walking out, Mr Bowen-Knowles throws a spanner in the works. He summons me into his office and assigns me two additional Saturday viewings: a cottage near Shepton Mallet, and a semi in Glastonbury.

'Great,' I lie, quickly doing the maths. Even if everything goes smoothly with the first two viewings, I'll still have to rush to make the two o'clock at Rosemont Hall.

'And Amy, I hope these viewings go well, because you've been here over a month and haven't made a sale.' He wrinkles his nose and gives a short laugh.

It's obviously his idea of a joke, but all the same, anger

surges in my chest. Everyone in the office knows I should have got the credit for the Blundell sale.

'By the way,' he adds with a little smirk, 'Fred Blundell was arrested two days ago for smuggling stolen artwork into the UK. The only property he'll be buying is an eight-by-ten cell in Wormwood Scrubs.'

'Oh no!' The moral high ground liquidates under my feet. 'Poor Fred and Mary – they seemed so nice. And keen.'

'Just as well,' he says. 'The vendors have decided to remarket the Bristol penthouse. Since the Blundells offered the asking price, they think they can get 3.5 in the new year.'

'Oh.' I turn away, unable to face him. I'm officially back to square one.

* * *

The Blundell incident is a setback (and, I acknowledge, more for them than for me) but I'm determined to bounce back – *and* I have a plan. I ring Mum from the car park and tell her not to expect me for dinner. Then I drive to Rosemont Hall.

Rain pelts the windscreen as I go through the gates and up the long drive, the trees skeletal in the beam of the headlights. From the top of the hill, I expect to see the dark silhouette of the chimneys against the sky.

Instead, the house is ablaze with light.

I slam on the brakes, imagining that the house is on fire. It takes me a second to realise that all the lights are on inside the house, glowing yellow out of the large symmetrical windows. Someone is inside. I should turn around and go home. But what if Mrs Bradford is wreaking havoc in advance of tomorrow's viewing? What if she or her huge dog, Captain, goes on a rampage inside?

A Mercedes is parked outside the house. Surely Mrs Bradford wouldn't drive a fancy car (and she looks too old to drive at all). Mr Kendall drives a Beamer so that leaves... who?

I park next to the other car. Rain lashes my face as I run for shelter beneath the door architrave. I ring the bell – if necessary, I can pretend to be lost. Inside, there's a faint echo of chimes.

No one comes; I ring again. It's all very odd. I should leave, but what if something really is wrong? As I'm about to peek inside the front windows, the door creaks open.

'Oh!' My hand flies to my mouth, and I stifle a scream.

# 21

It's her – the woman in the painting!

The orange rectangle of light inside the door frames her face as she stares at me with those huge blue eyes that I would recognise anywhere. She's even wearing dusty pink, though as reality dawns, I see that it's a cashmere cardigan rather than a silk gown. Her dark blonde hair falls loosely around her face in a long bob rather than curls. Her pink, bow-shaped mouth, outlined with dark lip liner, frowns at my shocked reaction. It can't really be *her*, so it can only be—

'Ms Flora?' I say.

'Who are you?'

Her voice is nasal and American, and I know I've guessed right: she's one of the two heirs of Rosemont Hall. The one who's come to strip it bare while her brother, Mr Jack, does a deal with the devil.

'I'm Amy Wood, the estate agent.' I make a half-hearted attempt to fluff my wet hair and hold out my hand. She doesn't take it. In my windblown, rain-battered state, I must look more like a tramp than a competent professional. 'I thought I would pop by to prepare for tomorrow's viewing. When I saw the lights on, I was afraid that Mrs Bradford, the housekeeper, might be making mischief. But I won't disturb you if you're busy. I can just leave...?'

The woman stares at me with her striking eyes as if unable to decide if I'm friend or foe. Warily, she opens the door. 'I guess you can come in, Ms Wood.'

'Please – call me Amy.'

Shivering, I step inside the hallway. It's just as cold inside the house as out. A little puddle of water forms at my feet on the grimy marble floor.

'You can call me Flora,' she says. 'I hate all that "Ms Flora" stuff the lawyer uses.'

'Sure. I'm pleased to meet you.'

We gravitate to the library. The window is propped open with a stack of old books. I notice she's placed little pink stickers on some of the furniture, books, and knickknacks.

'I'm selecting things to go to the special auction at Christie's,' she says. 'Before my brother arrives.'

'Oh, is Mr Jack coming here too?' I stifle a grimace, hoping I never have to meet him in person. He's probably planning a meeting with Hexagon to dispose of the property – like a modern-day Mr Jasper in *The Mystery of Edwin Drood* who secretly wishes to ravish his ward. But as I look around at all the pink stickers, I realise I've been handed a chance on a dusty silver platter.

'I'm sure you and your brother must be thrilled to have inherited this house,' I say. 'It's such an amazing place. A truly unique architectural gem. It will be lovely once there's a family to live here again and appreciate it. I'm so glad you've decided to let us market it rather than selling it to developers' – I purse my lips into an exaggerated cringe – 'who will only strip away its character, carve it up, and ruin it.'

She looks at me like I've got two heads. 'Didn't the lawyer tell you?' she says. 'The house needs to be sold quickly. The taxes are outrageous. And as for who buys it – I honestly couldn't care less as long as we get a good price. My brother says someone wants to build a golf course or something. Fingers and toes crossed that they make an offer.'

I try to reconcile this cold, mercenary woman with the young woman in the portrait. Looking closely, I note that Flora is older than I first thought – probably late thirties. Old enough that she ought to be able to appreciate what she's got, but clearly doesn't. Aren't Americans, of all people, supposed to be gaga over classic English houses? Lucky me to have found the two bad apples in the barrel!

'Besides,' she says, 'I think the house is hideous. So big and clunky. And cold. I can't imagine anyone wanting to live here. I plan to sell the furniture and Jack can deal with the rest.' She sticks a pink sticker on an antique mantel clock.

'The house may not be to everyone's taste,' I say through my teeth, 'but a developer will always try to lowball you. But if you find the right private buyer – well...' I shrug theatrically. 'Many people will pay a premium to get their hands on a place like this. The people I'm seeing tomorrow, for example.'

I'm talking knee-deep rubbish, that's for sure. But Flora looks interested.

'What do you mean?'

I give up all pretence of the truth. 'In England, you see, it's all about class. People will pay over the odds for a status symbol, even if the house is big and cold. Think of who might be interested – politicians, pop stars, actors, supermodels. I read somewhere that Kate Moss bought a house near here. Practically a neighbour.'

Flora's jaw creeps down.

'And then there are the foreign buyers,' I add. 'They're always looking for something unique and aspirational. Of course, you could make a quick quid – buck, I mean – by letting Hexagon take it off your hands for a song.' I shake my head and tsk. 'But you'd be leaving heaps of money on the table.'

'That's not what the lawyer says.'

'I expect his fee is the same either way.'

Flora looks around at the room as if seeing it for the first time. 'How much time would it take – to get all that money?'

'Hard to say. I've got several interested parties, but a special place like this might not sell overnight.'

'Hmm.'

Clearly my speech has made an impact, so I decide to push my luck.

'In fact, you might want to wait a bit before clearing everything out. The furniture and artwork might help sell the place – the little touches and homely feel might tempt the right buyer.' I secretly hope that the girl in the portrait appreciates my efforts to save her home. 'Though I'm all for you clearing out the clutter,' I hasten to add.

She purses her lips. I know I've got her.

'I suppose we could hold off until March,' she says. 'As long as my brother doesn't get some ridiculous notion of playing lord of the manor before it sells.'

*Lord of the manor*. From the little I know about Mr Jack, that seems unlikely.

'When is he coming over?'

'Who knows?' She rolls her eyes. 'Jack's in computers. He works in Silicon Valley and teaches up-and-coming tech geeks at Stanford. He's always working on some amazing gadget or another. Or meeting with investors, or shareholders, or helping out some charity. I have no idea when he's going to find time to come here.'

I reimagine Mr Jack in light of this new information. He must be intelligent and savvy to teach at a top university. I picture him: skinny with receding hair and pasty skin, wearing a turtleneck sweater, a blazer and cowboy boots. And little wire-rimmed glasses like Bill Gates. He'll drive a convertible accessorised with a lithesome blonde undergrad, and they'll spend their weekends living the California dream, playing eighteen holes at a seaside golf course. It's no wonder that a falling-down old house in England holds no appeal for him.

'All this must be very inconvenient,' I say.

'Inconvenient?' She scoffs. 'It's a big pain in the butt.'

I give her my best smile. 'I'm sure it will all work out. Just give me a chance. I won't let you down.'

'Why do you care so much?'

'It's my job to get the best price for my clients. But beyond that… this house is special. I used to teach English literature. It reminds me of all the old houses in the books I love. *Jane Eyre*, *Wuthering Heights*, *Rebecca*.' I blush. 'The great romantic classics.'

'We had to read some of those in high school. They were really boring.'

'They may be old-fashioned, but I love the fact that the houses are characters just as much as the people. They have personality, and history. It would be a shame if Rosemont Hall was lost to posterity just because of bad timing.'

Her blue eyes narrow.

'And the women in those stories dealt with great obstacles. It's fascinating to learn about the real people who lived here –

like the girl in the painting on the landing. You look a bit like her.'

'I do?'

'Yes, haven't you seen it?'

'No.'

'Let me show you.'

I lead the way, hoping I'm doing the right thing. I'm sure that when she sees the portrait, it will be like looking in a mirror. She follows me up to the landing, and I stand aside to give her space. She stares at the painting for a few seconds before shaking her head. 'I don't see any resemblance.'

'No?'

'Honestly, it's a little creepy.' She turns away from the girl in the pink dress. 'This place – it gets to you when you're here alone.'

'It does,' I agree, though obviously we mean it in totally different ways. We go back downstairs and I offer to turn off the lights and lock up. 'You must be dying to get back to your hotel for a nice hot bath,' I venture.

'Yeah, that would be good. The flight was so long, and then it took forever to drive here on the wrong side of the road.'

'And you're OK with the viewing tomorrow?'

'Yeah. I'm going to London to do some shopping. I've had more than enough of this place. It's so... dead.'

We walk together to the blue salon where she left her handbag. The room smells oddly of polish, and I practically trip over a hoover in the middle of the floor. Mrs Bradford must have done some cleaning. It seems strange that she's started doing her job when it no longer matters.

Flora locates her oversized Coach tote and Burberry scarf, her eyes watering from the chill.

'Can you find your way back to the hotel?' I say.

'Yeah, I think so.'

'Have a good night – and it was nice to meet you.'

This time when I hold out my hand, she shakes it.

'Thanks,' she says gratefully.

I wait at the door until she's back in her hire car. As the tail-lights disappear into the gloom, I return to the library. Rain is seeping in through the open window and pooling on the rotting windowsill. The books propping open the window (mostly spy and romance novels) are damp too. I dry them one by one with my scarf and put them back on the shelves. The last book intrigues me – it's a small leather-bound volume with no title or author. I open it gingerly, unsure of its age.

Inside, the pages are covered with doodles and drawings in black charcoal pencil. It's a sketchbook, though there's no name or date to reveal who the artist might have been. Many of the drawings are of people – young men, children, older women, pretty flapper girls, even a Spanish flamenco dancer. A few names are scribbled in the margin: Feldmann, Stein, Rabinowicz. There are also sketches of evening wear designs: beaded flapper dresses, 1930s bias-cut gowns, jaunty little 1940s suits, and Homburg hats.

At the very end, I find a spread labelled 'Windham'. There are sketches of a dour-looking young man with a thin nose, delicate cheekbones, and a curtain of hair falling half over one eye. On the next page, I find *her* – the girl in the portrait on the stairs! Her hair is different – it's tied severely back from her face rather than loose at her shoulders. But the eyes are the same, I'm sure of it. Rendered in charcoal, she looks exactly like Ms Flora. The rest of the pages in the book are blank. The girl in the pink dress was the last person to be sketched by the artist.

Closing the book, I sit down on a threadbare sofa with a trail of stuffing gnawed by mice. I know little of the Windham family, and nothing about the girl in the portrait. The letters I found mention an artist who was hired to paint Henry's portrait in the early 1950s. The date on the frame of the girl in the pink dress is 1899. That leaves two possibilities. Either the sketchbook dates back to the time of the portrait – unlikely given the fashion designs – or else the artist sketched the portrait itself, using the face of the girl as a basis for other designs. I feel proud of myself for solving that particular mystery, though I'm no closer to knowing the sitter's identity.

I slip the book into my bag for safe keeping – I can't risk Flora labelling it for auction. As I do, a piece of paper slips out onto the floor. I pick it up and unfold it. It's another letter.

*Rosemont Hall*
*1 April 1952*

*My dear friend,*

*I eagerly await your arrival. Has it really been more than a decade since we last met? When I close my eyes I can still smell the scent of gardenia, feel the warmth of the Andalusian evenings on my face, taste the wine and the salt of sweat on my lips. I've never felt so alive as when we were cheating death every day.*

*Now that you are coming, I must warn you that the years have not been kind. I have sold my treasures off one by one to maintain this house. Each time – another little death. Only you can help me now. This is my hour of need.*

*Be assured you will have a fine space in which to work, with beautiful views and light flooding in through the oriel window. It's everything an artist could want. And you, my friend, are so much more than that.*

*Please come immediately. I have enclosed money for the*

*fare. I will tell people that you are here to paint my son's portrait. Your work must be finished before the date we spoke of. I am planning a grand ball for the occasion. And maybe, a few fireworks...*

The letter isn't signed, but I deduce it was written by Sir George. I read through it again. The references to his time in Spain and the sale of his treasures is self-explanatory, but what did he mean by his 'hour of need'? And what about the portrait? There's no portrait of Henry in the house.

I refold the letter and tuck it back into the sketchbook. There's more here than meets the eye, and I want to keep collecting the pieces of the puzzle. A puzzle that no one else is looking to solve, and pieces that no one will miss. I tuck the letter and the sketchbook into my handbag.

As I'm about to leave, I climb the stairs to the landing and pay one last visit to the girl in the pink dress.

'I told her a few white lies to buy you some time.' I remove the pink sticker that Flora must have stuck on the frame when I wasn't looking. 'Don't tell anyone, OK?'

Just for a moment, I imagine that the girl in the painting smiles a bit more broadly – even conspiratorially – now that she's keeping my secrets as well as her own.

# 22

By the next morning, meeting the 'girl in the portrait' seems like an odd dream. But when I check my knicker drawer, the bundle of letters, the gold lighter and the artist's sketchbook prove it was real. I wish I had time to go through everything again; reconstruct the final hours before the ball and look for connections that I might have missed. But I don't have that luxury now – I have to hurry to prepare for the day's viewings.

'Three viewings?' Mum shakes her head as I'm leaving the house. 'You've been working six days a week. For what they're paying you, it isn't right.'

'But if I can sell a property and get a commission, it will be worth it,' I say. I'll be able to buy or rent my own flat and move out (though I don't tell her that). Although the Blundell deal fell through, that experience proved that, barring unforeseen circumstances, I can sell a property. And I can do it again. Today.

My first viewing, a 'character cottage near open country-side', proves to be a down-at-heel cottage with a higgledy-piggledy thatched roof that abuts a main road. My heart sinks as I pull up and see that my clients, a Mr and Mrs Wakefield, are there before me and look quite well-heeled in comparison to the surroundings. I introduce myself in my cheeriest voice, but it's obvious that the Wakefields are neither impressed nor amused. 'From the map on your website, we were expecting it to be off the main road,' Mr Wakefield says as a lorry whizzes by, practically knocking us down in its by-blow.

'And the particulars didn't say it was thatched,' Mrs Wakefield scolds. 'That's a bit of false advertising.'

'It costs a bomb to insure thatch,' Mr Wakefield chimes in. 'I should know – I'm in insurance. As was my father before me.'

'Of course.' I smile through my teeth. 'On the plus side, it is a lovely area. Shall we go inside?'

Before they can say no, I knock hard on the door.

Bolts and chains jingle, and a small woman in a tracksuit opens up, a cigarette dangling from her mouth. 'Mrs Chip?' I say, consulting my notes.

'Who are you?' she says.

'The estate agent.' I force a smile. 'Can we come inside?'

'Knock yourself out.'

She stands aside and we enter a room that smells distinctly of dirty nappies. Mrs Wakefield wrinkles her nose like a pug dog. In the main room, four children are screaming. Two little boys are fighting over a ride-on Thomas the Tank Engine, a half-naked toddler is watching CBeebies, and a little girl in an Elsa dress is literally swinging from the net curtains. The floor is crunchy with cereal and crisps. Mrs Chip oversees the chaos, smoking her cigarette as she folds a pile of laundry.

Mrs Wakefield takes one look around and begins to cough.

'Why don't we go upstairs,' I suggest. I lead the way up the narrow staircase.

At the top of the stairs, Mr Wakefield bangs his head on a low beam. 'Bollocks!' he roars, rubbing his head.

'Mummy, that man said bollocks!' a child yells.

I cringe inwardly. 'On the plus side,' I say, 'there are three good-sized bedrooms and plenty of built-in storage.'

The bedrooms are packed floor to ceiling with toys and oversized furniture. Everything reeks of smoke. As we peer into the grotty bathroom, Mrs Chip comes up the stairs. I'm about to suggest that we move on when Mr Wakefield decides to get chummy.

'Why are you selling?' he asks Mrs Chip. All of us ignore a blood-curdling shriek from downstairs.

'My scrote of a bloke ran off with some tart he met at the gym. Me and the kids got a two-bed council flat in Yeovil.'

'Oh,' the three of us say at the same time, for different reasons.

We head downstairs; at the bottom, one of the little boys jumps out at Mrs Wakefield waving a plastic gun. 'Bang, you're dead.'

'Good heavens!' she says.

'Piss off, lady,' he says.

'Well, I never.'

I herd my clients out of the house, slamming the door behind us. 'As you can see,' I say, 'there's lots of potential for the right buyer to put their own stamp on the place.' I hang my head. 'But I take it that it won't be you.'

'Chin up, young lady,' Mr Wakefield says. 'Keep us posted if anything else comes up.'

'I will – thanks.'

* * *

I comfort myself that the next viewing can't possibly be worse. The next house is located in Glastonbury, and as I enter the town, the mystical pull of the Tor works its magic. It's said that King Arthur and Guinevere are buried in the abbey. I imagine myself as a knight errant on a quest for the Holy Grail – my first sale.

The town centre is buzzing with shops selling crystals, love potions, indie music and goth clothing in all shades of black. But Google maps directs me onwards to a warren of less quaint streets lined with council blocks, chip shops, and a tattoo parlour. I pull up in front of the house I'm showing: pebble-dashed and decrepit, attached to another house with breeze blocked windows and a door crisscrossed with police tape. A squat and crack house all-in-one? My enthusiasm evaporates like a leaky balloon. I consider ringing my client, a Mr Patel, and calling the whole thing off. But just then, a large black car pulls up behind me and a man in a suit gets out. I have to risk getting out of the car. As I do, a booming beat starts up from inside the house. *Someone* is clearly at home.

'Hi, I'm Amy Wood,' I say, 'the estate agent. I don't want to waste your time, but I thought the place was vacant. Maybe we should reschedule...?'

He holds up his hand to cut me off. 'It is of no importance.'

It might be of some importance if we get killed, but it's obvious that he's not going to be put off. The front door is marked with a spray-painted biohazard symbol. I ring the bell, and when no one answers, I fish out the key and unlock the door. Before going inside, I shout hesitantly: 'Hello, anybody home?'

Mr Patel pushes past me. He pulls out a laser tape measure and starts zapping the walls with the little red light, tapping the measurements into his phone.

Cosmetically, the place is trashed – grimy wallpaper hangs off the walls, the carpet is black and ripped, the walls and ceiling are covered with spray paint. I glance at Mr Patel. He's making all sorts of satisfied noises. Surreptitiously, I rip up a tissue to make earplugs. They do nothing to drown out the din.

Mr Patel finishes in the hallway and opens the door to the main reception room. The room has no floor, just joists with rubble beneath. Steadying himself against the wall, he steps out onto the joists. 'Be careful,' I plead, but he ignores me. He skips across the boards, laser measure poised and ready in his fist.

'There are some fine features here that could be restored,' I shout half-heartedly. 'I'd say this house has loads of potential. The rooms are good-sized, and so is the garden. It could be a lovely family home, and it's a real bargain at the price.' It's almost true. Beneath the graffiti, the room does have some nice crown mouldings and an original fireplace.

A rat scurries between the floor joists. I let out a little yelp. Unfazed, Mr Patel keeps measuring. Then his phone rings and he proceeds to carry on a conversation for (yes, I time it) seven minutes. Each moment ticking away increases the likelihood that I'll be late for the Rosemont Hall viewing, not to mention the possibility of getting killed.

Finally, Mr Patel puts the phone away. 'Now the upstairs,' he directs.

Clenching my teeth, I go first up the rickety stairs. A board gives way beneath my feet and I nearly tumble to the bottom. Mr Patel goes past me, brandishing his laser. At the top of the stairs is a bathroom filled with pipes and tubes, resembling a home laboratory. The Chip cottage looks positively pristine in comparison. 'Lovely good-sized bedrooms,' I say. Mr Patel responds by zapping them. He walks to the door of the main bedroom. The music hammers like a ravenous beast trying to escape.

'I think we should skip that one,' I say. 'I can email you the dimensions.'

Mr Patel opens the door without knocking. For an instant, I'm terrified. Do I have some kind of liability if he gets murdered? He steps inside the room. I creep over to the door and look inside.

Four very large, very tattooed and pierced men are lying on various filthy sofas and chairs. My heart is in my throat until I realise that their eyes are all closed – they're drunk, or asleep, or stoned, or dead.

I rush over to Mr Patel. 'We need to go,' I shout.

Unbelievably, he takes out his laser measure and starts doing his thing. He stands on a sofa next to one of the passed-out men and measures a ceiling rose. The smell in the room of sweat and booze mixed with cigarette smoke and incense is making me gag. Just then, the CD comes to an end and everything goes quiet. Mr Patel goes to the bay window and measures it, knocking a syringe off the sill in the process. It clatters to the floor and rolls to the feet of one of the men. The man groans and opens his eyes. 'What the hell!'

'Let's go!' I grab Mr Patel's arm and pull him from the room. We successfully navigate a gaping hole in the floor, but Mr Patel pauses at the top of the stairs. For an awful second I think he's going to measure something else.

'Come on!'

We half tumble down the stairs together. I drag him through the hall and out the front door to our cars. A few seconds later, four hairy men come out of the house, shouting and brandishing beer bottles.

'Can I see the garden?' Mr Patel says.

'Ring the office!' I shriek. 'Schedule a second viewing!'

# 23

I put some miles between me and Glastonbury and pull over in a lay-by to catch my breath. I feel like I've aged a hundred years in the last two hours. The last thing I want to do is another viewing. Even – and especially – at Rosemont Hall.

Thanks to Mr Patel, his laser, and Saturday afternoon traffic, I'm running late. By the time I drive through the rickety gates and begin the ascent of the long, winding drive, my palms are sweaty and slick on the wheel. The towering monolith of Rosemont Hall looks lonely and forbidding. The east wing is like the skeleton of a vast, beached whale, the burnt rafters slicing the sky into jagged pieces.

The clients are due, but there's no car in the drive. A knot of tension tightens in my shoulders. Are they late too – or already come and gone? Or just not bothered to turn up?

After the events of the last few hours, I'm desperate for the loo. I dash into the house and up the stairs to the rose bedroom – which, I assume, was Mrs Windham's. According to David Water's report, it has the only working toilet. The bathroom has the same avocado-green suite as my parents' bungalow, and I feel right at home. Here, however, the tiles are mildewed and there's a large hole next to the bath where the floor seems to have collapsed under years of wet feet.

The sink tap is dripping like an excruciatingly arrhythmic Chinese water torture. When I go to wash my hands, the first tap doesn't turn, and the second tap turns on but won't turn off. Worse, the drain is blocked, and water pools in the basin.

I rush into the bedroom to look for a towel to mop up any overflow. The furnishings are dated and dreary: a seventies mismatch except for the huge canopy bed hung with rose chintz curtains. On the bedside table is a box of tissues and a tattered book: *The Tenant of Wildfell Hall* by Anne Brontë. I'm almost positive that it wasn't there on my previous visit. In addition, the bed clothes are rumpled. Has someone been sleeping here – in a dead woman's bed?

The water continues to drip. As a last-ditch effort to find a towel, I go over to the door cut into the panelling that David Waters said was a closet. I pull it open, anticipating the foul reek of dead mice or mothballs.

Instead, a flowery scent of potpourri wafts out. Curious, I flip the light switch and a bare bulb lights up. The closet goes back about two metres. It's full of clothing zipped in plastic garment bags, with an upper shelf full of hats and elaborately coiffed wigs. I'm reminded of an old-time pantomime: flouncy gowns, a clown suit, a gentleman's cloak and dagger, a pirate's outfit. A huge spider scurries away from my feet. To be honest, it's all a bit creepy.

Then I see it: a pink dress on a padded hanger with a boned, Victorian-style bodice and flowing skirt. It's either the same dress as in the portrait or a well-made replica. Unzipping the plastic, I run my fingers over the watery satin fabric. The scene in *Rebecca* pops into my mind where Mrs Danvers tricks the second Mrs de Winter into dressing up like one of the paintings for a costume ball, in a similar gown to that worn by the ill-fated Rebecca. The whole party is sent into an embarrassing uproar. And as for Henry Windham's party – that ended in a tragic fire. Was this gown a fancy-dress costume that belonged to Arabella Windham? Why would Mrs Bradford keep these garments in such good order when the rest of the house is a wreck? My neck crawls with goosebumps as I switch off the light and close the door. Clearly, I'm intruding on private memories and carefully kept secrets.

The tap is still dripping in the bathroom. I give it one last good twist – and it comes off in my hand. There's a deep gurgling noise, and the next moment, the whole thing erupts! I scream as brown water douses me from head to toe. Frantically, I try – and fail – to put the broken piece of metal back on. Luckily, the water fizzles out quickly and subsides to the original drip. If the house doesn't want its plumbing disturbed, then who am I to argue?

I'm about to leave the room, freezing and dripping, when I hear the crunch of gravel. My clients! I've practically forgotten about them.

I rush to the window as a silver Aston Martin pulls up in front of the house. Springing into action, I run down the stairs, rifling in my pocket for the paper with the client's name – a Mr O'Brien – leaving a trail of water behind me.

I reach the door; the car is moving again. It reverses in the drive, like they've taken one look and seen enough. Waving my arms, I run towards it. 'Mr O'Brien,' I shout. 'Stop! I'm Amy Wood, the estate agent!'

The car stops. The driver door opens and a man in a black hooded tracksuit gets out. He's about my age, and fairly nondescript. But the woman who gets out of the passenger side is anything but. Tall and bleached blonde, she's wearing a micro skirt, lace tights, and gold stiletto heels. On top, she has on a fitted leather jacket that augments her impressive, oversized chest. Everything about her – nails, make-up, lips drawn in a little red pout – seems in perfect fabricated order.

'Hello, Mr O'Brien,' I say. 'I'm really glad you came.'

'It's Ronan Keene, actually,' the man says as we shake hands. 'O'Brien's my agent.' The woman looks at me and sniffs.

'Oh, of course,' I say. Agent?

'And this is my girlfriend, Crystal.'

The woman beams me an irritated pout. Maybe she thinks I should recognise her, or act more impressed, or maybe she thinks I've no business showing a house when I'm dripping with rusty water. I rack my brain, but if they're celebrities, I don't recognise them.

'Nice to meet you,' I say.

I usher them in the door and begin my spiel. 'This house is truly special,' I say. 'It's one of a kind. And with a little TLC, it could be amazing. Every feature is a piece of history.' I point out some of the decorative plasterwork; Crystal sniffs in response.

In the great hall, I give them a moment to be awed by the faded grandeur of the house before enthusiastically launching into a brief history of the house. 'Rosemont Hall was built in 1765,' I say. 'It's one of the finest examples of Georgian Palladian architecture in the country. It's been in the Windham family for over two hundred years. The first Windham won the house in a game of whist.'

I watch them closely for any sign that they're impressed, awed, or overwhelmed – any emotion I can connect with. Crystal takes out a handkerchief and puts it over her nose as we go through the ground-floor rooms.

'Cracking place,' Ronan says. If anything, he looks puzzled by the surroundings.

'We've had a quantity surveyor around.' I persevere with my sales pitch. 'He's doing some costings on the renovations. I know it's a bit of a project right now, but just think how much value you could add.'

Ronan shrugs. 'Money's not really an issue, as long as we can do what we like, eh, cupcake.' He flaps his elbow at Crystal. 'We'll need to add an Olympic-sized swimming pool, sauna, and gym, and clear those fields to build tennis courts – and the football pitch, of course.'

'Of course,' I echo half-heartedly.

'And Crystal wants one of those big open-plan kitchen diners with bifold doors and a breakfast bar,' he adds. 'So we'd want to knock down some walls.' He swings an imaginary sledgehammer.

'The house is listed, so there are some restrictions,' I say through my teeth. 'But you could still put your own stamp on it without altering the basic structure...'

'Does that include bulldozing it?' Crystal pulls out a compact mirror and reapplies her lipstick. 'Because it's so dark and draughty – it would never do at all.'

'Crystal...' Ronan says. 'You said you'd keep an open mind.'

'Why?' She pouts. 'You know I loved that new-build mansion in Gerrards Cross. That pink marble Turkish bath was to die for. And the cinema wing...' She sighs. 'I hate these horrible old houses. I mean, someone else has *lived* here.'

My hand itches to tweak her surgically altered nose. I walk over to the window and look out at the parkland, trying to remain calm and professional.

'I mean, why did you have to sign with Rovers?' Crystal laments. 'Even Man City would have been better. Or Liverpool.'

'Crystal—'

'I'm sure there isn't a nail salon or a decent boutique for miles.'

It's a lost cause. I'm not proud to say it, but I allow a tiny little mean streak in me to come to the surface.

'Would you like to see the kitchen?' I offer, knowing full well that its old-fashioned grottiness will horrify her. 'It's in the basement. Very spacious, if a little dated.'

'Ugh,' Crystal says. 'No thanks. I'll wait up here.'

Too bad.

I lead Ronan down the stairs. 'It's a big space,' I say, 'you could do a lot with it.'

He seems almost to prefer the subterranean damp (or maybe he's just happy for a Crystal-free moment). 'It's a nice house,' he says. 'It reminds me of my nan's house in County Down. I see it's got lots of potential.'

'Yes.' I smile gratefully. 'It will be a lovely family home once it's restored. The previous owners were married for over forty years. It's a "together house" – a house for life.'

'Yeah, but that's not really what we want,' he says. 'I'm never sure where I'll be from one season to the next.'

'Season?'

'The Premiership. You know – football. I signed with Bristol Rovers. We're newly promoted this season.'

'Oh. Well, that is exciting. Maybe I've seen you when my dad... uhh... my boyfriend... watches *Match of the Day*.'

'Maybe.' We check out the exploded boiler. I try not to picture this lovely house as a football party pad. Hot-tubs, WAGS, gym, football pitch, nail salon. With enough room left over for Crystal's very own live-in plastic surgeon.

Upstairs, Crystal is nowhere to be seen. 'There's two more floors up above,' I tell him as we make our way back to the entrance hall. 'Would you like to see more? The attic might make a great home cinema.'

'Sure,' he says with more enthusiasm than I had expected.

We start up the stairs, stopping off on the landing before the portrait of the lady in pink.

'Wow,' he says, 'she's something.'

Renewed hope flickers in my mind. Maybe Mr Ronan Keene, Premiership footballer, is not an entirely lost cause.

'Yes, she is. I love the way she looks like she has a secret.'

I'm about to tell him that I met a real woman who is the spitting image of the girl in the picture, in case he wants to 'trade up', but suddenly from downstairs, Crystal starts screaming.

We both rush down.

'What is it, cupcake?' Ronan shouts.

In the library, Crystal is standing on an old sofa; her spike heels have ripped a hole in the upholstery and fluff is coming out.

'I saw a mouse! There!' She points to a tiny hole at the base of one of the bookcases. 'I hate this place. Let's go.'

'Now, cupcake, it's more afraid of you than you are of—'

'No! And stop calling me that. We're leaving – NOW!'

Ronan lifts Crystal off the sofa and carries her out to the main hall. Her heels skid on the pitted marble floor as he sets her down. Turning to me, he shrugs apologetically. 'I guess we'd better look at new-builds next time.'

'That's fine.' I'm relieved that Crystal won't be living here. 'There are lots of lovely properties out there. I'd like to help you find one that's right for you.'

'That'd be great,' Ronan says.

As we walk to the door I have a sudden brainstorm. 'In fact, if you really want modern, I know of a cracking penthouse flat in Bristol. All glass and chrome and views to kill for.'

'Hmm,' Ronan says. 'What do you think, cupcake? Could you live in Brissy, or is it too near your mum?'

'Anything's better than here,' Crystal moans.

I'm secretly pleased that it's started to rain and, as we leave the house, Crystal's gelled hair is going flat. She grabs the car keys from Ronan and rushes to the Aston Martin.

'Sorry this wasn't the house for you,' I say. 'But good luck in your search. Do ring the office if you're interested in the Bristol flat. And if I see any new build mansions come on, I'll let you know straight away.'

'Thanks.' He looks wearily at his car. Before getting inside, he pauses. 'Hey, Amy, do you think they'd sell that picture? The one on the stairs?'

I stare at him. He really is keen.

'I don't know. I think she stays with the house. But if I hear otherwise, I'll let you know.'

'OK.' He gets into the car and revs the engine, tyres squelching as they drive off.

I lean against my wet car and let the rusty water trickle down my nose. All my hopes for the day have dissolved like raindrops in the sea. Frankly, all I care about right now is getting back to the bungalow for a very long, very hot bath.

# 24

As if three terrible viewings aren't enough, the night holds in store an additional nightmare – the office Christmas party. I check my messages as I sink into the tub: two voicemails and three texts from David Waters asking me when and where to meet. I text him the details of the Glow Bar in Bristol, the venue for the dreaded event, and put my phone aside. Closing my eyes, I picture the costumes I found at Rosemont Hall. All lovely garments, carefully preserved and looked after. Something else floats to the surface of my mind. What did Fred Blundell say? A Picasso in a new frame like 'old wine in new bottles...'

I sit bolt upright; the sudsy water streams off my skin. All along I've assumed that the girl in the pink dress was painted in 1899 because that's the date on the frame. But what if the date on the frame is a deliberate misdirection? What if the portrait is, in fact, a modern painting done to look old?

Sir George's ledger listed his paintings that were bought and sold. I recall that one of them, a John Singer Sargent, was auctioned off in a frame listed as 'new'. It seems farfetched, but maybe the original frame was taken off that painting and used for the girl in the pink dress. For the painting itself, the artist could have skilfully replicated the varnish and cracks of an old painting. If it is a modern creation, then the girl could be just about anyone.

But there's one person it's most likely to be. Henry and Arabella were in love and secretly engaged to be married. The pink dress was hanging in a closet in her room. And the letters speak of a painter hired by Sir George to paint Henry's portrait. One by one, the pieces fall into place. Instead of painting Henry, the artist painted Arabella. The painting was left in the attic studio during the fire, so it wasn't destroyed or sold off. It makes sense that Arabella dressed up in a beautiful Victorian-style ballgown in honour of Henry's twenty-first birthday. Unlike my original idea, she didn't dress up like the portrait, but rather, she sat for the portrait. And putting it in an old frame lent it gravitas. It was *meant* to fool future generations of onlookers – people like me – into thinking that the painting was much older. Perhaps the painting is the 'birthday present' that Arabella mentioned in her letters to Henry. And when I asked Mrs Bradford if the woman was Sir George's wife or mother, it's no wonder she sniffed disdainfully – the young woman in the portrait is Arabella Windham!

I get out of the bath feeling pleased with myself. Everything fits, even down to Mrs Bradford. She was devoted to Arabella Windham and kept her things in good order, including her special dress. Though if the rumpled bed is any indication, maybe she was a little *too* devoted...

Dad's carriage clock chimes – I need to get ready for the party. Rummaging through my closet, I decide on a vintage pink satin shift dress with matching heels and pashmina.

Underneath, I bite the bullet and put on my only surviving pair of lacy knickers 'just in case'.

As I'm standing in front of the mirror wondering whether or not the outline of the underwear will be as visible in a dimly lit bar as it is in my well-lit bedroom, Mum comes in, setting a library book on my bedside table.

'That's a lovely dress,' she says. 'You look like a princess – Princess Di. You know, before she—'

'Died?' I wince. Mum means it as a compliment; she's only trying to bolster my post-Simon self-esteem. But why couldn't she have chosen Princess Catherine – or even Meghan Markle? Does my dress scream 'eighties'? I'm neither tall nor blonde, nor do I possess the statuesque elegance that Princess Di had back in the day.

'Well, yes.' Mum makes a pretext of dusting the knickknacks on my bureau. There's a long pause while I brace myself for whatever is coming next.

'You know,' she says, 'if you want to bring someone back here, your father and I are all for it.'

'Mum! Of course I don't.'

'We're both heavy sleepers. I swear we won't hear a thing. And we'd prefer to know you're safe rather than worry about you going to some stranger's flat.'

'Mum!'

'We want you to meet someone. Make hay while the sun shines.'

'Mum, I'm hardly going to bring some bloke back to sleep with me in a single bed on the other side of the wall from you.'

Mentally, I add up my savings plus my meagre wages. Unless I make a big commission, it will be March before I can afford the rent on a half-decent flat.

'OK, darling, I'm just trying to be helpful.'

'Great, Mum. I'm sure.'

She dusts for another minute and then leaves the room. I glance longingly at the thick Sarah Waters novel she's brought me. How I long to curl up under the covers and escape to a seedy, dimly lit Victorian world. But it's my fate to attend an office Christmas party in Bristol, escorted by a moderately handsome almost-stranger. On paper, that doesn't look too bad.

With a final twirl in front of the mirror, I put on a pair of diamanté earrings and get ready to go. I'm almost at the door when my dad, sitting in front of the TV watching *Eggheads*, notices me leaving.

'Wow, it's Princess Di.' He winks at me. 'Tell Prince Charles that we're dying to meet him.'

'Dad!' I seriously debate changing into something else. 'It's an office Christmas party, not a *date*. Besides, you're thirty-five years off the pace.'

He chuckles. 'Whatever you say, princess. But looking like that, maybe we'll meet your Dodi Fayed in the morning?'

'Dad!'

'Just kidding. Oh, and just so you know, we'll be out tonight. It's the anniversary of the night I met your mum. At your Uncle George's – ha! Can you believe she ever went out with that old todger?'

'No, Dad, I can't say I've ever given it much thought.'

He points to the television. 'Let's see if the challengers can oust them.'

I stand there patiently while the challengers miss an easy question about Dickens, and the Eggheads take the crown as usual. I leave my dad hemming and hawing. Just as I reach the door, he turns back to me.

'Well, princess, try to have a good time. And even if you don't – I'm sure your mum and I will.'

Of that, I have no doubt. The prospect of sleeping elsewhere is becoming more and more attractive. The walls really *are* thin. I do a quick recalculation to determine if mid-February might be possible for moving out.

'Bye, Dad.' I force a smile. 'I'll keep that in mind.'

* * *

I arrive in downtown Bristol right on time. Then I proceed to sit in the car for fifteen minutes staring at the cascading white Christmas lights hung between the buildings and fretting about going inside the bar. A thousand objections come to mind: I haven't really bonded with anyone in the office other than Claire; Jonathan and Patricia both hate me, my boss is annoying, and then there's the whole issue of David Waters. Unfortunately, absence has not made my heart grow fonder. It's given me time to conclude that inviting him was probably a mistake.

Eventually, I force myself to leave the car. The bar turns out to be a chic, swanky joint – all leather and chrome. As I'm about to go inside, a hand grabs my bottom. 'Hey—'

I shriek. My fist raised, I spin around. 'Stop that!'

The hand belongs to my boss, Alistair Bowen-Knowles. He stands there grinning at me like a Cheshire cat. Over his usual shirt and tie, he's wearing a tacky knitted snowman jumper with an embarrassingly phallic carrot nose. An attractive blonde woman is hanging onto his arm. Conveniently for him, she's peering into a tiny compact mirror and doesn't notice anything untoward.

'Tessie.' He turns to his companion. 'Meet our newest addition, Amy Wood.'

'Pleased to meet you.' My face burns.

'Charmed, dahling.' Tessie's voice is deep, her fingers claw-like as she shakes my hand. For a second, I wonder if she was once a man. 'Are you here all alone?' she warbles.

'No,' I say firmly. 'I'm meeting someone – he may already be inside.'

'Well, let's go and look for him, shall we?' Alistair says. 'First round's on me.'

We enter the bar, pushing our way through the crowd towards a cordoned-off area in the back. A banner trimmed with a gold garland is taped to the wall: *Happy Christmas from Tetherington Bowen-Knowles*. I spot Claire, dressed in a lovely turquoise sari, accessorised with a handsome Indian man in tow – her husband, I presume. Escaping my boss, I make a beeline over to her.

'Oh, hello, Amy.'

She introduces me to her husband, Raj, and leaves to go to the loo. Unfortunately, I can't remember anything she's told me about Raj other than that he's from Birmingham. I make an attempt at small talk, telling him how Simon and I once went up north to Edgbaston to do the Tolkien Trail, but he looks blank and says they live up near Walsall.

I'm concentrating so hard on the non conversation with Raj that the next thing I know, I'm holding two empty glasses of champagne, one in each hand. My quota for the entire night is gone in the first fifteen minutes. Raj commandeers a roving waitress and a second later I'm holding another full glass. Just then, a cold hand grabs my arm. 'Oh!' I scream. The glass goes flying, spilling champagne all over Raj's trousers before shattering on the floor.

Like a needle ripping across a vinyl record, all conversations stop. I look up at a horrified David Waters.

'Hi,' he says. 'Looks like I've made an entrance yet again.'

'Looks like you have.' A small army of bar staff rushes over and attacks the mess with towels and brooms.

We move away from the wreckage. David gives me a little kiss, but I turn my head and it ends up somewhere in my hair. 'You look great,' he says.

'So do you. Love the jumper.' Over his pink shirt he's wearing a kitschy red jumper with a knitted white beard and black vinyl Santa Claus belt attached.

'Yeah, seemed appropriate.'

Before I can reply, Mr Bowen-Knowles (sans Tessie) swoops over to us.

'David…' His tone is distinctly superior. 'Long time no see.'

'Hello, Alistair. Great party. Love the jumper.'

'Ditto. I didn't know you were Amy's guest.'

'Well, she was nice enough to ask me.'

'I see.'

They stand squared off against each other, Christmas jumper-clad chests thrust out – a pissing contest if I've ever seen one. I'm curious as to how far back these two go. Certainly, I'm not vain enough to think they're actually fighting over *me*.

'And how's your handicap?' Mr Bowen-Knowles says.

'Up to six now. You straighten out that left cut?'

'I'm working on it. But I don't believe you're at six.'

'Well, fancy a round to prove it? You can put your money where your mouth is.'

*Golf*. They're talking about golf. My boss and my plus-one are planning a golf weekend.

'Next weekend any good?' my boss says. 'You still a member at Minehead?'

'Yeah.' David leans away from me. 'It's still my favourite course – for now.'

'Brilliant.' Alistair raises his glass. 'Put it in the diary.'

Maybe it's a trick of the twinkling Christmas lights, but the room has positively started to spin. There may be other golf courses in Minehead, but the only one I know is Golf Heritage.

'Amy?' David grabs my arm as I teeter away a few steps. He steers me to a chair and sits down opposite, keeping hold of my hand.

I pull it away. 'I didn't know you and Alistair were such good golf buddies.'

'Oh, not really.' He shrugs. 'We play from time to time. That's how we met.'

'And I suppose you'll be happy when Hexagon guts Rosemont Hall to build another Golf Heritage and you can run your golf buggies through the wreckage.'

His boyish face hardens. 'That's not fair, Amy.'

'No?' I inhale sharply. 'I read your report line by line. You're right, someone will need to find buried treasure to fix it up. Whereas a golf course – now there's a good option.'

He shakes his head. 'I'm just doing my job, Amy. You know that. And if it does become a golf course, then at least the site will be open to the public. You should like that.'

'I've read the articles about Hexagon and their "sustainable developments". I'm sure you have too.' I stare him down.

'Look, babe,' he says. 'Do we have to talk about this now? This is a party. Let's go dance.'

He points to a cleared space across the room where Alistair is in the process of mauling Tessie to the tune of *It's Raining Men*. Claire and her husband step into the fray and join them.

I shake my head. 'I'd rather not.'

He purses his lips, obviously taking my refusal as a personal rejection. 'Why did you invite me tonight?' he asks. 'Because you needed a plus-one for your work party, or because you wanted to grill me about my report? It's obvious that you weren't seeking the pleasure of my company.'

He's got me, and I feel ashamed. David Waters came here in good faith, as my guest. I'm the one who's putting a damper on the evening. 'I'm sorry,' I say, smiling shakily. 'I'm a little too tipsy to dance. But we can sit and chat, and a glass of water might help.'

'Fine. I'll get you one.' He heads to the bar; I go to the loo to splash cold water on my face. As I enter, I find I'm not alone.

Alistair Bowen-Knowles is standing at the sink – in the *ladies'* loo – rubbing at a spot on his tie.

'Ah, Amy,' he slurs. 'Just the person I want in a crisis. Can you help me with this stain? It's red wine.'

With some trepidation, I walk over. Instead of showing me the tie, he leans in and kisses me, holding me by the shoulders. The snowman's nose flattens against my chest. I have the overwhelming urge to laugh out loud – this can't possibly be happening. For a second, I go limp, which catches him off guard. I push him away.

'Not a good idea.'

'Why not? It's Christmas. No strings attached, right?'

Anger and alcohol mix in my veins. I grip the edge of the sink; he's still standing too close. 'Two reasons really. One, I don't want to, and two, you're my—'

Tessie enters the loo, takes one look at the proceedings, and lets out a blood-curdling scream. People rush in – a blur of colleagues – pointing at me; I point at Alistair. My face in the mirror is as red as Rudolph's nose. And Jonathan is laughing and David swoops up and grabs me by the arm.

Cold air hits me in the face. I'm outside a fire exit being dragged away by David and, I notice, Claire.

'Are you all right?' she asks me.

'Yes, but it wasn't my fault – Mr Bowen-Knowles—'

'Don't worry,' she says. 'That happens sometimes when he gets drunk. Don't take it personally.'

'But how can he just... do that? It's awful. What if no one had come in?'

'I don't know,' David says angrily. 'What if no one had come in?'

I stare at him. 'What? You think I led him on? That's ridiculous.'

'I think the evening's over.'

'Yes,' I snap. 'I'll call a cab. I want to go home.'

'I'll drive you,' he says.

'Whatever.'

Claire retrieves my handbag and coat and bundles me into David's car. He's angry, and I'm angry; we drive in stormy silence all the way to Nailsea.

The outside of the bungalow is trimmed with a riot of multicoloured Christmas lights, white icicle lights, and this year, Dad's outdone himself with a tableau of near life-sized light-up plastic figures: Santa Claus, Rudolph, and – oddly – the baby Jesus, next to the door. As David pulls up in front, I feel quite sober and more than a little sorry. I put my hand on his arm. 'Sorry about tonight,' I say. 'You've every right to be angry. But since we're here, would you like to come in for a hot chocolate?'

'OK,' he says.

I remember too late that my parents are out on their anniversary night, and we'll have the house to ourselves. As we walk to the door, the automatic light flicks on like it's caught me in the act of doing something untoward. Next door, the curtains in Mrs Harvey's kitchen window twitch – no doubt she'll ring her friends at the Scrabble club to tell them that Amy Wood brought a bloke home when her parents were out.

The wreath wobbles precariously as I open the door and usher David inside. I'm suddenly aware of things I usually don't notice: the smell of English Leather soap that says 'ageing parents'; the tacky fibre optic tabletop Christmas tree; the fading floral three-piece suite in the sitting room that is not ageing gracefully. I feel ashamed of being ashamed. Not for my parents – they can live however they want – but rather, for myself. I'm the well-educated adult woman, being escorted back to her parents' house by her plus-one.

Once we're inside, David Waters approaches me with a come-hither look on his face. Clearly, he's looking forward to the 'kiss and make up' part of the evening. I teeter backwards. All of a sudden, everything feels wrong.

He reaches out for me.

I sidle away towards the kitchen and start babbling over my shoulder. 'I'm so cold – I'll just put the kettle on. Chocolate, I thought, unless you'd prefer coffee? I'll make one for Mum and Dad too. I'm sure they'll be home any minute now. You can meet them... or, if you don't want to – which I completely understand – we can do this another time and—'

'Amy.' He comes into the kitchen. 'I don't want any chocolate or coffee. I didn't want to talk to those people at the party, and I didn't want to dance or chat at that bar. I just want to be alone with you.' Drawing me close, he kisses me full on the lips while simultaneously unzipping my dress. I will myself to melt into his embrace, but my body automatically stiffens. He stops kissing and fumbling.

'I'm sorry,' I say. 'I'm just feeling... well, I did have a lot to drink.'

'Oh.' He holds me at arm's length. 'You're feeling sick?'

'A little. Plus...' I take a breath. 'This is all going a bit too fast for me.'

'Fast? We've been out exactly twice.'

'I know.'

'What is it?' His voice rises. 'The golf? That damned house?'

I wince. 'No really, it's not that. It may sound like a cliché, but it's not you... it's me—'

'Save it.' He holds up a hand. 'I get it. I'll go—'

'Amy, is that you?'

*Mum's voice.*

To my great horror, she appears in the kitchen doorway with Dad at her side. David looks flushed and dishevelled like he's *coitus interruptus* instead of *coitus rejectus.* My dress is hanging off me, my bra showing, and the kettle starts to boil furiously.

I rush over and switch it off.

'So sorry we interrupted you,' Mum coos to David, drawing him conspiratorially by the arm. 'Love the jumper, by the way.'

'We're so pleased that Amy's met a nice chap,' Dad chimes in.

'Actually, Dad,' I say, 'David was just leaving. His dog needs—'

'Don't worry, Mr and Mrs Wood.' Clearly, David means to torture me. 'The dog will be fine. I've been looking forward to meeting you – and dying for that chocolate.'

'Yes, Amy, please be polite.' Mum addresses me like an overgrown toddler. She draws David away into the sitting room. Dad follows them, humming *Some Enchanted Evening.*

Resigned to my fate, I load a tray with hot chocolate and biscuits, stalling as long as I can. Unfortunately, by the time I bring everything into the sitting room, Mum, Dad, and David are getting on famously, talking about light displays, holiday plans, Christmas jumpers, and party games, specifically Scrabble – my parents' favourite. Before I can voice an objection, the single-malt Scotch is out and the Super Scrabble board is on the table.

'No,' I groan. No one pays any attention.

We draw tiles to see who goes first. My head is half-nodding in sleep and I just want to crawl into bed – alone. But everyone else is going strong, and Mum gives me a little kick under the table.

I draw the high tile which goes first, and take six more terrible letters – ending up with a J, Z, E, two U's, an S and an X. All I can come up with is SEX on the double-word score.

'Ha!' Dad jokes. 'I guess you kids'll be up to that later, eh?'

'Dad!' I want to curl up in a ball and die.

'We'll have you both beaten in no time and then you can get on with it,' Mum says. 'Will you be all right on the sofa bed?'

'Just write down my twenty points, OK?'

David makes a crack about my parents' bed being more comfortable and everyone laughs but me. The three of them come up with a spontaneous new rule – extra points for every naughty word.

Mum has the next clincher with 'TOSS' and David manages somehow to make 'SHAG'. I'm hoping that at least all the S's are gone when Dad makes a coup using one of Mum's S's and the next thing I know, 'PENIS' has entered the fray.

The three of them rollick with laughter, slapping each other on the back. I silently palm a few tiles, hoping to make the game go faster.

My next turn, I make 'BANKER' and everyone frowns. I'm obviously a party pooper. When someone offers to trade me a 'W' for the 'B', I push my rack of letters away and stand up. 'That's it!' I say. 'I'm going to bed.'

The laughter fades. Mum looks embarrassed. Dad and David both look annoyed.

'I've had a rough day and a lot to drink. I need sleep.'

David stands up. 'I've had a lovely time. But I should be going.'

'No,' Dad practically pleads. 'Finish the game. I haven't had this much fun since Amy's boyfriend... I mean – ex-boyfriend... heh, heh... took me go-cart racing...'

'Well, if you insist.' Smiling triumphantly, David sits back down. I give him an obligatory peck on the lips.

'Thanks for an interesting evening,' I manage.

'Sure,' he says. 'See you around.'

He doesn't look at me as he lays down his next word: 'SUCKS'.

# 25

Driving to work on Monday, I amuse myself by trying to decide which weekend debacle was most humiliating. From the three disastrous viewings to the Christmas party and its aftermath, it's impossible to pick a winner. When I enter the office, immediately I sense a collective flashback to the shenanigans at the party. Jonathan gives me a fake 'come hither' look, and Claire asks me if I made it home all right after the party. 'Yes, thanks,' I say, my cheeks hot with embarrassment. I sit down to check my emails. Before I've even deleted the day's spam, Mr Bowen-Knowles's office door bangs open. He blusters out, without a hint of regret or apology, and gets straight down to business.

'Amy,' he says sternly, 'I've just had a Mr Patel on the line. You showed him a property?'

I shudder at the memory of the fourth most humiliating experience of the weekend: getting chased out of a crack house by squatters.

'That's right,' I say.

'He's just rang with an offer. Sounded fairly genuine. He wants to exchange this week, if possible.'

Though I recall Mr Patel's enthusiasm with the laser measure, still, I'm stunned.

'He said you convinced him it had great potential.'

'I did?' I practically choke. 'I mean... yes, I did.'

Mr Bowen-Knowles's lip curves up in what might be construed as a smile. Not the wolfish, lecherous grin I've seen from him before, but one that is almost genuine. One that, despite his behaviour at the Christmas party, almost smacks of respect. And I realise that, for better or for worse, this job is for real, and I can do it. I look around: Claire is smiling; Jonathan is glaring; Patricia is putting on lipstick.

Mr Bowen-Knowles shakes my hand and returns to his office. I sit back in my chair, my hand smarting from his firm grip. I may never get to the top of the sales chart. I may have sent a decent bloke packing without so much as a proper good-night kiss. I may be living with my parents and causing them perpetual disappointment because I haven't inherited the Scrabble gene. But none of that matters right now...

I've made a sale. That's something to be proud of.

* * *

At lunchtime, Claire and I sit outside the Assembly Rooms watching the tourists, and she fills me in on the Christmas party antics that occurred after I left: Mr Bowen-Knowles moved on to snog Patricia under the mistletoe; Tessie left in tears and got her own taxi; Jonathan punched someone from the Cardiff office over a slur about his rugby team. I decline to fill her in on the later events of my evening. I like the way she sees me as a co-conspirator rather than just an object of gossip. By the time we return to the office, my sides hurt from laughing, my hands are freezing from sitting outside, and the day has a general winter glow about it.

Until about an hour after lunch when once again, Mr Bowen-Knowles bursts forth from his office and summons me.

I sense that my good luck has run out.

'A Nigel Netelbaum phoned from Hexagon,' he says, perching on the edge of his desk. 'They're going to send through the offer for the Rosemont property. If we do the legwork, we should be able to pocket the commission even though Kendall's client – that idiot "Mr Jack" – negotiated the deal. At least, you'd better hope we can, or else it's all been a colossal waste of time.'

I open my mouth but can't speak as the cracks in my heart steal my breath.

'They're sending someone round to look at the house. See what it will take to transform it. Clubhouse, pro shop, fine-dining restaurant, cigar parlour, members-only VIP lounge.' As he gleefully outlines the possibilities, I imagine that he's mentally practising his belly putt for his first round there with David Waters.

'But if that doesn't fly with the antis and the blue-hair brigade, they'll build the clubhouse on the other side of the property. The planners have hinted that they can leave the house to crumble – as long as they fence it off so no one gets hurt. Then they can crack on with everything else: the floodlit driving range, car park, buggy rental, and so forth. The planners seem pretty happy just to let them run with it.'

'But what about my three months to find a buyer?' I croak. 'Someone to restore it as a family home? Or... or even flats?'

Mr Bowen-Knowles laughs in my face. 'Come on, Amy, get a grip. As long as we get our commission then it's a success. You've had plenty of time to come up with other alternatives.

Your efforts to date have been... let's be frank... industrious, but also ineffectual.'

'That's not exactly true—'

'You've had what – two viewings?'

'One,' I mutter. Cinderella's clock has short-circuited and all too soon struck midnight. Her dress shreds to rags; the golden coach turns back into a pumpkin.

He shrugs like he's not surprised. 'Anyway, someone from Hexagon will ring to arrange the viewing – probably mid-Jan. Start pulling everything together: the site plan, the surveyor's report, the probate petition. Let's be ready to move quickly. Oh, and get in touch with Kendall – make sure his "Mr Jack" agrees in writing to our commission. These Americans can be such hard-arses...'

I stop listening; what's the point? Just this morning I was celebrating my success, but now the party is well and truly over. Once Rosemont Hall is gone with me failing to save it, I'll be left, if I'm lucky, with the odd Mr Patel or two in between failures like the Blundells—

'Amy? Have you heard a word I've said?'

Given that 'no' is not an acceptable answer, I settle for a hoarse laugh. 'Of course, Mr Bowen-Knowles,' I say. 'I'm happy to help out in any way I can.'

* * *

I seek the sanctuary of the disabled loo to hide tears that appear from nowhere. When I emerge, Claire is in the kitchen. 'Are you all right, Amy?' she asks gently.

'Fine.'

'Did he say something about the Christmas party?'

'No. It's Rosemont Hall.'

She opens the cupboard, pushing aside the 'I'd rather be... GOLFING' mug. 'That was always going to be a long shot,' she says.

'I know. It's just all got away from me so quickly, and I really wanted to make a difference—'

'Amy,' Mr Bowen-Knowles bellows.

Good grief, what now?

'Yes?' I say wearily.

'Go back to the house in Glastonbury,' he orders. 'The police are on their way to clear out the squatters. Make sure they don't damage the house – we need to preserve Mr Patel's investment.'

And just like that, the day goes from bad to worse: an afternoon spent ducking thrown beer bottles and dodging police crossfire (in truth, all I do is sit in my car while the police arrest the four thugs, do the paperwork, and take a statement from me and my new best friend Mr Patel).

And once again, I rue the day that I ever set foot in the offices of Tetherington Bowen-Knowles.

# PART III

As I stood there hushed and still, I could swear that the house was not an empty shell but lived and breathed as it had lived before.

Light came from the windows, the curtains blew softly in the night air, and there, in the library, the door would stand half open as we had left it, with my handkerchief on the table beside the bowl of autumn roses.

— *DAPHNE DU MAURIER – REBECCA*

# 26

*A—*

*God forgive me – I have been such a fool. He means to ruin our plans, but I will not let him! We must play along with this little charade for tonight, but tomorrow—*

# 27

In real life, there are no happy endings. Only ups and downs and new beginnings, loose ends, a few laughs, and many tears. This I realise during the course of the next few weeks, which fly past in a blur. Christmas comes and goes (my parents and I exchange gifts of socks and bath smellies), then New Year (my parents lament my poor taste in having jettisoned the most willing Scrabble player they've had in years).

As a break from the festivities, I transcribe the letters I found. The hours leading up to the ball and Henry's cryptic last letter niggle in my head like an itch I can't quite scratch. I look for clues in the sketchbook as to the identity of the artist, but find none. All I know is that he was most likely Spanish, and was captivated by the image of Arabella Windham in her pink dress.

The keys to Rosemont Hall remain at the office, locked in a desk drawer. Early in January, I ring David Waters (who hasn't called me since our Scrabble night) and apologise for my behaviour. Admittedly, it's a relief when it goes to voicemail, but

I also experience a tiny flicker of doubt – did I let him go too easily?

Eventually, he rings the office. We make the obligatory small talk and harmless flirtations, and I wonder if he's calling to see if I've changed my mind about seeing him again. I almost do change my mind. But then, he asks to speak to Mr Bowen-Knowles. I realise that he's not pining after me, and didn't even ring to speak to me at all.

'Oh, so you want to schedule another round of golf, then?' I joke to hide my embarrassment.

'Actually' – his tone is deadly serious – 'it's not a golf round that we're planning, but the golf course. I'm going to work on some costings. I'd love to get more business opportunities in golf course development.'

'Just a minute,' I choke, 'I'll see if he's available.'

In a way, I'm relieved as I transfer the call to my boss. I'm now convinced that I no longer require the services of David Waters on either a personal or a professional level.

Things begin to look up when, a week later, Mr Patel completes on the Glastonbury house. My name goes straight to the top of the sales chart on the door of the disabled loo. The winter days gradually begin to lengthen, and although I have several promising client viewings of 'character cottages', 'charming semis', and even a 'top-notch barn conversion', I'm not one jot closer to finding anyone to rescue Rosemont Hall.

The long shadow of the meeting with Hexagon's representative hangs over my head. As the days pass, every phone call to the office, every email enquiry, kindles my fears. Each night when I go home, I feel a sense of relief like a prisoner who's received a stay of execution. Each morning when I enter the office, I experience the same creeping dread that today might be the day.

On a grey Wednesday afternoon, the last week in January, the axe falls.

I return from a lunch hour spent browsing the last of the sales to find a telephone memo on my chair.

*Meeting confirmed for Rosemont Hall, Saturday 31 January 11 a.m. Mr Faraday.*

Hexagon. Mr Faraday. At least now the demon has a name. I drop my other work and make one last Herculean effort to find an alternative buyer. I phone and re-phone anyone who has shown even the slightest interest. But thanks to David Waters and his repair estimate, everyone has been put off. As a last resort, I ring up Ronan Keene, the footballer. I'm surprised when he answers himself, and even more surprised when he remembers me.

'Hullo, Amy,' he says. 'I'm glad you called. In fact, I've been meaning to ring you.'

'Oh, well, that's nice.' A splinter of hope pricks my heart.

'We looked on your website at that penthouse flat in Bristol. Crystal's very excited. She thinks it might be just the place for us. What was it you said? Our "together home"?'

'Great.' I cross them off as 'possibles' for Rosemont Hall, but business is business. There's a right home for everyone, and I want to find it for them.

'You know the one I mean? The penthouse?'

'I certainly do.'

I picture Fred Blundell sitting in jail. He and Mary had been so excited to find their 'forever home' before promptly losing it. Criminal or no, I feel sorry for them. I wish things – a lot of things – had turned out differently.

'It's a showpiece flat,' I tell him. 'Ultra-modern, lots of light, great for entertaining. And brand new,' I emphasise. 'Not pre-lived in. I'm sure you and Crystal will love it.'

I gush a little more about the roof terrace and the views. He seems delighted, and we make arrangements for a viewing. By the time we end the call, I'm confident that I can match up Ronan Keene and Crystal with their perfect flat. But as for Rosemont Hall, I've singularly failed.

# 28

The dreaded day dawns bright and clear with a dusting of snow on the ground. The roads are slick, so I give myself plenty of extra time to drive to Rosemont Hall. I arrive early enough to stop off in the local village for a coffee and muffin to calm my nerves. There's a twee little tea shop called the Cup o' Comfort that looks welcoming and smells delicious. I park the car in a loading zone and run in. The tea shop is nearly full with pensioners and families taking advantage of the £3.95 full English advertised on a blackboard outside. A harried, elderly woman in a calico apron serves me a huge scone that's dripping with fresh butter on a willow-patterned plate. There's an embarrassing moment when I remind her that I've asked for it to take away, and she purses her lips and chucks it into a paper bag. The Cup o' Comfort doesn't have any takeaway cups either, so I decide to skip the coffee.

Outside, the sun has disappeared, and the sky has turned a bruised purple-brown colour that means more snow is coming. I dare to hope that Hexagon's stooge will be put off by the weather and not turn up.

With the hour upon me, I drive the rest of the way to the house. The avenue of trees is covered with a few inches of snow, but my car ploughs through it easily. If I can make it, so can Mr Faraday.

I sit in the car, fogging up the windows with my breath, shivering a little in the chill. Ten minutes go by, then twenty. Mr Faraday is late. If I left now, surely I'd be in the clear. At the very least I could cause inconvenience by making him schedule another viewing.

Before I can execute my plan, a vehicle approaches: a blue Vauxhall Corsa – a newer model than mine. Not the flash sports car or monster SUV I'd have expected a Hexagon executive to drive.

The car parks next to mine. A man jumps out – I glimpse a red ski jacket and dark hair. I walk a few steps towards his car.

'Mr Faraday? I'm Amy Wood, the—'

I stop.

He stops.

Our eyes meet.

'—estate agent...' I finish to break the remarkable silence. In an instant, the world has shrunk into a bubble around me and this stranger. He stares back at me, his sharp-chiselled face framed by soft, dark brown hair. I shiver again, but not with the cold.

'Hello,' he says, his voice deep and penetrating. 'I'm sorry I'm late. Thanks for coming out in this weather.'

I blink hard and time comes rushing back. I remember who I am and what I'm doing, who this man is, and why this can't possibly be happening.

'Oh, no problem,' I stammer. 'It's my... pleasure.'

I can't meet his eyes – a soft blue-grey like the winter sky. Looking past him, I hold out my hand. He takes it and our fingers touch. He's smiling at me; the puffs of our breath mingle as he speaks. 'To be honest, I wasn't expecting this snow. The rental car's not really cut out for this weather...'

A few things register: Accent = American. Our hands = still together.

Hexagon.

I jerk mine away.

# 29

I don't like him. He's anathema to everything I believe in. He's an unfeeling Neanderthal who's come to ravage a piece of history. I'm *determined* not to like him.

It's just...

I'm acutely aware of his presence as we trudge through the snow towards the front door. I don't speak – I can't speak. I know I should start talking my spiel about the house. Try to appeal to his humanity, if he has any. But the words won't come.

As we reach the front door, he points to the frost-caked lintel.

'Is that the family crest?' he asks.

'Yes.' I look up at the carved stone to avoid glimpsing the face that might bewitch me. 'The house came into the Windham family in the early 1800s, not long after it was built. I believe the owner added it then. It's a dog and unicorn.' I press my lips together. He can't possibly be interested.

'A dog and unicorn?'

'It stands for fidelity and virtue.'

'Hmm,' he muses. 'How odd.'

'Odd?'

He turns towards me. I take a quick step back.

'I guess that's the wrong word,' he says. 'It's just that I wasn't expecting the place to be quite so...'

A wave of relief passes over me. The place is way too rundown for anyone – even Hexagon – to bother with. They'll build their golf course somewhere else. I'll go home and try to forget that I ever laid eyes on this man who's—

'...beautiful.'

'Beautiful?' Warmth oozes through my veins. 'You really think so?'

'It's obviously a fixer-upper, but the outside is pretty amazing. I guess maybe because you're English, you see these things every day and don't notice them any more.'

'Well actually...'

'Where I'm from, ancient history starts about 1900,' he says. 'I was never that interested in exploring Europe. It's a typical American attitude, I'm afraid. We've got our own history, and lots of interesting things in our own country. And when I learned about European history at school, all they really focused on were the wars, the beheadings, and the six wives of Henry VIII. None of it seemed very "real", if you know what I mean.'

'No... I mean – yes.' I fumble for the keys. 'And I suppose people can play golf anywhere.'

He raises an eyebrow as if studying me. What does he conclude? Why do I care?

'I guess that's true,' he says. 'Though I don't play myself.'

'Really?' I assume he's joking.

'No, I never got into it. What was it that Mark Twain said? "Golf is a good walk spoiled"?'

I stare at him in surprise. 'Yes, that's right.' I unlock the door. This must be a ploy – some dirty little trick of Hexagon to catch me off guard, lull me into a false sense of security.

We step inside the great hall. It's freezing, but the air seems heavy and close. I remove my pink cashmere scarf and drape it over the staircase banister. Mr Faraday looks around the room and lets out a low whistle.

'This place must have been really something in its day,' he says. 'Can't you just picture it? Ladies in silk gowns, gentlemen in top hats. Servants scurrying about... Amazing. I mean, you see places like this on TV and read about them in books. But to actually be here... it's completely different.' He smiles wistfully. 'If the house could talk, I bet it would have some interesting things to say. You can practically feel the history crackling in the air, can't you?'

'Well...' No. *This* man, of all people, cannot possibly be the one person who understands.

'But I think the surveyor hit the nail on the head,' he says. 'It would cost a small fortune to fix up. No – make that a *large* fortune.'

'I definitely agree. The place is a money pit.' I raise my hands in futility. 'A huge, unwieldy white elephant. And although the surveyor's report says it would cost at least three million pounds just to get it to comply with building regs' – I lower my voice – 'I happen to know that he was just being kind. I'm sure Hexagon would be better off building their golf course somewhere else. The only way this place is going to be saved is if someone buys it to fix up as a labour of love.'

I take a breath and gear up to lie in grand Tetherington Bowen-Knowles fashion. 'Besides,' I say, 'no matter who your friends are in the planning department, you'll be tied up in red tape for ages. There's an army of old ladies in the village ready to challenge any change of use. They'd rather see it crumble to the ground than have a golf course here. And I've heard there are some protected insects near the village. And bats – there are loads of bats that live up in the eaves. Your plans will be nothing but hassle and headache, let me tell you.'

'I guess that's good to know.' He gives me a puzzled frown. 'But aren't you supposed to be selling the place?'

'Oh.' I laugh coyly. 'Yes, I am. But I don't want to lead you up the garden path. I think it would make someone a fantastic family home. Someone who loves it and has the wherewithal to restore it. It's just the merits as an investment that I question.'

'All property is an investment,' he says. 'If you live in it, develop it, rent it out – whether you keep it or sell it, it all has financial consequences. And this place' – he waves his hand to take in the great hall – 'it *is* a money pit. I did some research of my own when I first saw the surveyor's report. Apparently, with a listed building, it's incredibly hard to make any alterations, and every material used for restoration has to be authentic and in keeping with the original. That will put most people off. I seriously doubt you'll find someone to take it on as a "labour of love".'

'You never know.' I smile. 'There's a right house for everyone, and a right owner for every house. Someone who belongs to the house as much as the house belongs to them. I'm working on finding the right combination for this house.'

'You're like a house matchmaker, is that it?' His eyes dance with amusement.

'Precisely.'

He walks into the first drawing room off the main hall and opens the curtains; a cloud of dust engulfs us. Mr Faraday looks around the room and goes over to the table where someone – Mrs Bradford, I assume – has left a pile of papers and newspaper clippings. He picks up the top one: a page of obituaries.

'Sorry for the mess,' I say. 'The housekeeper, Mrs Bradford, is a bit shaken by everything that's happened. It's too bad really, but she's gone a bit barmy.'

'A bit barmy?' He laughs. 'I like that.' He skims over the paper and sets it back on top of the others. 'Do you know if Mrs Windham died in the house?'

'Oh yes.' Actually, I have no idea, but I seize the opportunity to put him off. 'Right upstairs in the main bedroom. The body was here for days before anyone discovered it. Luckily, the smell has dissipated.'

Mr Faraday doesn't respond. Instead, he walks through to the blue salon. He touches things – marble mantels, old books and photos, the carved panelling – almost reverently. He's lost in thought. Maybe he's picturing all the rich men in collared shirts drinking whisky and smoking cigars in the parlour after their eighteen holes. But somehow, I don't think so. Nonetheless, he is who he is, and we are where we are.

We finish downstairs and return to the great hall. 'Interested in seeing the upstairs?' I ask cheekily. 'It's even more of a tip.'

'Sure,' he says. The warmth has gone out of his voice. I feel an odd sense of guilt – like I'm the one betraying the house, not him.

I lead the way up the stairs and pause before the portrait of the young woman. I rub my fingers along the frame as if to say 'Hello again'.

He stops beside me, looks at the painting, then at my hand, which is still touching the frame. Sheepishly, I withdraw it.

'Who is she? Do you know?' He leans in and studies the brushwork.

'I'm fairly sure it's Arabella Windham.'

'Those eyes...' he says. 'She looks familiar somehow. And what's that in her hands? Paper, or letters, maybe?'

'I don't know,' I say. 'Maybe you'll discover the answer when you start ripping the house apart piece by piece.'

As soon as the words come out, I can't believe I've said them. Mr Faraday's face hardens.

'I'm sorry,' I say, 'that was totally out of line.' Turning away, I go to the edge of the landing and look out over the elegant hall. 'You must think I'm the barmy one. I've obviously grown too fond of this place...' I can't even finish. It sounds so silly, and it's pointless to try and explain. But something about this man seems to demand it. 'It should be nothing to me,' I say. 'I'm just the estate agent. But this house is special. I'd love to see it go to a family that loves it, or else see it preserved and opened up to the public. I hate the idea that yet another great English house is about to be changed into something beyond recognition. I'm sorry.'

I look at him out of the corner of my eye. He's staring at the picture like he hasn't heard me.

Unable to bear his presence, I leave him there and go into the first bedroom. This one doesn't have a working loo or a closet full of fancy-dress costumes, but it does have the same clutter spanning decades, even as far back as the 1930s. On the mantel, there's a photograph of a young couple standing on either side of the queen, and a photograph of the same man standing next to Winston Churchill. I pick up the photograph and blow the dust off the frame.

Mr Faraday comes into the room after me. His eyes seem to pierce my skin and see inside the depths of my soul. To my great shame and dismay, I almost hope Hexagon does pursue their development – so I might have a reason to see him again.

'I admit that things are not quite what I had expected,' he says. 'I can almost see where you get your romantic notions from. But unfortunately, reality is something quite different. The public will get to enjoy the estate, or at least, the members of the golf club. There are worse results, surely.'

I set the photograph back on the mantel. 'I just wish I had more time.'

'Unfortunately, that's something you don't have,' he says. 'You're obviously a passionate person, Miss Wood, and I admire that. But maybe you're also too quick to judge a book by its cover.' He smiles like he's won a victory over me, and at that moment, I do hate him a little. I maintain a discreet distance as he walks through the other rooms. He seems lost in thought, touching a damp spot here, a crumbling window frame there.

Eventually, we go up to the attic. I stand beside him, looking out of the huge round window to the parkland that stretches as far as the eye can see. Far below us, the fountain crumbles and the long tree-lined avenue snakes downwards from the house into a little valley. A cloud of dust rises – I can almost see Mr Rochester riding furiously towards Thornfield, his horse wild-eyed and lathered, straining at the bit, when all of a sudden, he encounters Jane Eyre on the path—

'Damn,' Mr Faraday says, pulling me back to my senses. There is no horse and no lord of the manor, but a car is coming up the drive, scattering snow in its wake.

'If you want to keep looking around, Mr Faraday,' I say, 'I can go see who it is.'

'Fine. Thanks.' When he smiles at me, I sense that he sees everything – from my ridiculous fantasies with him in a starring role to how much I wish they could be true. And I can't bear to think that he might be laughing at me, thinking I'm pathetic and eccentric – or worse.

I leave the room, breaking the spell he's cast over me. I rush down the stairs two at a time. The last thing I need is an ill-timed visit from Mrs Bradford and Captain, and I want to head them off at the pass.

But as I reach the bottom, I see that it's not Mrs Bradford.

'Oh, hello,' I blurt out.

It's the Windham heir, Ms Flora, looking polished and perfect in her dark green Burberry coat, black stiletto boots, and black pashmina. I had no idea she was back in town.

'Hello, Miss Wood.' She unbuttons her coat. 'How are you?'

'I'm well,' I say, returning the smile. 'I'm just showing around an executive from Hexagon. We won't be much longer – is that OK?'

She arches an eyebrow. 'Hexagon? You must be joking.'

'No—?'

'Actually, Miss Wood,' she interrupts, 'you can go now. I'll lock up. I need to speak to my brother in private.'

# 30

Brother?

As soon as Flora says the word, the penny drops. Mr Faraday is not, in fact, an executive from Hexagon, but the second American heir – Mr Jack – and now that I know the truth, it seems blindingly obvious. I rewind the sequence of events, from my boss telling me that an executive from Hexagon wanted to schedule a viewing, to me jumping to the conclusion that Mr Faraday was said person. But although wires were crossed, Jack Faraday must have guessed my mistake. How dare he deceive me like that?

Finally, I have a good reason to hate him.

But when he comes down the grand staircase, his sheer *je ne sais quoi* hits me all over again. I feel like Jane Eyre after she's been half flattened by Rochester's horse and lashed with his whip. His blue-grey eyes flick from me to his sister.

'Hi, Flora. Glad you could join us.' He sounds anything but.

'Sorry to blow your cover, Jack, but I don't want you to get too comfy playing lord of the manor.' Tension crackles in the air between them. She turns to me like she's dismissing a servant. 'Can you see yourself out?'

I look from her to Jack. He shrugs like Flora's in charge, and it's nothing to him anyway. 'Thanks for showing me around, Miss Wood,' he says. 'It's been interesting. I'll call your office tomorrow, OK?'

'Sure, no problem,' I say through clenched teeth. I hurry to the door and practically run to the car.

* * *

'Bloody hell!' I bang my fist on the steering wheel. How could I have said those things? *Luckily, the smell has dissipated*!

And to be fair, while Mr Faraday didn't come clean and say that he was co-owner of the house, in fact, he never denied it either. He might even have assumed I knew. *Aren't you supposed to be selling the place?*

God. I drive off in a spray of snow and gravel. The view of Rosemont Hall in the rear-view mirror is sure to be my last.

# 31

After two sleepless nights and a miserable Sunday afternoon spent helping Dad demolish the old garden shed, when Monday morning rolls around, I still feel furious, embarrassed, and every other negative emotion in between. I seriously debate taking a sickie. But in the end, I can't stand the thought of sitting at home stewing in my juices while Mum potters around and Dad waits for the Argos delivery of a new prefab shed. Besides, since I'm obviously going to have nothing more to do with Rosemont Hall, I may as well give Jack Faraday a piece of my mind when he rings the office.

Jack Faraday. I think back to all my ludicrous imaginings of him: fat and middle-aged, a New-York ball buster, Bill Gates – all golf-playing, and all based on nothing at all. Whereas in reality, I now know that he's devious, underhanded, and... beautiful. Every nerve in my body tingles when I recall the sound of his voice and the electric moment when we shook hands.

Which is just ridiculous.

How could he, of all people, be the one person who feels a

connection to the house? And feeling that connection, how could he betray it? He's even worse, much worse, than I thought.

And so much better.

I change my outfit three times, but I'm no less distracted. Then, as I'm about to leave the house, I can't find my pink cashmere scarf, which was an end-of-term gift from my students from the one and only class I taught. I'd be sorry to lose it. I've a vague recollection that I wore it to the Rosemont Hall viewing. It's another freezing morning, so I grab one of Mum's chunky knit snoods instead. I'll call Mr Kendall to arrange to get it back. Sometime when I know for sure that Jack Faraday won't be there.

Jack Faraday. I'm not going to think about him. Full stop. I get to the office and check my emails. There's one from my former graduate thesis advisor, attaching an advert for a job in Edinburgh teaching literature at a private school for girls. *Happy to put in a word for you*, his note reads. I stare at the screen, conscious of how much my life has moved on since I lost my teaching job. I think of the Blundells, David Waters, Hexagon, and Rosemont Hall. For all the slings and arrows I've encountered at Tetherington Bowen-Knowles, I have a strange notion that, for the first time, I've been experiencing life – not just reading about it. And then there's Jack Faraday. I shiver at the memory of the brief, fleeting *realness* of him.

*Get a grip!* I reply immediately to the email: 'Thank you! The job sounds perfect. I'll definitely send in my CV.'

The phone rings. I stare at the blinking light on the switchboard. It's *him* – I just know it.

The light stops blinking but doesn't go out. From the bowels of Mr Bowen-Knowles's office, I can hear his muffled voice. He's picked up the phone, and I've missed my chance to do damage control. But that's fine, because I'm not going to think about Jack.

The phone rings again. My heart leaps into my mouth. Maybe *this* is him.

I jerk the phone off the cradle. 'Tetherington Bowen-Knowles, Amy Wood speaking.'

It's Ronan Keene ringing to schedule a viewing at the Bristol flat. We go through all the details and arrange it for that same afternoon. Which is fine by me. Anything to get my mind off *other things*.

When I hang up the phone, Mr Bowen-Knowles's line is still lit. The suspense is killing me. I stand up. 'Anyone for Starbucks?' I say. Over the last few months, my willingness to do the coffee run has somewhat defrosted the hearts of my colleagues, but today, I just need to clear my head.

Everyone orders their usual (skinny decaf latte for Patricia; Earl Grey tea for Jonathan; Americano for Claire) and I leave the office practically at a run.

The day is grey and foggy, but nonetheless, Bath is buzzing with tourists and shoppers. The traffic crawls by, people push past me, and I feel like I'm in a bad dream where I'm being chased through the woods but my feet are too heavy to run. The dreadful mistake I made on Rosemont Hall continues to loom in my mind. As does the delicious and unscrupulous Jack Faraday.

As I'm waiting for the order to be prepared, I'm startled by a tap on my shoulder. 'Amy Wood? Is that you?'

I turn around. It's Mary Blundell. She's gives me a smile that's homely and open, and if I didn't know better, I never would have pegged her as someone who's married to an art thief and dreams of living in an ultra-modern penthouse flat.

'Hi, Mary,' I say with real enthusiasm, 'how are you getting on?'

'Fine – we're fine.' By some unspoken cue, we both collect our drinks and sit down together at a little table by the door.

'I can only stay a few minutes,' she says. 'I'm on my way to London to visit Fred at Holloway.'

'And is Fred doing… OK?' I figure I can ask since she brought him up.

'Yes, he's good. He's using his time inside to write a business plan for a new gallery we hope to open.'

'Really?'

'Yes. The prison has a good library, and he's making lots of good contacts.'

'Oh,' I say, a bit less enthusiastically. 'How interesting.'

'We were gutted to lose the Bristol flat,' Mary adds. 'As soon as Fred's out, I'll ring you. We'd still love a flat like that, but on a bit of a smaller budget.' She winks.

'Sure.' I smile. She may have criminal associations, but still, I'd like to help her and Fred find their perfect 'remand home'. I decide to come right out and ask her how her husband got into his… 'business'.

Mary sips her coffee thoughtfully. 'Fred always loved art,' she says. 'Did you know – he studied to be a painter in Madrid?'

'Really?'

'Yeah. But he was rubbish at it. His flatmate had an uncle who was an artist. Tio Francisco. The uncle was a hero during World War Two. He helped wealthy Jewish families smuggle their art to safety from the Nazis.'

'Wow,' I say. 'That *is* interesting.'

'But after the war, Tio Francisco went back to more mundane things. Art smuggling and that sort of thing. He taught his nephew, Fred's flatmate, the tricks of the trade. They started a business together.'

'And it's been... lucrative?'

'No risk, no reward, Amy,' she says good-naturedly. 'Fred sees it as his mission to make sure great art gets appreciated.'

'Umm... how exactly?'

'Well, who do you think will appreciate a great work of art the most – a collector who loves it and is willing to pay for it, or your average Joe, day-tripping through a museum?'

'I've never thought of it that way.'

'It's all a matter of perspective.' She grins. 'You say "tomato" and all that—'

Her phone beeps in her pocket. She rummages for it and frowns at the screen. 'Sorry, Amy, I should go. Flipping French postal workers – always striking when you need them.'

I don't dare ask. With a conspiratorial grin and a little wave, she walks briskly out of the café.

* * *

Everyone's coffee is cold. Back at the office, I dole out the goods and collect money (today I end up short-changed by 22p). Mr Bowen-Knowles's phone line is still lit and his muffled voice seems louder than usual. Meeting Mary Blundell was temporarily distracting, and it was interesting to hear about Fred's art 'career'. But I still have the Jack Faraday debacle to deal with. I sit down at my desk and wait for the inevitable to happen.

The inevitable takes exactly seven minutes to occur. I'm sipping the last of my hot chocolate when Mr Bowen-Knowles's door opens with a smack against the wall.

'You' – he points at me – 'in here.'

I am thus summoned.

All eyes are on me as I embark on the familiar walk of shame. Though the Christmas Party incident has never been discussed, mentioned, or repeated, fleetingly, I wonder if my colleagues think I'm putting in a little 'overtime' behind closed doors.

'Sit down.'

I thus obey.

He sits down opposite me, steeples his fingers, and frowns.

'Ian Kendall rang about Rosemont Hall. I hear there was quite a mix-up.'

'Yes, you could say that.' My anger simmers. 'But you could also say that the viewing was arranged under false pretences. I may not have the right accent, or have gone to the right schools, but my time is not worthless.' I stare him boldly in the face. 'Saturday was a waste of time. I'm hardly going to sell a property to someone who owns it already, am I? So if you or Mr Jack are annoyed with me – well...' I stop just short of telling him where to go.

Mr Bowen-Knowles sits back in his chair and appraises me. I furiously calculate the odds that his next words will send me packing. I'm too angry to care, although I *do* care – more than I want to – about a great many things.

'Jack Faraday would like you to ring him,' he says. 'I gather he wanted to see the house and didn't have a key.'

'You said that Hexagon was sending someone around,' I say heatedly. 'But no one's rung me. I assumed that this Jack Faraday was their rep. It was an honest mistake.'

'Look, "Mr Jack" is a moron – that's obvious. I'm as annoyed as you are.'

I doubt that, but I'm surprised he's taking my side.

'You've done as well as could be expected. That old pile was never going to sell. And most importantly, you *looked* like you were doing your job.'

'Oh?'

'Yeah. Kendall said that Hexagon came in with a formal offer this morning. It's on the low side, but Mr Jack talked them up from the original figure. He's going to accept it and cut his losses.'

I wring my hands together, struggling to stay composed.

Mr Bowen-Knowles fiddles idly with his cufflink. 'But because we did the viewings, we're going to get partial commission. The Hexagon rep will email you to sort out the paperwork. I doubt he'll bother to go round the place now. It's down to numbers, plans, and cash.'

'I see.' I stand up. 'Thank you, Mr Bowen-Knowles. I appreciate your telling me.'

My chest aches and my breathing is shallow as I walk out of his office feeling like I've been diagnosed with a fatal disease. I grab my handbag from my desk and leave through the back door, desperate to get away from the office. There's the Ronan Keene viewing in Bristol, but it's not for several hours yet. I get in the car and start driving.

As I leave Bath, I think of the literary heroines I've encountered over the years. All of them had to cope with bad things happening – tension is a necessary part of good literature. I wonder if I'm an Elinor Dashwood in *Sense and Sensibility*. Even when she thinks she's been jilted by Edward, she bears her sorrows with a stiff upper lip. Or maybe I'm a Jane Eyre – she votes with her feet when she discovers that Mr Rochester already has a wife locked away in the attic.

I honk the horn at a lorry that's overtaking another lorry. At least I've no penchant to be an Emma Bovary or Anna Karenina. The ends they chose were extreme, not to mention messy.

Instead of heading to Bristol, I take a detour. To Rosemont Hall. Surely no one would mind if I pop inside quickly to find my scarf.

I drive slowly through the gates, savouring what is bound to be my last visit. I try to memorise the details and the view of the house when the road tops the crest of the hill. The huge silhouette against the sky always makes my heart beat faster.

But today, the view is marred by another huge silhouette: a removals lorry backed up to the front door. I slam on the brakes, skidding across the verge.

In addition to the removals van, there are two cars – Jack Faraday's hired Vauxhall and Flora's Mercedes. Two burly men are loading something heavy into the back of the lorry.

I do a swift three-point turn and floor it back to the main road. Once I'm outside the twisted iron gates, I discover once and for all which kind of romantic literary heroine I would be. The kind who, when faced with adversity, pulls her car over to a lay-by, puts her head against the steering wheel, and cries.

* * *

I may have lost both battle and war, but I still have a flat to show in Bristol. Maybe if I sell enough penthouse flats to footballers, someday I'll be able to afford a little flat in a historic house conversion next to a golf course.

Perish the thought.

While the car is stopped, I remember that I'm supposed to ring Jack Faraday. I dig in my handbag, throwing out the contents on the seat. At the bottom, I find the yellow sticky with the information for the 'Hexagon viewing' – Mr Faraday's mobile number.

Knowing that he's busy directing removals men to bin his deceased relatives' precious belongings lends me courage to dial the number. Courage that immediately evaporates when he answers the phone, and instead, I experience a very strong, very unwelcome surge of adrenalin through my body.

'Oh, hello,' I stammer. 'It's Amy Wood. The estate agent.'

'Amy...' His brusque tone warms. 'I'm glad you called.'

'Mr Bowen-Knowles said you asked me to ring you?'

'Yes, yes. I... just a second.'

A commotion erupts in the background (a woman's voice yelling: 'No! The one with the sticker, not that old thing!').

'Sorry, Amy,' Jack says a moment later. 'It's not really a great time for me to talk, but listen, is there any chance you can come over to the house tonight? Say, around seven?'

I hesitate; the blood rushes in my ear. 'I could,' I say, 'but I'm not sure—'

A loud crash echoes in the background.

'Damn!' Jack's voice. 'Sorry, Amy – did you say yes or no? I think you left your scarf here.'

'Well, yes, but—'

'Great, I'll see you around seven.'

'But—'

The call ends.

I roll down the window to let in the cold air. The lay-by reeks of urine. A car whizzes past.

Jack Faraday wants me to stop by so he can return my scarf – nothing more, nothing less.

So why are my palms clammy, and why do I feel like I might hyperventilate?

I should ring him back – tell him to give my scarf to the solicitor and take his lovely, ruined house and stick it somewhere unpleasant.

But I do nothing of the sort. Instead, I put the phone away and drive off towards Bristol with a silly grin on my face.

# 32

The idea of seeing Jack Faraday again – even if it's only to get my scarf – fills me with a guilty, thrilling terror. Despite my best efforts, he's there in my mind, drifting just below my conscious thoughts. There was a spark there when we met; an understanding on some primordial level. It's ridiculous; it's annoying – and it's incredibly distracting.

When I meet Ronan Keene at the Bristol penthouse (this time with the right keys), I'm so on edge that I even greet Crystal with a friendly kiss on the cheek. She instantly stiffens – like I've mussed up her carefully applied foundation, but her bee-stung lips lift in a smile. 'How've ya been?' she even asks (though she clicks off in her stilettos before I can answer).

They both like the flat – the building, the location, the view, the floor-to-ceiling glass walls.

Of course, Crystal finds fault with a number of things: the double-wide bathtub is too small; the carpet on the top floor is a hideous beige (and 'wouldn't white look so much better?'); the alcove in the master bedroom is only big enough for a 72-inch screen rather than a custom home cinema. But overall, she's much more enthusiastic than I'd expected.

Ronan doesn't say much, but I get the feeling he's eager to end what must be a very painful search with Crystal in tow. As for me, I don't have the same buzz I had when showing the flat to the Blundells, but if it turns out to be the 'right now' home for Ronan and Crystal, then who am I to argue?

I praise the place to the moon, downplay the defects in grand Tetherington Bowen-Knowles style, and eventually, leave them on the roof terrace mulling things over. I flop onto the ultra-chic cowhide sofa in the main living space to wait for them.

My mobile phone rings; it's Claire checking to make sure that I'm OK. She goes a bit quiet when I tell her where I am (keen clients being hard to come by). But she wishes me luck.

Ronan and Crystal stay outside for a long time. At this rate, I won't have time to go home and get changed before the evening. On the other hand, maybe that's for the best. I really don't want to face my parents and their over-zealous questions about where I'm going, who I'm meeting (and whether he or she plays Scrabble). I even debate going back to the office – anything to get my mind off seeing Jack Faraday again.

Finally, Ronan and Crystal return. 'This place has given us a lot to think about,' Ronan says as we ride down the (newly replaced) lift. 'We'll definitely be in touch soon.'

'Great,' I say. 'I'll look forward to hearing from you.'

We shake hands and go our separate ways. I check my watch – it's five o'clock.

Two hours to go before...

# 33

I grip the wheel with sweaty palms as I pull up in front of Rosemont Hall. The lights are on downstairs, the windows glowing like the eyes of a jack-o'-lantern.

The removals lorry and the Mercedes are gone, but the blue Vauxhall is still there. I park next to it, gathering my courage. My knees are so shaky that I can barely totter in my heels through the mucky gravel. I manage to make it up the cracked stone steps to the front door and ring the bell.

The door opens. Jack Faraday's smile has an air of amusement; his blue eyes are sharp and intelligent, and I feel like they could penetrate the fog of my deepest dreams. I experience a stirring in parts of me that were previously unknown.

'Hi, Amy. Here you go.' He holds out my scarf. My heart plunges – is that it then?

'Would you like to come in? It's freezing out there.'

'Sure.' I tuck the scarf in my handbag and move past him into the great hall. At the foot of the stairs, a folding table is set up with paper plates for two and a large brown bag that smells of Chinese food. Two electric radiators, stretched to the end of their electrical cords, pump out heat at either end of the table.

I stand there, stunned.

'I wanted to apologise,' Jack says. 'I should have told you who I was right away. But by the time I realised that you thought I was someone else, it seemed too late to tell you. Besides' – the laughter is back in his eyes – 'it was interesting to experience your sales technique.'

'It's me who should apologise. I had no right to say those... uhh... things.'

He smirks; I blush. 'Anyway,' he says, 'I hope we can call a truce. And do some damage to this Chinese takeaway. I'm told it's the best in the village.'

'You mean, the *only*.' I can't help but smile; I'm tingling all over, and not just from the warmth of the radiators.

'Since you love this place so much, I thought we could have a picnic in here,' he says. 'Unfortunately, as you know, cooking anything in the kitchen is out of the question. And as far as I can tell, there isn't a supermarket for miles. Otherwise I would have whipped up my special chilli con carne, extra spicy.'

'Do you like to cook?' I ask, pleasantly surprised. I hang my coat on the newel post and sit down in one of the chairs.

'Sometimes. But nothing too fancy. I can do Mexican pretty well – that's all in the sauce. And I like making Italian food with homemade pasta. And I live near the ocean, so I like making things with fresh fish. Anything seasonal, really. That's the secret – fresh ingredients.'

'I can make chicken curry,' I say. 'But that's about it. When I lived in London, I did a lot of takeaway, I'm afraid.'

'Sure, makes sense. I don't bother to cook when I'm working late or eating alone.'

Alone as in no wife or girlfriend? I can't bring myself to ask. 'And where is it that you live?' I say instead.

He rummages in the bag and takes out a bottle of wine and two glasses.

'California,' he says. 'I've got a nice Victorian house in a little town called Carmel-by-the-Sea. The house was built in 1899. Practically ancient – for California.' He smiles. 'It's painted light green with dark green gingerbread trim. There's a holly tree out in front that's as old as the house. It's trimmed in the shape of a bell. And from the top floors, you can see a little strip of ocean. There's a balcony in front called a widow's walk. It was built for a sea captain's wife – so that she could go out and see if her husband's ship had returned.'

'It sounds lovely,' I say truthfully.

'I thought you'd like to hear the details. So you can see I'm not a complete architectural and historical neanderthal.'

'Thanks.' I risk a little laugh. 'I guess I was wrong.'

He opens the bottle of wine and pours it.

'Your sister said you teach at Stanford,' I say. 'That's impressive.'

'Is it?' He hands me a glass of wine. I take a little sip.

'Well, I think so. Stanford is a great university and all.'

'Yes, it is. And I'm lucky to have the job. It's fun. Some of those kids are so smart that I'm not sure who's teaching whom. We're working on a new design for micro-processing board circuitry.'

'What's that?'

'Basically, components found in all microchips. That's what my company did before I sold it. Now I'm mostly freelance.'

'I'm not quite sure what to say.'

He laughs. 'Don't worry. I don't expect you to be interested in computer chips. Business is business, and I make a point not to mix it with pleasure.'

He looks at me intently; my cheeks flare with warmth.

'What most people don't realise is the creativity that goes into even simple devices. It's that creative part that I enjoy now more than anything. If my team succeeds with this patent, it could be revolutionary.'

As I'm trying to take this all in, he clinks his glass to mine.

'But I must be boring you silly,' he says. 'Sorry about that. It's just habit. We computer geeks don't get out much.'

'I'm not bored.' How can I be when each detail adds to my mental picture of him? I want to know everything about him. I want—

'Good.' He smiles like he's read my mind.

'And what do you do when you're not working?'

'Well' – he takes a sip of wine – 'after my wife died, I kind of shut off from everyone and focused on work. It's only in the last year or so that I've enjoyed doing anything again. I suppose most of my hobbies are solitary – art galleries, walks by the sea, reading books – nothing too exciting. A geek is as a geek does.'

'I'm sorry about your wife,' I say. 'Not that sorry is any good in these situations.'

He swirls the wine in the glass. 'Maybe not. But I'm getting past it. It was cancer. She's been gone for three years now.'

Frowning, he takes a handful of plastic cutlery out of the bag. I want to reach out and grab his hand – comfort him somehow. His story has plucked a chord that resonates inside of me. My loss was nothing compared to his, but still, I know what it's like to have one's world and one's life turned upside down. I feel like I've known Jack Faraday for much longer than just hours. It's strange and implausible, but it's like he's been part of me all along.

'It was awful, of course,' he says, 'and time isn't the great healer that people say. Every day you're waiting for something to happen. Some days, you're waiting for the person to come back. Other days, you're waiting to forget. Months pass, then years.' He sighs. 'And then one day, out of the blue, a stranger with an English accent called up looking for a "Mr Jack and Ms Flora". I thought it was a wrong number. When he told me that we'd inherited a crumbling mansion in England, it didn't sound like the thing I was waiting for... In fact, it sounded like a damned nuisance.' He passes me a plate. 'But the lawyer, Mr Kendall, seemed like a decent guy. He told me he'd met an estate agent who was passionate about the house and finding a buyer who would restore it. I admit, I was sceptical.' He gives a little laugh. 'In fact, I pictured Miss Marple – tweed suit, pearls, sensible shoes.'

'Really?' I laugh too.

'So you can imagine that when I finally met you, I was pleasantly surprised.'

'Me too,' I say. 'I won't even go into what I thought you might look like.'

'Bill Gates, maybe?'

'Something like that.'

'I guess we were both wrong. But enough about me. Tell me about Amy Wood.'

'Oh... uhh...' Nerves commandeer my body. I should make up something interesting about myself – pretend I'm an Olympic triathlete or studying to be a barrister or a brain surgeon, or campaigning to save polar bears. But Jack has been honest with me, so I decide to tell him the truth.

'I used to teach in London...' I tell him about my former job, and then move on to the juicier bits: finding my perfect flat, discovering the truth about Simon and Ashley, getting sacked, and moving back in with my parents in their 1970s bungalow. My life… warts and all.

Jack listens, slowly sipping his wine. I take a little sip to moisten my throat, determined not to get too tipsy to drive.

'Sounds like you've had a hell of a time,' he says.

'Oh.' I shrug breezily. 'It did hit me pretty hard. But it feels like ancient history.' With him sitting across the table, that feels true.

'Sounds like you're better off without your ex, but it is a shame about your job. English literature…' His eyes twinkle. 'I should have guessed. This place is straight out of a novel, isn't it? Maybe *Jane Eyre* or *Pride and Prejudice* – something like that?'

'You've read those?'

'Hasn't everyone?'

'No,' I say. 'I don't think so.'

'My wife had all those books. After she died, I went through a phase of reading the classics. They may be old-fashioned, but the themes still resonate today, don't they?'

I nod.

He leans in on his elbow, staring at me as if something doesn't compute. 'And then you became an estate agent?'

'I didn't plan on it. I mean, who would? I don't know what it's like in America, but over here, they have a certain… reputation.'

He laughs. 'Tell me.'

'I'm afraid there's a certain tendency to, shall we say, overstate the good and downplay the bad.'

'You mean they lie in order to get a sale? Yeah – they do that everywhere.'

'I guess so.' I sigh. 'And while it wasn't what I'd envisioned, when the solicitor called about Rosemont Hall on my very first day, it seemed like fate. I saw the house and immediately wanted to find someone who would make it live and breathe again.' I shrug. 'It sounds naff, but I feel a strong connection with Rosemont Hall.'

'I can tell. Even though you tried hard to make me hate the place.'

'Well, that's because...' I stop.

His smile fades. 'Shall we eat?' He takes the food containers out of the bag.

A cold wave of reality hits me. This man may not work for Hexagon, but he is not some kind of romantic hero. He is not going to restore and nurture the house that's been handed to him on a silver platter. In fact, he's the one who contacted Hexagon in the first place. In between creating his revolutionary microchip, cooking chilli con carne, reading the classics, and taking walks by the sea, he's been dealing with the devil. Whatever happens to Rosemont Hall – if it becomes a golf course, or crumbles away to dust – it will be entirely down to Jack Faraday.

He opens the cartons of steaming food. 'I got chicken, beef, and vegetarian. A little of each?'

'Sure.' I no longer feel hungry as he scoops the food onto my plate and hands it to me.

'Flora and I are selling the house.' He looks at me intently, judging my reaction. 'To Hexagon. It seemed the best result under the circumstances.'

I push the chicken chow mein around on my plate. The whole evening is a pointless charade, with any romantic happy endings purely the product of my imagination. Not that I had the right to expect anything different. For one evening, as Flora said, Jack Faraday wants to play 'lord of the manor'. I've let him play me in the process.

'I don't agree it's the best result,' I say. 'If you gut this house and turn it into a golf clubhouse or flats, it will be lost forever. It will, Jack...' I set down my fork. 'And all the computer chips in the world won't be able to save it once it's gone.'

He rests his chin in his hand. 'OK, Amy Wood, you're the estate agent. Tell me – what's the alternative?'

I should have the perfect answer prepared. I should have the perfect buyer lined up. But I don't. The failure doesn't rest solely with Jack Faraday. I'm responsible too.

'Once it's fixed up it could be self-supporting.' I grasp at straws. 'Lots of houses like this are. It would make a lovely home for the right person, or maybe opened up to the public.'

Jack Faraday looks for a second like he's about to laugh in my face. Instead, he folds his arms and sits back. 'And how do you propose that it gets "fixed up", as you say? I'm sure you've seen the figures just to get it watertight, not to mention the rest of the work, plus the annual upkeep. Then there's the inheritance taxes and other debts of the estate.'

'There are grants and bank loans, and things...'

I trail off, completely embarrassed. After all, if *I* had inherited Rosemont Hall, even with the best will in the world, I couldn't afford to restore it.

Jack swirls the wine in his glass and sighs. 'Tonight before you got here, Amy, I spent a couple of hours here in the house, just walking through the rooms. As I told you before, I never had much time for history. My life was all about the future. But being here, it feels like something inside me has shifted. This house – it gets under your skin, doesn't it?'

'*You* feel that way?'

'Don't get me wrong – it sounds crazy. I don't think you can just turn up at a place and have it feel like home.'

'But it does, doesn't it?' I whisper.

There's a long moment. My heart begins to kindle and flare up with a dangerous fire – that thing called hope.

But then Jack turns away, severing the connection. Slowly, he turns back. 'I admire your passion,' he says. 'But real life is more complicated than fiction. In this case, there are no heroes or villains. I hope you can see that.'

The lid on Pandora's box shuts firmly. Hope? Silly me. 'You're right, Jack,' I say. 'Life is complicated. I'm sorry I've wasted your time.' I push my chair back and get ready to leave. It's the right thing to do—

The lights flicker overhead. We both look up at the cobweb-laced chandelier. There's a loud popping sound and the whole room goes dark. The hum of the heaters stops. Everything is deathly quiet.

'The heaters must have blown a fuse.' I reach for the table to orient myself.

'Amy... wait,' Jack says softly. His hand finds my arm.

I jump up. 'Thanks so much for dinner, Jack. It's been great.' I take a few steps in the direction – I think – of the newel post with my coat. 'I don't think there's much you can do about the lights tonight. The cellar's a bit of a maze, so it's probably best to leave it until tomorrow. Oh, and the housekeeper, Mrs Bradford – I think she might still be living in the house some nights – just so you know.'

'Really? She told me she'd moved out.'

'Oh, you've spoken with her? Well, then you know more than I.'

My heels echo on the marble. The staircase isn't where I thought it was.

'Let me help you.' Jack flicks on a tiny pen-sized torch.

'I'm OK—'

My heel catches in a crack. The next thing I know, the cold marble floor comes up fast and hard against my face.

'Owww!' I yelp. The darkness is spotty before my eyes.

Strong arms help me into a sitting position.

'Amy! Are you hurt? Your ankle?'

I can just make out the outline of my heel, half-twisted off. But nothing is seriously damaged other than my pride – and my foolish illusions.

'I'm fine,' I say. 'I just need my coat.'

'Sure, I'll get it.'

His arms release me, and he gets my coat. I will myself to leave, but my ankle *does* hurt – a little. But more than that, there's an elemental force deep inside me that's battling for me to stay.

Jack wraps the coat around my shoulders and plunks down beside me. I'm acutely aware of his proximity. He flicks the tiny beam of his torch absently over the floor.

'It's bad timing,' he says with a little laugh. 'After all this time, I finally meet someone, invite her to dinner, and forget the candles just when they would have come in handy.'

I process the salient piece of information: *meet someone*.

'Don't worry, Jack. It was a nice surprise – thank you. I hope I haven't offended you.'

'No, Amy, you haven't. I hear what you're saying about the house. And part of me agrees with you. But it isn't just about the money for repairs and upkeep. There are other things – other people in my family who have been hurt over the years. I can't explain it to you. Not in a way that would make any sense. But I think it's best if our family is shot of this house.'

'What do you mean?'

The circle of light from his torch begins to fade. His hand

brushes my cheek as he leans very close to me and whispers in my ear.

'It's a long story. But know this – I'm sorry if you're disappointed about the house – and disappointed in me. I'm sorry for a lot of things... but not for this—'

And there in the darkness, his kiss sends lightning bolts of electricity through every nerve in my body. I melt into him; our lips mould together like they were made to stay that way. His fingers are magic as they slowly trail down my neck, and my body longs to end what seems like years of drought. But, at the same time, my mind whispers that this can't happen. It will end in tears, I'm betraying Rosemont Hall, *and*...

He stops and draws back. My hands are on his chest and I've pushed him away.

'I can't...'

I put on my coat and scramble to my feet. I whip off the offending shoes and run stocking-footed across the cold marble.

'Amy, wait. I didn't mean to—'

The slam of the door drowns out his words.

# 34

I haven't just made the biggest mistake of my life. I haven't ruined a perfect evening. And I know this because...

Reason eludes me as I nearly slam into the back of a lorry at a roundabout. Certainly, I've made lots of mistakes before – too many to count. Mistakes like not having a candid discussion with Simon about where our relationship was headed; or committing an assault with mobile phone; or moving back to Somerset; or kissing Frankie Summers at age fourteen when he was at home with chickenpox. But running away from Jack Faraday is not another disaster of my own making.

The more I think about it, the more I'm certain that I made the right decision. I was bowled over by the moment. It was right to step back before I was swept into the abyss of... what I really wanted to happen.

The miles flash by. Jack Faraday is no friend of mine – or Rosemont Hall. Ultimately, he's responsible for the fate of the house. He's the one choosing to turn it into a golf course for the gleeful enjoyment of people like David Waters, Alistair Bowen-Knowles, Simon, and Ashley. Jack said himself that it's not about the money for repairs and upkeep. He's got a lucrative business and teaching job. He could save Rosemont Hall if he wanted to.

When my mobile phone rings, my hands jump on the steering wheel. Should I pull off the road, answer it, and if it's Jack, give him a piece of my mind? Or should I turn around, rush back to the house, and pick up where we left off? The call goes to voicemail; I drive on. The lights of Nailsea shine cold and white in the distance.

Jack Faraday is nothing to me, and it's going to stay that way. He'll go back to America and his nice life in Carmel-by-the-Sea.

Leaving me...

Here.

My mobile rings again. I screech to the side of the road and scramble for it in my bag. It rings off before I can grab it. I turn it off, my hands unsteady as I drive the rest of the way home.

Mum and Dad are up watching the news when I get back. I refuse the offer of a cup of tea, have a quick shower, and get into bed. I try to read a little, then turn out the light and put a pillow over my head. It doesn't matter who called. I toss and turn and pop in my earplugs.

The suspense is killing me. I sit bolt upright, creep out of my room and grab my handbag. I smuggle it back into my room and take out my phone. Three missed calls. Holding my breath, I check the number.

*Yes!* My heart does a jig of glee. I turn off the light and lie in bed, trying hard to recover the mixture of confusion and outrage I'd so carefully concocted on my way home. But it's no use. I close my eyes and snuggle into the duvet, my body still tingling from the memory of his kiss.

* * *

After a night of pleasantly disturbing dreams, I wake up the next morning in a fog of disbelief. How could I have run away from Jack Faraday? How could I have been so utterly stupid?

It takes a cold shower and most of the drive to work before I can once again muster the anger I feel towards Jack. What did he mean about his family having been hurt over the years? Why didn't I find out more? Why on earth didn't I stay?

The day gets worse when I reach the office. I have an email from one Nigel Netelbaum, Director of Regional Development for Hexagon UK, asking about the paperwork for Rosemont Hall. I hit delete.

Mr Kendall has also left a message asking me to ring him as soon as possible. I stall – make some coffee, run out and grab a muffin, eat it slowly at my desk while googling Jack Faraday.

There are a lot of hits. Jack Faraday is officially a rich and successful computer geek. There's a picture of him in the *San Francisco Chronicle* giving a $100,000 cheque to a cancer charity. Another article details the sale of his company with figures involving more noughts than I can count on two hands. The articles prove one thing: Jack Faraday has the money to save Rosemont Hall.

But he isn't going to.

The phone rings. It's Mr Kendall again. When I answer (telling him that I was just about to ring him, and it's like he read my mind) he sounds cordial as usual, if a little chilly. He explains that he's dealing with Hexagon himself, and I don't need to respond to Nigel Netelbaum. All he needs from me is the keys back as soon as possible.

'Sure,' I choke, 'I can drop them by your office.'

'Fine, if—'

'You know, Mr Kendall, I tried to convince Mr Jack that he

should keep the house, because it's part of his family heritage.' I give a weak laugh. 'But I couldn't persuade him.'

Mr Kendall sighs – he obviously thinks I've got way too big for my knickers. 'Not everyone is like you, Amy. Why should Mr Jack and Ms Flora – two people who have their own lives in America – want to do that?' He sounds perturbed. 'You may not know it, but they're running out of time before they will have to pay the estate debts and the first instalment of a whopping inheritance tax bill.'

'Oh.'

'Besides, not every family history is a happy one. The Windhams owned a grand house, but in the end, it's just a house. What about the people who lived there? Aren't they more important? And believe me—' He pauses as something beeps in the background.

'Yes…' I coax. 'Please… I'd really like to understand.'

'Sorry, Amy, I must take this call. And actually, don't worry about dropping off the keys. I'll send someone round later today.'

'No really, it's—'

The phone clicks off.

My chest feels like a black hole, but for the rest of the morning it's filled with other matters. Ronan Keene phones and (miracle of miracles) puts in an offer on the Bristol flat. I ring the vendor myself and come back with a counter offer, engage in some toing and froing on the price, and finally reach an agreement. Once again, my name is heading to the top of the sales chart on the door of the disabled loo.

That *should* make me happy. I *am* happy. So why don't I *feel* happy?

I check my mobile, hoping Jack might have rung again. He hasn't. I debate ringing him. I don't. After all, what's the point?

Jack Faraday will go back to America. Rosemont Hall will be sold. I'll still be here at Tetherington Bowen-Knowles.

Unless I do something about it.

Perhaps the universe has sensed my wayward path and now wants to catapult me in the right direction. Perhaps it's telling me that I've been playing estate agent for long enough. It's time for me to go back to my true vocation. If nothing else, teaching literature is much less painful than real life.

I spend the rest of the morning dusting off my CV and applying for the teaching job in Edinburgh. I wax lyrical about how I've always been inspired by setting as a 'character' in fiction, and how I'm looking forward to a romp through the literary wilds of Scotland – *Rob Roy, Ivanhoe,* the poetry of Robert Burns. I almost manage to convince myself. *Almost.* My throat is tight as I press send.

At lunchtime, I grab a sandwich with Claire, desperate for someone to talk sense into me. I tell her the latest on Rosemont Hall (leaving out certain relevant details about my dinner with its reluctant heir). She's less than sympathetic to my plight. 'God, Amy,' she says, 'you've really got to get a grip.'

'Yes – I want to. But how?'

'Start facing the facts. If the house is sold, then it's sold,' Claire says. 'It may be a shame, but no one's died... I mean, other than the last owner. But *you* need to move on. The heirs have every right to sell it.'

'I know, it's just...'

'It's just what?' She cocks her head, frowning. 'There's something you're not telling me. Is it the old lady who's been turfed out? Or something else?'

Someday, Claire is going to make one hell of a barrister. 'Well, there is one other thing worth mentioning.'

'Yes?'

'The heir. Jack Faraday.'

'What about him?'

'We had dinner. And a long talk.'

'Dinner?'

'I think I might be falling for him.'

Claire's mouth forms a lip-lined 'O'. 'Please say you're joking.'

'I certainly didn't plan it! I despise him! He could save the house if he wanted to. *We* could save it.' I tell her what Jack Faraday said about the house and its history seeping into his bones. That he feels a connection just like I do.

'But he's not going to save it, Claire. None of it makes any difference.'

'That's his prerogative. But for the record, did he say why not?'

'He said that people in the past had been hurt.'

'Which means what?'

'I've no idea.'

'Then ask him! Come on, Amy, this isn't the nineteenth century. You have to stop thinking like Jane Eyre and start thinking like the Hotel Inspector. Make a business plan for saving the house and present it to him. And if he still says no, then you can always get down on your knees and beg.'

A business plan? Why didn't I think of that before?

'Get the facts down on paper,' Claire says. 'Crunch some numbers. Show him how the house can make a profit on its own – if it can. Convince him that he's better off keeping it than selling. If he's a techie, he'll appreciate that.'

'Yes,' I say brightly. 'Numbers. That's what I need. But how do I get them?'

Claire rolls her eyes. 'Haven't you learned anything from

our delightful boss? Make them up. Create a spreadsheet. Something that will get him thinking.'

'I've never done anything like that before, but I can give it a try.'

'Go to the library and find a book. There must be loads. I'll tell the boss you're on a viewing.'

'Thanks, Claire. I owe you big time.'

'I won't forget.'

* * *

Claire is a genius. After lunch, I go to the tourist information office and pick up some leaflets on historic homes that are open to the public. Longleat House, for example, has a zoo and a safari park, loads of activities for kids, eateries, gift shops – the place is definitely paying its way.

Maybe Jack and I could go there together to check out the possibilities. I picture us in a little open-top car, driving through country lanes, my hair tied up in a scarf, him wearing his red jacket and sunglasses. We'd visit Longleat in the morning and Sudeley Castle in the afternoon, stopping for lunch at a rambling little country pub where we'd sit outside in the garden and Jack would sample the local bitter. And at night when the sun went down, neither of us would want the day to end. We'd have supper together in the restaurant of his hotel and make plans for the future of Rosemont Hall. And we'd plan other little trips we could take, other places to see... and one thing would lead to another, and—

'Hey, watch it,' someone yells.

I look up realising that I'm in the middle of a crossing, about to get run down by a 'Hop on, Hop Off' open-top tour bus. A group of Japanese schoolgirls snap me with their iPhones. At least if I'm flattened, there will be plenty of witnesses.

My fantasy in tatters, I go to the public library and find a book called *Business Plans for Complete Idiots.* I sit down at a table and tackle chapter one – *Brainstorming*.

I jot down a long list of things that could be developed at Rosemont Hall to turn a profit. A tearoom with locally sourced organic produce, a children's adventure playground, garden walks and treasure hunts, paintball boot camps, and the real money-spinners: weddings, corporate away-days, film shoots.

It's a good start. The next section of the book covers budgeting, double-entry accounting, and profit-and-loss statements. My eyes glaze over. Writing a credible business plan is going to take longer than one afternoon, and I'm already on borrowed time. My 'can-do' mood deflates rapidly. I put the book back on the shelf and wander through the library to the local history section. Being surrounded by history books makes me feel better, and there's a whole shelf on places of architectural interest. In one of the books I find a three-page section on Rosemont Hall. The publication date is 1950 – before the fire, I note.

The print is minuscule, and I have to squint to read it. Much of the information on the architecture I already know, but I'm intrigued by three black and white photos printed with the blurb. The first shows two men in a mountain pass. The caption reads, 'Sir George Windham and Francisco Walredo, Spain 1937'. I stare at the photo. I've no idea who Walredo might be, and the text doesn't say. In the photo, Sir George is smiling, but his eyes are as dark and murky as pools of ink. What had Mrs Bradford said? *The eyes of a demon.* The back of my neck prickles with goosebumps.

The second photo I've seen before. It's of the inside of the great hall at Rosemont Hall, circa 1939, the walls covered with paintings. The caption describes the famous Rosemont Hall art collection. 'Most of the artwork was sold off after the end of World War Two to pay for repairs to the house,' it reads. 'However, a few key collection pieces, including *Orientale* by Rembrandt, were retained by the family.'

The final photo shows a painting, dim and shadowy except for a few shimmering rays of light that reveal the figure of a man dressed in a Chinese-style robe. The Rembrandt! Even in miniature, the details – the folds of the fabric, the brocade on the jacket, the fall of light on the planes of the man's face – are vivid and otherworldly. It must have been a stunning sight to see that painting hanging in a place of pride at Rosemont Hall. It's no wonder that Sir George wanted to keep it even after all the other art was sold off. It must have been his pride and joy. But in holding on to it, he unwittingly contributed to its destruction.

I return the book to the shelf. The Rembrandt was lost in the fire, and the house is about to suffer its own sorry fate unless I can conjure up a miracle. And maybe even then...

My mobile vibrates in my bag – I find I have four missed calls from the office. I rush back to work, hoping Claire has covered for me.

'A Mr Kendall was here, Amy,' Claire says as I return to my desk. 'He came for some keys, but we couldn't find them.'

'Sorry, I forgot.' I give Claire a wry smile. In fact, I did forget Mr Kendall was coming for the keys to Rosemont Hall. Keys which are currently safe and sound at the bottom of my handbag.

'He says someone will be at the house tonight and wondered if you could drop them there on your way home.'

'I'll do that.'

*Someone*. My heart thumps in my chest.

# 35

In the early evening, I drive to Rosemont Hall. My pulse is pounding as I turn off the road and drive between the sagging iron gates. While my previous visit far exceeded expectations, tonight, I'm expecting no miracles.

The sky is streaked with pink and gold, and the outline of the house looks lonely and forbidding. Two vehicles are parked in front: Mr Kendall's Beamer and a gargantuan black Range Rover. No Vauxhall Corsa – no Jack Faraday. As much as I want to want to forget him, I taste the sharp bile of disappointment.

I park next to the Range Rover and walk to the front door. As I'm about to knock, it opens. Mr Kendall is standing there (apparently he doesn't need my keys *that* badly) along with a short man in a pin-striped suit. Something about him looks familiar, and everything else – from his ginger hair (looking suspiciously like a comb-over) to his golf club print tie and rhinestone-chip cufflinks – makes my hackles rise. A single word comes to mind...

Hexagon.

'Hello, Ms Wood,' Mr Kendall says. 'Thanks for stopping by.

We were lucky to catch Mr Jack before he left for the airport, and he let us in.'

'Oh.'

Jack is gone. I'm suddenly awash with anger – at myself. Why didn't I return his calls? Why did I let him go?

Mr Kendall turns to the ginger-haired man. 'I don't believe you two have met,' he says. 'This is Amy Wood, the estate agent.'

The man's fleshy lips lift into a smile. 'Hello there,' he says. 'Nigel Netelbaum, CEO of Hexagon plc.'

'Hello,' I croak, realising why he looks familiar. I've seen him before – in a photo in David Waters's flat. The two of them were standing together holding up a golf trophy. I force myself to shake his hand.

'We're just finishing up,' he says. 'Helluva place, isn't it? Must have really been something once upon a time.'

'It's still really something,' I say. 'For now, anyway.'

'Yeah, OK.' He raises an eyebrow like he's humouring me, then turns back to Mr Kendall and asks him something about the paperwork. His accent is American, like Jack's and Flora's. The conspiracy theorist in me begins to wonder if it's all some kind of nefarious transatlantic plot. The two men talk and I stand there feeling like a tatty piece of furniture cluttering up the room. I should hand over the keys and go – there's no reason for me to be here. But I keep a tight grip on the key ring.

'Right then,' Mr Kendall is saying, 'that all sounds good. We'll send over the draft contracts early next week.'

The two men shake hands. Mr Netelbaum gives me a little wave and a 'cheerio' as he goes down the steps and climbs into the Range Rover. The vehicle roars to life and he reverses in a three-point turn. I watch the vehicle until it disappears into the gloom.

'So that's it, then?'

'That's it.' Mr Kendall lets out a long sigh. 'He's just doing his job, Amy. We all are.'

I shrug like I'm not bothered. 'Sorry I wasn't in the office earlier. I guess subconsciously, I don't want to hand these over.' I place the heavy ring of keys in his hand. They're no use to me now.

'Thanks.' He tucks the keys into the pocket of his overcoat. 'Jack and Ms Flora are on their way back to America. You just missed them. I doubt either of them will be back.'

I don't trust myself to reply.

'Would you like a last look around?' Mr Kendall offers. 'Since you love the place so much?'

He stands aside so I can enter. For once, I have no desire to go inside. The house seems cold and dead: an empty shell where my heart once lived. And I can't even pretend that it's all down to meeting Mr Netelbaum and seeing him seal the deal.

Jack is gone.

Mr Kendall raises an eyebrow expectantly. 'Unless you need to be somewhere—'

'No, I don't.' I go inside with a heartfelt sigh. I'll see the house one last time, say goodbye, and start the process of forgetting.

He flicks the light switch and the chandelier illuminates (minus the bulbs that blew out during the power surge). I take a last look at the grand staircase, the marble floor, the cool stone walls, the exquisitely decorated ceiling. Despite everything that has – or hasn't – happened, I want to remember every detail.

Everything from my evening with Jack has been cleared away, as if it never was. Even the heaters are gone. Last night, I didn't notice that in the other rooms off the great hall, most of the furniture and bric-a-brac have been removed. More than ever, a once-loved home feels cavernous and forbidding. I peek into the library. Even the books have been cleared off the shelves. All that's left is dust and mice droppings.

But one thing still remains – the painting of the lady in the pink dress. As long as she's hanging on the staircase landing, I feel a tiny flicker of hope that, somehow, Rosemont Hall can be saved.

Mr Kendall follows me up the stairs and we stand together in front of the painting. 'She's quite stunning, isn't she?' he says.

'Yes. It's Arabella Windham, isn't it?' I half turn to him. 'All along it's been her, watching as everyone tramps through her house, talking about her things like they're just some old lady's rubbish.'

'Arabella? Is that who you think she is?'

'Yes.' I explain briefly about the costumes I found. I avoid mentioning the sketchbook and the letters, which are still safely ensconced in my knicker drawer. If anyone misses them, I can always post them back.

Mr Kendall frowns. 'I've always assumed the painting was old. It says 1899 on the frame.'

'But frames can be changed, can't they? Like old wine in new bottles.'

He shakes his head. 'I don't know, Amy. I've been their solicitor for about twenty years – Arabella was well into middle age when I knew her. But she had light brown hair and brown eyes.' He points to the face of the girl in the painting. 'Not blue like hers.'

'Oh.' I take a step back. The only photo I've seen of the young Arabella was the blurry black and white wedding photo, where it wasn't possible to make out the colour of her eyes. But now, I realise that it's obviously not the same girl. All my sleuthing – thinking I was so clever to discover the historical joke that Henry and Arabella must have played – has been pointless. If there is a mystery as to who the woman is, I haven't solved it.

'Whoever she is,' Mr Kendall says, 'most likely she won't be going far.'

'What do you mean?'

'All the art in the house was left to Mrs Bradford, not Flora and Jack,' he explains. 'That's why that painting is still there. When the house is sold, Mrs Bradford will have to take it away.'

'Oh. Is she going to sell it?'

'I've no idea.'

Mr Kendall turns and walks the length of the landing, as if he too is trying to imprint the house on his memory. 'If this place does become a golf clubhouse,' he says, 'at least Hexagon will be required to keep the fabric of the building. Maybe it won't be so bad. Lots of people will be able to enjoy the house, not just one family.'

I shake my head. 'You don't believe that.'

'Of course I'd prefer it to be left intact. It's a national treasure – too bad the National Trust didn't want it.'

'You checked too?' I smile wryly.

'Yes, a while back, when Mrs Windham was ill. I was told that the Trust has its hands full.' He leans over the railing to look down at the great hall. 'And this place needs too much work. It's a money pit.'

'With the right business plan, Rosemont Hall could be self-supporting,' I say. 'A wedding venue, a tea shop and restaurant, organic garden shop – the whole estate would draw in loads of people if it was advertised properly.'

'That requires a huge outlay of cash. No bank will lend on a wing and a prayer, and as I mentioned before, there's a large inheritance tax bill that the heirs are responsible for. The first instalment is due next month. Eighty thousand pounds. And that's only the beginning. The total bill is closer to a million.'

'A million pounds in taxes?'

'Yes, that's right.'

The truth seeps through my veins like freezing water. I remember what David Waters said: *It will take buried treasure to save this house.* No amount of number crunching about tearooms and adventure parks will make any difference.

'The crown always gets paid first before the rest of the estate can be distributed,' he says. 'The house and land are the only assets with any value. If the heirs don't sell, they'll still be liable for the IHT. Imagine getting a phone call that you've inherited a crumbling mansion in England. And by the way, can you please pay a million pounds for the privilege.'

'It's hopeless,' I whisper to the woman in the portrait.

She smiles back, keeping her secrets.

'The heirs were very relieved to get an offer from Hexagon,' Mr Kendall says. 'At least they can walk away with the debts cleared.'

'Of course.' I turn away from the painting, my head hung low. It was ludicrous of me to think that Jack might want to keep the house even if he could afford to. He must be so relieved to be shot of the whole inheritance palaver, and everything and everyone associated with it. Everyone – including me.

Mr Kendall and I stand together, leaning against the carved railing. It helps to know that he too feels sad about the fate of the house. But ultimately, he's right – we both have a job to do.

A noise from below breaks the silence. Keys rattle; the front door opens and closes. Whistling echoes in the vast room.

Mr Kendall goes back downstairs just as Mrs Bradford enters the great hall, clunking her stick in time to the music.

Behind her, she's dragging a plastic trolley full of grocery bags like she's setting up camp in the house.

'Hello, Mrs Bradford,' he says loudly. 'You're keeping well, I trust?'

The last note peters out. Looking past Mr Kendall, she lifts her gnarled hand and points her cane at me. 'What's *she* doing here?'

'She's with me. I'm sure you remember Amy Wood. The estate agent.'

I go down the stairs, keeping a smile drawn on my face. I'm sure we both remember all too well our previous encounter when she and her dog ran me off the property, and then she called the solicitor to complain about me. But I'm determined to take a charitable interpretation – she's an old woman going through hard times, and I'm going to be polite.

'Hello, Mrs Bradford. It's nice to see you again.'

'Is it?' Her blue eyes look hollow and haunted.

'I noticed you've been doing some cleaning. The house is starting to scrub up well.'

'Well, it's high time,' she says. 'Now that *she's* finally gone. Out with the old and all that.'

The thinly veiled reference to Arabella's passing is somewhat disturbing.

'I hope you're not tiring yourself out, Maryanne,' Mr Kendall says. 'After all, it's a big house.'

'Pah,' she says. 'I've never felt better.'

She drags her trolley towards the kitchen stairs. Mr Kendall and I exchange a look.

'There was a problem with the electrics,' I say. 'I'm not sure if it's been sorted yet. In case you were planning on doing any cooking.' I point to the trolley.

'Well, you would know, wouldn't you,' she says snippily.

'Since you're always here snooping around, poking your nose where it doesn't belong. Taking a few souvenirs for your trouble?'

'Really, Mrs Bradford—'

Mr Kendall steps forward and cuts me off. 'Amy is doing her job. And Ms Flora had a removals van around to take away some things. But everything that belongs to you is still here, so don't worry about that—'

'Oh, I'm not worried.' With a pointed look at me, Mrs Bradford plods onwards. At the edge of the great hall, she trips on a cracked tile. Her stick quavers like she's about to go down. I run over and help to steady her.

'Here, let me help you with the trolley,' I say.

I expect her to lash out and tell me where to go. So I'm surprised when she leans on my arm and says: 'All right. Hand me that bag, will you?'

I do as she says. The bag is full of cleaning supplies, not groceries. Regaining her balance, she takes out a can of Mr Sheen and sprays it on an old rag. Leaning on her cane, she goes two-footed up the steps, dragging the rag over the banister.

The whole thing is ridiculous and heartbreaking. She loves this old house – and so do I. Grabbing another rag out of the bag, I spray on some Mr Sheen and start to polish the white marble balusters.

'Amy...' Mr Kendall says. 'We should go now.'

'I'd like to have a word with Mrs Bradford first, if you don't mind.' I set my chin firmly. 'Alone.'

'I have to be back at the office for half six.' He checks his watch. 'So you've got five minutes.'

'I'll meet you out by the cars.'

* * *

I continue to polish as Mr Kendall walks out the front door. The only sound is the thud of Mrs Bradford's cane on the stairs and the swish of the dust rags.

'They're going to turn Rosemont Hall into a golf course,' I say. 'I couldn't find a buyer to save it. It will go to Hexagon.'

Mrs Bradford tsks. 'A house is just a house,' she says.

I steel myself, determined to find a chink in her armour. 'Is it? So you don't mind leaving here for good? I'm glad to hear it – because I was worried you might be upset.'

She's reached the top of the stairs and has stopped polishing; I focus intently on the baluster I'm working on.

'What does it matter what I want or don't want?' she says. 'I'm just an old lady who was looking after another old lady.'

'Good. I'm glad you don't mind having to relocate. Silly me...' I give a deliberate little laugh. 'I was worried that Rosemont Hall might feel like home to you.'

She mutters something under her breath. It sounds like, 'More than you know.' Her knuckles are white as her hand reaches for the banister; she strokes it like the smooth cheek of a baby. Mrs Bradford does care about the house – I knew it all along.

'Anyway, I wanted to make sure you knew what was happening. Once the probate decree comes through, things are bound to happen pretty quickly.'

'I did everything I could,' she says. 'But I knew in my heart that it wasn't meant to be.'

Her eyes are clouded over. She's not answering me but talking to herself.

'And the worst part was all those years of nothing. Not a letter or a how d'ya do.'

She wheels around suddenly to face the painting. My heart almost stops as she brandishes her stick at the girl in the pink dress.

'Stupid, that's what she was. Stupid.'

'Oh,' I say, alarmed. 'Why was she stupid, Mrs Bradford?'

'She fell in love with the wrong person.'

I consider this. 'And who is she?'

Mrs Bradford turns away from the painting. The demon passes; she goes back to polishing the dado rail like nothing is amiss.

'My daughter thinks it's a good idea for me to leave here.'

I look up at her trying to decide if she's speaking to me. Her daughter? She seems like such a lone, stalwart figure – I hadn't even considered that she might have family other than the sister in the village.

'She thinks it was a bad idea that I ever came back here at all. But then again, what does she know?'

'Does your daughter live locally?'

'No, of course not,' she says sharply. 'She lives in America. She's Jack and Flora's mother.'

'Their mother?' I look up in surprise. 'So you're their grandmother?'

'You worked that one out, did you?'

'Sorry. I had no idea. Mr Kendall said that the heirs were distant relatives. I didn't know you were related to the Windhams.'

She shakes her head like I'm an idiot child. 'Of course *I'm* not related to them.'

'But the house...?'

'Who else were they going to leave it to? They had no children and no relatives.'

'I don't know. But you have to admit that it sounds like

something out of a fairy tale – a faithful servant inherits the castle…'

She wrinkles her nose.

'Not that you're a servant,' I add quickly.

'It was no fairy tale,' she snaps. 'It was payback. And *I* didn't inherit it. Unfortunately.'

'Amy?' Mr Kendall's voice is icy as he calls up to me. 'We need to go now.'

'Just one more minute,' I shout back.

'You heard the man – off with you now.' Mrs Bradford flicks her dust cloth in my direction.

'I will, but just one more thing.' I gesture at the painting. 'What are you going to do with *her*?'

'Nothing.' She leans against the wall like the weight of years is pressing upon her.

'I suppose she belongs where she is,' I say with an uncomfortable little laugh. 'Stupid or not, she fits that spot so well – the spot where the Rembrandt used to hang. Right?'

Mrs Bradford doesn't answer.

'Maybe Hexagon will buy her and let her stay.' I brush the heavy frame with my fingers. 'But if not, I had kind of a silly thought. If you were thinking of selling it, maybe you'd let me know. I have a little money saved up.' I wince. 'Not much, and actually, I'm supposed to be using it for a down payment on a flat. My boyfriend dumped me, you see, and I'm living with my parents.' I prattle on in a last-ditch effort to shake some information out of her.

'Anyway, it's such a beautiful painting, and you only live once, don't you? No harm in asking, right? Though I'm sure it's out of my league. I'm a nobody too, you see. And I've also fallen in love with the wrong person.' I can feel my cheeks growing flushed. 'Just like the girl in the picture. Maybe that's why I'm drawn to her.'

Her stick is still as she peers down at me. I can't tell what she's thinking.

'Anyway, I'd better go now.' I go down the stairs hoping that she'll stop me. She doesn't.

Until I reach the bottom step.

'Why do you care so much?' she says. 'What is it you want? The painting, or something else?'

'I wanted to save the house,' I say. 'But I failed. The only thing I still might be able to do is preserve its memories. The woman in the portrait is part of that, surely.' I sigh. 'I thought that maybe you of all people might understand.'

She sucks a breath in through her teeth. 'All I know is that Rosemont Hall is my home.'

'Not any more, Mrs Bradford.' I shake my head. 'I'm really sorry, but not any more.'

* * *

The freezing rain mirrors my mood as I close the heavy door behind me. Mr Kendall is sitting in his car, the windows steamed up. He rolls one down and gestures for me to get in the passenger side. I do so.

'Well, Amy,' he says, 'it's been great working with you. I'm sorry things didn't work out the way you wanted, but...'

'...That's life,' I finish for him.

'I'll give you a call when the probate decree comes through. If you can send through your invoice for fees, I'd appreciate it.'

'Of course,' I say. 'But what about Mrs Bradford?'

'What about her?'

'Should I come back tomorrow? Check that she knows what's happening and has really moved out?'

'No.'

The single word is final; the judgement is passed. My involvement with Rosemont Hall has ended. We shake hands, and I get out of the car.

'Goodbye, Amy,' Mr Kendall says, 'and good luck.'

I open my mouth to reply, but the words are lost on the wind. I get into my own car and follow him down the dark, winding drive. I'm leaving Rosemont Hall...

For the last time.

# PART IV

Restore to me that little spot,
With grey walls compassed round,
Where knotted grass neglected lies,
And weeds usurp the ground.
Though all around this mansion high
Invites the foot to roam,
And though its halls are fair within—
Oh, give me back my HOME!

—*ANNE BRONTË – 'HOME'*

# 36

It's over. There's nothing I can do.

Except, there is one little fingernails-gripping-the-edge-of-a-cliff thing I can do. I can phone Jack. After all, I did have three missed calls from him after our... meaningless and never-to-be-repeated encounter. He wanted to talk to me before he flew off into the sunset.

I could phone Jack; it's rude not to.

But I'm not going to.

This becomes my new mantra each morning as I check my emails to see if there's any word about the Edinburgh teaching job. Mr Kendall is right: I need to move on. I need to forget all about Jack Faraday and Rosemont Hall, turfed-out old ladies, mysterious paintings, buried secrets, and happy endings. The reality is I'm a thirty-one-year-old single woman working in the profession that everyone loves to hate. I've shown that I can adapt to and even excel in a new environment. I've proved myself at Tetherington Bowen-Knowles. But it was never going to be my 'forever job'. I need to create an alternative future, starting as soon as possible.

By Friday morning, I've made very little progress getting Rosemont Hall and Jack Faraday out of my mind. I've tried everything – even attempting to raise the ghost of what I once thought I felt for Simon in the early days. But all I can muster is disappointment with myself for not seeing the wood for the trees. What I feel for Jack is totally different – and totally pointless. I must banish Jack Faraday from my head. At the office I go about my morning tasks trying to focus on the mundane here and now.

*THIS IS MY REALITY.*

By late morning, I've had it.

I sneak out to my car, take out my phone, and dial the number. *His* number.

On the third ring, the dashboard clock catches my eye – it's 11.30 a.m., UK time, which means that in California it's—

I fumble frantically to end the call, but it's too late. A groggy male voice answers: 'Hello?'

'Uhhh.'

'Who is this?'

'Jack?' My voice is a squeak.

A long pause.

'Amy? Is that you?'

'I'm so sorry, Jack, I didn't realise it's the middle of the night there. I'll ring another—'

'Why didn't you return my calls?'

I hear movement like he's sitting up, then a click – a light switch? Just hearing his voice makes me dizzy with desire. Which is stupid. *Stupid.*

'I didn't know you were going back to America so soon.'

'Yes, but I did try to call you. Something came up and I had to get back for work. Otherwise, I might have stayed a few more days.'

*A few more days*. But then he would have been gone just the same. In a way, I'm probably lucky. Except, I don't feel lucky – not one bit.

'I wanted to apologise.' I limp along. 'I heard about the inheritance tax. Of course you couldn't keep Rosemont Hall with so much debt hanging over it. I was vain and naïve to think otherwise. I'm sorry.'

'The inheritance tax? Yes – great business for the state, or the crown, or whoever.'

'Yes, and I also didn't realise that Maryanne Bradford was your grandmother.'

'Really? I assumed you knew. But the truth is, we're far from close. I never really understood her obsession with Rosemont Hall.'

'To be honest, I'm worried about her,' I say. 'I think she's more upset than any of us realise. Change can't be good at her age.'

'She's moved in with her sister,' he says. 'Aunt Gwen has a nice cottage in the village. When I last talked to her, she seemed fine.'

'Of course. And you know best, I'm sure. Besides, no matter who you sold the house to, she'd have to leave, wouldn't she?' I laugh sadly. 'Vacant possession and all that. Mr Kendall has the draft contracts drawn up for Hexagon. I met Nigel Netelbaum – the man you were in contact with. I'm sure your grandma will be fine and I've bothered you for nothing—'

Jack laughs softly. 'Amy Wood, I must say – you're so different to anyone I've met before.' His voice is warm, like a purring cat. 'The night we had dinner, I felt very strange – like I'd known you for a long time. I felt like a door was open before me. To some imaginary place that's totally different from my real life. A place full of passion and mystery – and just a little bit of the – what was your word? – "barmy" about it.'

I don't dare to breathe.

'For a minute I thought that maybe things happen for a reason. That in order to get my life back on track I had to travel halfway around the world to a crumbling old house in England. That maybe some things aren't rational, but we still just have to go with them.'

'Yes?' I say breathlessly.

'And then you slammed the door in my face.'

'I'm sorry. I didn't mean it like that. I was just... overwhelmed. Scared too. It was so unexpected. But I wish... well...' I can't bring myself to say it.

'I thought a lot about things while I was on the plane back to San Francisco,' he says. 'How I'd like to experience the world, get outside the sunny little bubble I live in. I had this crazy fantasy that you and I could go around and explore England together – maybe in one of those nippy little English cars. What are they – Minis?'

'Yes,' I whisper. 'And?'

'And... part of me wishes that things had turned out differently.' He sighs (or maybe it's a yawn). 'But when I got home, reality hit pretty hard. I realised that my life may not be extraordinary, but at least it's familiar. My one regret is that I didn't get to know you better.'

'Me too.' I feel like a punctured balloon.

'Anyway, I'll deal with Gran. You don't have to worry about her. And I'll call you next time I'm in town. I'll plan a longer trip – maybe in the summer.'

'OK, Jack. I'll... I'll talk to you. Sometime.'

'Goodbye, Amy.'

I end the call and sit there staring at nothing.

## 37

The devil makes work for idle hands (or in this case, it's Mr Bowen-Knowles masquerading as said demon). The next morning I arrive late at the office (terrible traffic, long line at Starbucks) and find a stack of papers on my desk. My boss is hovering in the waiting area, straightening the *Country Life* magazines on the table – my job. As soon as I sit down, he comes over to me.

'Amy...' His tone is brusque. 'I need you here at 9 a.m. – not ten past. You need to get your skates on.'

'Sorry.' I sip my latte, hiding behind the cup.

'There's a couple who want to view some properties this afternoon. The details are there.' He indicates the papers on my desk. There are two brochures, and two Google Map printouts. Like a proverbial bad penny, both of the properties are within a few miles of Rosemont Hall. By the time I leave for the viewings at noon, I glance at Cinderella's glass slipper and calculate that I've survived three more hours of life-without-Jack. Only a countless number left to go.

Outside in the car park, I run into Claire. 'Oh, Amy, I think

I've just sold a whopper of a flat.' She grins from ear to ear. 'This could be the one I've been waiting for. They want to exchange this week!'

I give her a quick hug. 'That's great, Claire. I'm so glad.'

'Do you want to have lunch? On me?'

I shake my head. 'I'm off to do some viewings.'

'Well, you go knock 'em dead. The market really is picking up.' She beams. 'Maybe it'll be your lucky day too.'

'Maybe. Thanks, Claire.'

I don't spoil her mood by telling her the truth – it would take more than luck to turn my day around. It would take a miracle.

* * *

Things do not improve when I discover that the house-hunters are my old friends the Wakefields: Mr and Mrs 'It-costs-a-bomb-to-insure-thatch', from the ill-fated visit to Mrs Chip's cottage. As I get out of the car, I'm about to make a joke about main roads and thatch, but it's immediately clear they don't even remember me. I don't bother to remind them of our previous encounter.

Remarkably, the viewing goes off without a hitch. The two cottages I show them both have solid slate roofs and substantial front gardens on quiet country lanes. Mrs Wakefield makes the appropriate noises that she's pleased, and her husband seems happy enough to follow her lead. By the time we leave the second property, I even find myself thinking that if the job was like this all the time, it would be almost enjoyable.

Feeling brave, I invite them for a cup of tea at the Cup o' Comfort, which happens to be walking distance from the second property. As we approach, I can almost taste the homemade bread with a touch of cinnamon, scones fluffy and thick with strawberries and mounds of fresh cream. After days of not feeling very hungry, suddenly, I'm starving.

A bell tinkles as we go inside and sit down at a table by the window. The curtains and tablecloths are matching chintz, and little doilies nestle underneath the willow-patterned cups. The elderly woman, who I assume is the owner, takes her time sauntering over to us, and we order tea and scones all around.

The Wakefields are familiar with the local area, and they show me their favourite villages on Google Maps. I promise to keep my eye out for new properties coming to market. Then, Mrs Wakefield points to a big green patch on the map – one that I know all too well.

'There's a big country estate here,' she says. 'The owner's widow died a few months ago. Winford? Winslow? Something like that. Maybe it will open up to the public – it looks like a great place to walk the dogs.'

'It's Windham,' I say. 'The house is called Rosemont Hall. Unfortunately, it's destined to become a golf course – unless you can find a Good Samaritan with a spare million or four...'

'I'm afraid not.' Mrs Wakefield sips her tea.

'I know that place,' Mr Wakefield says. 'I've been in insurance for forty years, and so was my father before me.'

'Really?' I act surprised.

'Dad worked for Lloyds in their Bath office. He investigated all kinds of claims – flushed out fraudsters like a flock of grouse.'

'Oh?'

'He always said that Sir George was one of the worst.'

'Sir George Windham?' I lean forward in my chair. 'What do you mean?'

'He was a war hero, so no one was going to doubt his word

officially. But it was common knowledge that he was a wily old bastard. Dad couldn't prove it, but he thought Sir George set that fire himself.'

'The fire in the east wing?' I breathe a little faster.

'You know your stuff, don't you?' He takes a bite of his scone. 'Sir George tried to pin the blame on some poor servant. But no one believed that.'

'Why would he set fire to his own house?'

'The house wasn't insured but some painting was. A Renoir, I think.'

'A Rembrandt?'

'Maybe. It was the only one he'd kept when the rest of his collection had to be sold off. The painting was destroyed in the fire – so he said anyway. He made a hefty claim under the insurance.'

'What do you mean by "so he said"?'

His wife checks her watch. 'Peter, we should be getting home to the dogs.'

'OK,' he says to his wife. 'But it's not often I get a captive audience.'

'But what about the painting?' The puzzle pieces swirl around in my head faster and faster, refusing to come together. Sir George planning something. Henry and Arabella assuming it was the ball and unveiling Henry's portrait. But what if it was something else entirely?

Mr Wakefield chuckles. 'Search me. The funny thing was, no one at the party remembered seeing it hanging in the ballroom that night.'

'The Rembrandt wasn't in the ballroom? Well, I suppose that makes sense. I saw an old picture of the great hall. That's where it usually hung, right?'

'Sorry – I don't know.'

I think aloud. 'They might have moved the Rembrandt out of the great hall, if that's where Henry's portrait was supposed to go. Except, there is no portrait of Henry. Just the girl in the pink dress.'

Mrs Wakefield taps her husband on the shoulder. 'Peter, we need to—'

'What did your father find?' I press. 'Was there any wreckage – some kind of fragments of the painting?'

'The whole place was a wreck,' Mr Wakefield says. 'I believe they found a gold cigarette lighter. Sir George said the servant used it to start the fire.'

'A gold lighter!' My mind stops whirling, centring in on the first time I met Mrs Bradford. The insurance people must have returned the lighter to 'H', then it got mislaid and ended up woven into a bird's nest.

'In the end,' he says, 'Dad held things up in red tape. We're kind of good at that in my business. Heh, heh, heh.' He winks. 'Sir George died before anything was paid out. I don't think the burnt bit of the house ever did get fixed up.'

'It didn't.'

'The insurance company never did settle the case. Declared it an open verdict.'

'And what about the servant? Did they arrest anyone? Why would someone do that? Why would *Sir George*, of all people, do that?'

'Peter…' his wife says again. 'Sorry, Ms Wood. My husband can tell his stories all day.'

'Really, I'd love to know more.'

'You'd make a pretty good investigator yourself, young lady,' he says. 'You ask a lot of questions.'

'Sorry.' I am sorry – that I won't be finding out anything more from him today.

'No worries.' Mr Wakefield stands up. 'And we'll ring you about those cottages.'

'Oh, yes.' I get to my feet realising that I'd completely forgotten about my day job and their property search. 'And I'll keep you posted if anything similar comes on the market.'

'Sure, great.'

We shake hands, and the bell tinkles as they leave the café.

* * *

I sit back down at the table to consider what I've just learned. Sir George was planning something – something that involved his Spanish artist friend. It wasn't Henry's portrait, because as far as I know, no portrait of Henry was ever done. And the portrait of the girl in the pink dress: Arabella, or whoever she is – I still don't know for sure if the painting was done in 1899 or the 1950s. All I know is that those eyes are familiar somehow. I tap my fingers restlessly on the table. Rosemont Hall hasn't given up its secrets, and pretty soon it will be too late. I have to find out more. But how?

The white-haired woman comes back to my table, and I ask for more hot water. I should go back to the office, but the gas fire is warm and cosy and if I can just think it through—

'I heard what that man was saying.'

Startled, I look up. The woman sets a pot of hot water down on my table.

'He was talking about Rosemont Hall.' She stacks the plates of crumbs left by the Wakefields. 'About the fire, and Sir George.'

'Yes, he was.'

'He doesn't know the half of it.'

'What do you mean?' I shift eagerly to the edge of the chair. Maybe it's my lucky day after all.

The woman puts her hands on her hips. 'When I was a girl, my mother worked up at the house. Sometimes we used to play there, and when I got older, I worked there when they needed extra help for the parties. They were the most fancy parties and balls you could imagine. Sir George liked to recreate the old days before the wars.'

She stares at the flickering gas flame. I swallow back a thousand questions, afraid that I might put her off.

'There were so many beautiful people. My sister and I were mad about the men – ex-soldiers and officers, bankers, politicians up from London. But we were nobodies – only the hired help. Sir George ran the house like it was the 1850s rather than the 1950s. Everyone knew their place.'

She wipes down a nearby table, frowning with the memories.

'Sir George was a devil,' she says. 'So was his son, Henry. People like us meant nothing to them.'

'What do you mean?'

The old woman clams up like she's just remembered she's talking to a complete stranger. She glares at me. 'Why are you so interested anyway?'

'I'm interested in local history.'

The bell on the door tinkles and a woman with a pram comes inside. Silently, I curse.

The owner greets the newcomer. They chat for ages about the village bake sale. I pour more hot water into the teapot, and wait.

At last, the pram woman leaves. The owner flips the sign on the door from 'open' to 'closed', letting out a relieved sigh. Turning around, she looks startled to see that I'm still there.

'I'm closing up now, will you be wanting anything else?'

'I'd like you to tell me more about Rosemont Hall.'

'Why?' She wrinkles her nose.

Why indeed? At that very moment, an idea strikes me.

'I thought I might write a book about the history of the house,' I say. The words sound so *right*. 'I'd like to record the things that aren't mentioned in the archives. Tell the stories of the nameless women who lived and loved there. I'm a teacher – or, at least, I used to be. I can't save Rosemont Hall, but I can preserve some part of its history. The thing is, I need more information. A story that will really bring the place alive.'

The woman looks at me like I've sprouted a second head. I don't care. My chest fizzes with excitement. I want to go home and start right away.

'I'm not the one you should be asking,' she says. 'If you want colourful detail, my sister knows a lot more.'

The bell on the door tinkles again. We both look up.

'This must be your lucky day. Here she is—'

I barely hear the words. I stare at the old woman who's just come in. She looks at me and frowns, her eyes – her forget-me-not-blue eyes – sharp and piercing. And suddenly I guess the truth. It's been staring me in the face all along.

# 38

Mrs Bradford hobbles in leaning on her cane. The huge Saint Bernard, Captain, pads in behind her. When she sees me, her face remains impassive and she nods almost politely. Captain comes over and licks my hand like today I'm friend, not foe.

'Hello,' I say, staring at her wizened face like I'm seeing it for the first time.

'This is my sister,' the owner says. 'As I say, she's the one you should be asking your questions.'

'We've met, actually.' I feel like I've been flattened by a very large bus.

The cane points in my direction. 'Amy Wood,' Mrs Bradford cackles, 'estate agent.'

The dog lays down at my feet and I scratch his shaggy head, still staring at the old lady.

'Estate agent?' The owner looks at me with suspicion clouding her face. 'You said you were writing a book.'

'Um... yes. In my spare time.' I grip the edge of the table, bracing myself for an outburst from one or both of them about 'poking my nose where it doesn't belong'.

To my surprise, Mrs Bradford laughs. 'A book, is that it?' She hobbles over to a table across the room from me and manoeuvres herself into the chair. The stick waves in her sister's direction and clatters to the floor. The dog growls and picks it up in his mouth to give it back to her. 'What is it? Some kind of two-penny romance with you as the heroine, I suppose.'

'Actually,' I say through my teeth, 'it's a history book.'

'A history book.' She raises a bushy white eyebrow and chuckles again. I've no idea what could possibly be so funny. 'Get another cup of tea for Miss Wood, will you, Gwen.' She gestures for me to join her at her table. I move over to the empty chair as her sister goes off with an irritated tsk.

'Please, call me Amy,' I say.

She waves off my request with a gnarled hand. 'So, what is it that you want to know today? Let me guess – all about that painting on the landing. Who that girl is and what her life was like. You want to know all her secrets.'

'It's a stunning painting,' I say. 'And the artist has really captured the subject. She's beautiful, certainly, but there's more to her than that, isn't there?' My eyes lock with her familiar blue ones – or rather, with those of a girl, many years younger – in a pink dress.

The laughter fades from her face. 'So you've finally guessed, have you, Amy Wood?'

'It *was* you all along, wasn't it? How silly of me not to have seen it.' Of course it's her. All along she's been right in front of me, staring me in the face. No wonder Jack thought she looked familiar. And Flora – her granddaughter – is her spitting image.

Mrs Bradford sighs. 'Maybe the resemblance isn't so obvious now when you look at her pretty face – innocent chit that she was. But give yourself another sixty years and the trouble I've seen and see how you fare.'

I lean forward on my elbows. 'Tell me the story, Mrs Bradford. How did you come to be painted like that?'

'You mean, how did a lowly girl from the village come to be hanging on the wall in the big house? Just say it, Amy Wood. You won't be the first.' She purses her lips like a sphinx.

'OK,' I say. 'If you like.'

Her sister returns with a tray and sets it on the table. With a cursory frown, she takes up the story. 'A trunk full of costumes was delivered,' Gwen says. 'Sir George wanted everyone to dress up in period costumes for the ball – even the hired help. We were supposed to dress as kitchen servants, but then we found a whole room of beautiful dresses and costumes that belonged to Sir George's late wife. We couldn't resist trying on the beautiful gowns. They were fabulous – made of silk and satin, taffeta and chiffon. Trimmed with pearls, lace and sparkly beads – what girl could possibly resist?'

'Not me,' I say. 'It sounds wonderful. When was this?'

Gwen looks at her sister before answering. 'It was a week or two before the last ball,' she says. 'The one for Henry's twenty-first birthday. Sir George had an artist friend there – some Spanish chap. Handsome too. He was working in the studio in the attic. He was there to paint Henry's portrait, I think. But he had an eye for the ladies. He took a shine to Maryanne. He sketched her, and then did that painting.'

'The sketchbook.' I steal a glance at Mrs Bradford. 'I found it in the library the night that Flora was there. I, umm... took it for safekeeping. It's at home in my drawer along with the lighter.'

'I thought as much.' Mrs Bradford crosses her arms. Other than the sunken blue eyes, her pudgy, lined face bears little or no resemblance to the girl in the painting.

'I just can't believe it was you...' I trail off, barely realising I've spoken aloud.

'Well, Amy Wood, it's the truth,' Mrs Bradford says. 'I was the girl in the pink dress – and a hot and scratchy thing it was too, let me tell you.' She chortles. 'And those fancy-dress costumes are still there in the closet off the Rose Bedroom. But of course, you found them too.' She lifts her chin. 'Oh yes, I noticed.'

I smile uneasily. At least I was right about the pink dress. It wasn't a replica of the dress in the painting. It was the real one.

'Anyway, now you know.' She shrugs. 'No big secret.'

'But when I asked before, Mrs Bradford, why didn't you just say it was you?'

She sniffs. 'You asked if she was Sir George's wife, or his mother, or Arabella – someone posh and important. You never dreamt it might be a nobody like me. Though that's what I told you the first time you asked.'

'Well, you have to admit, it's a little strange. I mean, if the artist was there to paint Henry's portrait, then how come he never did?'

'He said Henry was no picture,' Gwen says with a laugh.

'Even so, it seems odd that he didn't fulfil his commission.' I try to recall the words of the letter I found – something along the lines of 'I will tell people that you are here to paint my son's portrait'. 'But maybe Sir George wasn't all that bothered?'

Mrs Bradford snorts like I'm stating the obvious.

'And what about the Rembrandt?' I say. 'It used to hang in that space, didn't it? I spoke to someone who said it wasn't in the ballroom the night of the fire. Do either of you remember seeing it there?'

The obnoxious ring of my mobile cuts off my question. I fumble to silence it, but it's too late. Gwen looks at her watch, then at me. 'I'm closing up now,' she says. 'We've got choir practice.'

'Wait.' I jab the mute button. 'You can't go yet.'

Nonplussed, Mrs Bradford whistles through her dentures. Captain jumps up, his head and tail high, like he's standing to attention.

The phone rings again. Cursing under my breath, I check the screen – my parents' number is blinking on the display. It rings and rings; I have to answer it.

'Amy!' Mum shouts frantically in my ear. 'Please come home right away. Your dad's had an accident.'

The blood drains from my face. 'I'll be there in twenty minutes, Mum.' I end the call and jump to my feet.

'I have to go now,' I say to Mrs Bradford. 'But will you please finish the story another time?'

Ignoring the question, Mrs Bradford hoists herself up and hobbles off towards the loo in the back, thumping her stick and chuckling.

# 39

I prepare myself for the worst. Dad's been hit by a car, or had a heart attack, or a stroke, and I'm too late and he's dead. I should have been a better daughter: provided them with grandchildren, or at least have done something with my life that they could brag about to their friends at the Scrabble club. All the way home my heart is in my throat. I turn into the lane expecting flashing ambulance lights, wailing sirens, and gaggles of curious onlookers.

When I rush into the house and find Dad sprawled on the sofa watching a repeat of *Antiques Roadshow* with Mum holding a packet of frozen peas on his ankle, I'm relieved – of course! – but also a tiny bit perturbed.

'Dad fell off a ladder putting pigeon spikes on the shed,' Mum explains. 'He fell into the lilac – otherwise, he might have broken something.'

I kneel down beside the sofa and kiss Dad on the cheek. 'I'm glad you're OK—'

'Shhh' – he waves a hand – 'let's hear the valuation.'

I look at the TV. Fiona Bruce is wearing a green leather coat and tight red jeans. Beside her is a rotund bearded man whose face is pouring with sweat.

'The good news is the vase does have the mark from Occupied Japan...' the bow-tied valuation man says.

'That man is hoping he can sell that vase to build an extension so his mum doesn't have to go to a home,' Mum says. 'Isn't that sweet?'

'But I'm afraid that the chip in the base means it won't fetch much more than two hundred at auction.'

The rotund bloke looks crushed. Standing up, I offer to make supper.

'That would be nice,' Mum says. 'I've thawed some sausages; plus these peas.'

Sausages! Peas *à la* Dad's ankle!

'Actually, I was thinking I might do something different, like... uhh, chilli con carne—'

'Shhh.' This time Mum holds up her hand. 'This one looks interesting.'

I roll my eyes and head to the kitchen.

'I've had my eye on this painting all day...' the valuer says. 'Tell me how you came by it.' The camera pans to a painting of two children playing at the seaside.

I hover at the door – I do love *Antiques Roadshow.*

'My grandmother died, and I inherited it...' a young woman is saying. 'She was Jewish and she lived in Germany before the war. Luckily, she got out.'

'You could make one of those curries,' Dad says, struggling to sit up.

'Shhh. Dinner can wait. I want to hear this.' I grab the remote and turn up the volume.

'A genuine Mary Cassatt!' the valuer says. 'And a lovely one at that. But you said there's more to the story?'

'A friend of a friend put my grandmother in contact with a Spanish artist who was also an expert smuggler. Walredo, his name was. He helped her hide it. Here's a photograph of her house...'

*Walredo* – the man in the photo with Sir George. I never did look up the name. My pulse quickens; I move closer to the TV. The woman holds up a black and white photo of a painting. But it's not the Cassatt. It's—

'That's fascinating. You mean, they hid the Cassatt to smuggle it out of Germany...?'

—A portrait of a Spanish flamenco dancer. Her dress swirls from a black background, her eyes dark and dominating. I've never seen the painting before, but I know the style all too well.

'Yes, that's right.' The woman smiles. 'The Nazis never found it.'

A painting that hides a secret.

'It was pure genius to hide it so well...'

Buried treasure that could save a house.

'...And the story you've told me makes it worth even more...'

And at this moment...

'I'd say you could easily be looking at seven figures...'

I know where it is.

# 40

Sir George might have been a devil, but he was also devious and shrewd. His beloved Rembrandt wasn't sold or destroyed in the fire – it was carefully hidden. Unfortunately, he died without letting anyone in on the secret. It's been right in front of me – and everyone else – all along.

In fact, the day I had coffee with Mary Blundell, I should have started putting two and two together. But I didn't, and now I've lost precious time. The sale to Hexagon will complete as soon as the probate decree comes through, which could be any day now. But if I can find the painting, maybe there's still a chance to stop the sale.

There's only one little problem niggling in my head – I no longer have the keys to Rosemont Hall.

* * *

Of all the things I thought I might be doing as an estate agent, breaking and entering did not figure high on the list. Nevertheless, the decision comes easily. After supper and a quick game of three-handed bridge (Dad pulls the invalid card so I can't refuse), I settle my parents in front of the TV and go to my room saying I need an early night. I change my clothes, sneak out to the garage and find Dad's torch, and drive off.

I reach my destination shortly before ten. But as I'm about to turn off the main road, I have to slam on the brakes. The old stone pillars have been reinforced with new brickwork and the ornate iron gates have been rehung. They now meet firmly in the centre, shut with a heavy chain and padlock. Obviously, someone's decided that leaving Rosemont Hall vacant is a security risk – from people like me.

I park the car in a lay-by and turn off the lights. Disguised in my black leather jacket, leggings, black trainers and knit woolly cap, I blend in with the darkness. But as I'm about to cross the road, a police car approaches, its blue lights flashing. I flatten myself against the prickly hedgerow until it whizzes past. There's nothing to fear – I'm not here to steal anything, and I haven't done anything wrong.

Yet.

The gates tower over my head, black and imposing. I try to climb the iron scrolls but can't get a good foothold. The old stone wall is overgrown with ivy. I walk along until I find a place where the top stones have collapsed and I can scramble over. I *thunk* to the ground on the other side into a nest of brambles.

The moon breaks through the clouds as I brush myself off and walk up the long avenue to the house. The wood is dark, the bare trees spindly and sinister like skeletons. It takes the better part of twenty minutes before I top the last hill and Rosemont Hall is before me. The windows shine black in the distance like glassy pupils – seeing all. Seeing me.

The front door of the house is locked. I circumnavigate the

perimeter looking for a loose window or broken pane, but none are on a level where I can reach them. On the back terrace, I shine the torch over the French doors that lead to the green salon. Clenching my teeth, I knock the torch hard against a cracked pane near the handle. The glass shatters. I unlatch the door and slip inside the house.

I'm now officially a criminal.

Inside, darkness swallows the beam of the torch. The parquet floor creaks and groans as if protesting the illicit entry. I grope my way through the green salon to the great hall, not daring to turn on the lights. I tiptoe up the main staircase and stand before the portrait.

Now that I'm here, I'm not quite sure what to look for. I half wish that I'd brought Mary Blundell along for some tips. I shine the torch over the painting. The oil paint glimmers, accentuating the folds of the pink dress that emerge from the shadows like moonlight. The subject truly is beautiful (though I still find it hard to believe she's a young Mrs Bradford). In my mind's eye, I conjure up the grand ball: the east wing lit by candlelight, well-coiffed ladies swirling around with handsome men in old-fashioned costumes. The portrait painter sketching a young woman as she tries on costumes, her neck long, shoulders soft and white, the silk clinging to her body like a second skin.

The frame is thick and ornate, but the gold paint is partly rubbed off, and the crevices are grimy with dust. I shine the light over the date on the plaque that was meant to fool everyone: 1899. The frame originally belonged to the John Singer Sargent painting that Sir George sold at auction. It seems so simple. But the best deceptions usually are. On the *Antiques Roadshow*, the valuable Cassatt painting was hidden behind another canvas – one stretched over the other. The top canvas was painted with a flamenco dancer – accomplished, but not a masterpiece. My hunch is that the same thing was done here. But what can I do to prove it?

I set down the torch and try to lift the painting off the wall. But it's almost as tall as me and very unwieldy. Something thuds to the floor from behind the heavy frame. For a second I'm worried that I've broken something. I let go of the painting and shine the light over the object that's dropped from behind the frame. It's a bundle of airmail envelopes bound together with a pink ribbon. I pick it up, squinting in the dim light. The envelopes are addressed to a 'Miss A Reilly'. I haven't heard the name Reilly before, but surely it must be Arabella?

And then I hear it: gravel crunching, and the noise of an engine. Headlights sweep over the windows; the blood freezes in my veins.

Someone is here.

I pocket the bundle of letters and switch off the torch. Flattening myself against the staircase, I creep down step by step, my heart thundering. If I can just make it to the east wing corridor then I might be able to keep out of sight until whoever it is goes away.

A cracked piece of marble gives way beneath my feet. I tumble down the last few steps; the torch clatters to the floor of the main hall, splaying batteries. The car engine goes off. Terror grips me – is it Mrs Bradford? Or the police who drove past earlier? I'm not sure which is worse. Abandoning the torch, I tiptoe across the main hall to the front windows.

The car's headlights penetrate the darkness like the eyes of a cat, then go off. A door opens; a pencil torch flicks on. A dark figure opens the boot, takes something out, and closes it again. Another tiny light goes on – a mobile phone. The intruder pauses on the way to the door, texting someone. Definitely not Mrs Bradford or the police.

I leg it to the east wing door and pull the handle. Nothing. It's locked. Panic rises in my throat. I'm trapped in the open. A key turns in the lock; the door groans open. My mobile beeps loudly in my pocket as a text comes in. I stifle a gasp, but it's too late.

The beam of the visitor's torch jerks across the floor towards my feet. A deep and familiar voice cries out.

'Who's there?'

# 41

*Jack Faraday.*

Oh my God, it's Jack Faraday! It can't be. But it is.

I cower against the wall, gripping my phone. Escape is impossible. The beam of light flicks upward to my face. I put my hands in the air – I'm guilty!

'Amy? Amy Wood? Is that you?'

I shield my eyes with my arm. 'Oh, hi, Jack. I left my, uhh...' I lower my hands. His skin glows like marble in the near darkness; my body liquefies in all those unmentionable places. Unfortunately, I have seriously cocked things up. Jack and I have no future, but I hate the idea that now he'll think I'm at worst a criminal or at best a nutcase – or the other way around. The one saving grace is that I didn't throw my phone at him.

'Amy, what are you doing here?' His voice chills the air.

I slump to the floor, defeated. 'I'm breaking and entering with an intent to poke my nose where it doesn't belong.'

He frowns – probably deciding whether or not to call the police.

'It's the girl in the pink dress,' I say. 'I had a hunch that I needed to follow up…' I swallow hard. 'I'm sorry.'

He's silent for a moment, his eyes shiny and penetrating. 'Any idea where the light switch is?'

'By the door, left side.'

I dust myself off as he goes to the door and flips the switch. Harsh light from the dusty, bare-bulbed chandelier floods the hall. But a second later, a loud pop makes us both jump. The chandelier goes out and everything is black. Unlike last time when the sudden darkness promised everything, this time he keeps his distance.

'Another damn fuse,' Jack says. 'We'd better get out of here. And you can tell me what the hell is going on.'

# 42

The atmosphere is glacial as he drives me to the main road where I've left my car. I try – and fail – to make a bit of idle chit-chat: 'When did you arrive?' 'Early this morning.' 'How was your flight?' 'Fine.'

I'm heartbroken over the unspoken questions I want to ask: 'What are you doing here?' 'Why didn't you ring me?' 'What next?'

Things improve marginally when he drops me off at my car. 'Now, I still want that explanation,' he says gruffly, 'and you can buy me a drink for good measure.'

'Sure.' Hope kindles inside my chest.

'You can follow behind.'

'OK.'

He rechains the gates as I get into my own car. Hands clenched on the wheel, I follow him to the White Horse Inn – a traditional Elizabethan country hotel with diamond-pane windows and wisteria vines twisting up the front. As we park our cars and go inside, I'm conscious of his proximity – and his distance. We find a table in the corner near the open fire.

'What would you like?' I say.

Jack shakes his head. 'I was joking about you buying.' His tone is anything but light. 'What would you like?'

'Red wine, please.'

He goes to the bar; I nip to the loo. My reflection in the mirror is appallingly dishevelled: my eyes have dark circles underneath, my hair is dusty, my lips are chapped from the cold. I look less like a cat burglar and more like something the cat dragged in. Not that it matters. The disappointing reality is that there's nothing between Jack and me. I'll explain myself and then leave. I've only got to endure his painfully attractive presence for maybe half an hour, max.

Back at the table, Jack arrives with the drinks, his face like carved stone. 'OK, now start talking. And you'd better make it good.' He crosses his arms. 'Convince me not to call the police – and your boss.'

I grip the stem of my wine glass. 'It's the mystery of the girl in the painting. I've solved it... or, at least, I think have.'

'What mystery? What are you talking about?'

Jack Faraday is judge and jury as I sum up the details of my research. I recount what Mrs Bradford and her sister told me about how young Maryanne came to have her portrait painted, and finish with my hunch about the painting. He listens in unreadable silence.

'So I went there tonight,' I finish. 'But I'd already given back the key.'

Jack frowns. 'Let me get this straight. You saw something on television – what was it again – *Antiques Roadshow*?' His raised eyebrow says it all. 'It made you think there might be a missing Rembrandt hidden somewhere in the house. A painting that everyone thought was destroyed in a fire? And no one's discovered it over all these years until you came along?'

'I know it sounds—'

'Crazy?'

I hang my head.

'So you felt the need to dress like a burglar and break a window to get inside the house?'

'I wanted to look for the painting. I wasn't going to steal anything.'

'And did you find this priceless missing Rembrandt?'

'Well... no. I didn't really have a chance to look. But I did find these.' I reach into my pocket and set the bundle of letters on the table. 'They were in the gap between the frame and the wall. I just wanted... I don't know... to find something worth saving before Rosemont Hall was lost.'

'Lost?'

'It's my fault.' A sob catches in my throat. 'It was my job to sell it. My job to find someone who would bring the house back to life.' I stare at the letters and the untouched wine in my glass, dark red like old blood. 'You said once that I was like a house matchmaker. Only, this time, when it was most important, I failed.'

He picks up the bundle of letters and stares at the name on the front: Miss Reilly. He tucks them away in his jacket pocket and looks at me in silence.

'I'm not some kind of deranged nutcase, Jack. Really, I'm not.'

Having said my piece, I await sentence.

He drains his pint and turns the empty glass around in his hand. 'You wanted a happy ending,' he says.

'Sorry?'

'A happy ending, like in one of your classic English novels.'

Hearing those words, every cell in my body shivers and

realigns itself, like leaves growing towards the light. How can he possibly know me so well? How will I ever get over the ache of sitting across the table from him knowing that there's no future? Tears spring to my eyes.

'Yes,' I say. 'That's it exactly.'

And I pray that he'll make it happen, but instead, he stands up and goes to the bar. The tiny part of me that isn't in love with him hates him a little. By rights I should leave. But I don't.

He returns to the table with two glasses of water. 'You could have just called me,' he says. 'If you'd told me about your "hunch", maybe you could have saved yourself the trouble of breaking and entering.' He fiddles with the beer mat. 'In fact, when I saw you there, I thought maybe' – he hesitates – 'maybe you got my text.'

'Text?'

'I sent you a text earlier. You didn't get it?'

'No.' I reach for my handbag – my phone must be somewhere.

'Never mind,' he says. 'I'll just tell you. It was to let you know that I was in town. I wanted to surprise you. I guess I did.'

'But when we spoke, you said that your life was familiar. I thought that meant you were gone for good.'

'I was.' His aquamarine eyes bore into me. 'I had some important work on the patent that couldn't wait. I flew home, just like I'd planned. But as soon as I got there... and you called me in the middle of the night...' He shakes his head.

'What?'

'I went to my home, I went to my meetings, I went to work. But *familiar* was no longer enough. Nothing felt right. Something happened when I was here. Something completely unexpected.'

I sit frozen in my chair.

'I realised I had unfinished business. Something more important than computer chips or patents. Much more important. So I booked myself on a flight to London. I didn't know if you'd even see me, after the last time.'

'Me?'

'Yes, Amy. You.' He stares at me intently. I can feel a flush creeping up my neck. 'And then you didn't respond to my first text. I figured that was my answer. I paced the room for a while but I couldn't sleep. So I decided to visit the place that most reminded me of you – Rosemont Hall.' He shrugs. 'When I got there I sent you another text. You know – the tell-tale beep.' He gives me a half smile. 'When I saw you there with your torch, I thought you'd come after all.'

He narrows his eyes beneath his long dark lashes. 'But now, I realise you were a burglar.'

'No, Jack! I didn't get your message.'

'So the question is' – he pauses, probably to make me sweat a little more – 'if you had read my text asking to see you, what would you have said?'

'I would have said that I was a complete idiot before to run away like that. And I've regretted it every moment since.'

He leans closer and takes my hand.

'Spoken eloquently, like an English teacher.' His soft laugh sends delicious shockwaves through my body. And at that moment, my appetite for mystery disappears, leaving room for nothing except him.

'No, Jack, I'm just an estate agent.'

He smiles and draws me close, his breath ruffling my hair. 'In that case, Amy Wood, *just* an estate agent,' he whispers in my ear, 'I'd love to hear more about your sleuthing. But maybe we can continue this little chat upstairs.'

He stands up and takes a room key from his pocket. This time, I can't even imagine running away. I leave my glass on the table and follow him out of the bar.

# 43

From the moment I enter his room, I'm lost. We come together with the urgency of two travellers in a desert seeking an oasis. His kiss is hard and searching, his hands delicate as they remove my clothing and explore my skin. The bed is a large four-poster, and we fling ourselves onto it. I pull him over me and he shudders as I run my fingers through his hair and over his chest, desperate to discover all of him. 'Amy,' he whispers, and the words are lost as our lips come together and speak their secret language.

Finally we lie still in each other's arms. 'I didn't think I'd ever find this again,' Jack says, his face soft and luminous.

'I can't believe it either.'

'Well, believe it,' he says, and after that, neither of us speaks for a while.

* * *

Tennyson wrote that it's better to have loved and lost than never to have loved at all. I spend the night and all the next day with Jack. Somehow, the logistics get sorted: I phone in sick to work, breakfast arrives on a tray and we eat it together at the little table in his room that overlooks the village green. Then we're back in bed and the duvet is warm and Jack's skin is warm, and his mouth is soft and yielding, his hands confident and demanding. I want it to last, but of course it won't. I know that there's no future and that when we say goodbye, it will be forever. There are still unanswered questions and unspoken topics between us: the house, the painting, the family secrets. But cocooned in his hotel room, a universe of two, I put all that out of my mind.

Finally, we sleep for a few hours, tangled in the sheets and each other's arms. When I wake up, it's late afternoon. A cold fear grips me. I don't want this to end.

Jack feels me stir and rolls over.

'Amy…' He strokes my thigh under the blankets.

'Hmm?'

'We should go while it's still light.'

'Go?' My heart freezes.

'I assume you want to have another look for that painting. We can't count on the lights working.'

'You mean… you don't mind?'

I roll over. His face is grave.

'I don't know anything about lost paintings, portraits, old letters, or anything like that. You have to admit that it sounds pretty farfetched. And the house will be sold, Amy, make no mistake. I don't want you here under false pretences. But if you need to go back there one more time – to say goodbye or whatever – then I'm not going to stop you.'

I shiver with regret. The hands of the clock are winding down so fast. I don't want things to end. But that's precisely what's going to happen.

'I don't know, Jack.' I run a fingernail delicately over his chest. 'Maybe it's better if I don't go there. You'll return to America, and I'll go back to my life. I might wish that things were different, but the truth is' – I turn away so he can't see the tears in my eyes – 'you've already given me more of a happy ending than I ever could have hoped for. I just want to enjoy *this* – while it lasts.'

He brushes a piece of damp hair off my face. 'That's not the Amy I know,' he says. 'What about your hunch?'

'In the end, the house will be sold.' I choke back a sob. 'As you've pointed out, it's really none of my business.'

Jack sighs. 'It's complicated, Amy. And I don't know how much Gran has told you.'

'Not a lot. Just snippets here and there.'

'I don't know the whole story either – far from it. But I do know that for her, bygones are not bygones.'

'What do you mean?' I prop up on my elbow.

He looks at me with his arresting blue eyes. 'When Flora and I were kids, Gran used to come and visit us every Thanksgiving and Christmas. Sometimes we'd sneak out of our bedrooms at night and sit on the landing, listening to the adults. Gran would have a few drinks and then start talking about England, where she came from. Something about a big mansion, and how something happened to her there.' He pauses. 'She always said that America was the land of opportunity. There wasn't all this business about class and family heritage.'

He fingers a lock of my hair, but his eyes are far away.

'Her story was a bit garbled and pieced together, but I gather that when she came over to America in the fifties, she was pregnant with our mom. It was just like something out of one of your classic novels. She'd been seduced by Henry Windham.'

'Seduced?' I pull away, stunned. 'By Henry? But... I thought, I mean... the letters! He was in love with Arabella. Wasn't he?'

'Probably, I don't know,' Jack says. 'Or maybe all that came later. All I know is that Gran was a nobody – just a girl from the village. But incidentally, her maiden name was Reilly. She could be the "Miss Reilly" on the letters you found behind the painting.'

I sit bolt upright as the possibilities explode in my mind like fireworks. I'm thinking not of the letters behind the painting, but about the original letters I found in the library. Reilly. Maryanne Reilly. 'A'—?

'Did your grandma ever go by "Anne" by any chance?'

He furrows his brow. 'I don't know. Once when we were little, Flora called her "Granny Annie". She flew off the handle and said never to call her that again.'

The fabric of time that I've carefully constructed in my mind rips apart. All along I assumed that the original letters I found were between Henry and Arabella. I never considered another possibility. All those benign, innocent love letters that I thought were written between a future husband and wife. A couple who were married to each other for over forty years. *They never had any children.* Now the truth glimmers in the distance like a mirage. The great love story of Rosemont Hall never existed. Not between Henry and Arabella, at least.

'The other letters I found were between "H" and "A". Arabella, I'd assumed. But maybe I've been wrong all along. Could they be between Henry and your grandma?'

'No idea.' He frowns, as if it's all too much to process. 'I'd like to read them, though. Are they still at the house?'

A blush rises to my cheeks. 'Actually, they're at home in my knicker drawer.'

He laughs. 'Of course they are.'

I laugh too, but my brain is still firing. 'The letters I found stopped just before Henry's twenty-first birthday party – the night of the fire. That must be significant. Do you know much about your grandma's past? How she ended up in America, for example?'

'As I'm sure you can imagine, she's not really the type to be open about that kind of thing.'

I *can* imagine.

'I don't know all the details,' he says, 'but she gave birth to my mom not long after she arrived in America. She settled in New York and found work in a big hotel. She told them she was a widow, I think, to avoid the stigma. It must have been difficult with a baby, and really, I don't know how she managed it. But she ended up marrying the hotel manager, Tim Bradford. Grandpa Tim. He was great.' He grins. 'Taught me how to ride a bicycle and build a tree house – stuff like that. We even took apart an old RadioShack computer together. They were married for a good many years before he died.'

'He sounds like a good guy.'

'They didn't have children of their own. But my mom grew up and married my dad. Then Flora and I came along. That should have been the end of it – a happy ending, if you like. But it wasn't.'

'What do you mean?'

He stares up at the beamed ceiling. 'Gran always talked like she hated her life in England. So you can imagine how surprised we were when she pitched up one Christmas and said she was moving back there.'

'Did she give a reason?'

'Just the usual. She said she was homesick for her own country and left just like that.' He snaps his fingers. 'We didn't hear much from her – just cards at birthdays and Christmas. But once or twice I heard my mom arguing with her on the phone. Later on, Flora and I found out that her main reason for going back to England was to confront Henry Windham. All through the years she'd been so angry. He got her pregnant, dropped her, and never even tried to contact her.'

'I can see why she'd be angry. I recall her saying something about "never a letter or a how d'ya do".'

'But it didn't stop there. She wanted him to rewrite his will leaving Rosemont Hall to her. Arabella was unstable, I believe, and paranoid because she hadn't given Henry an heir. Gran threatened to tell her about Henry's child.'

'So she blackmailed him!' I try to picture Mrs Bradford as a villain; it's not hard to do. On the other hand, maybe she was justified.

'Henry was senile by that time,' Jack adds, 'but he didn't doubt her word. I don't know if he ever loved her or not, but he'd never forgotten her.'

'Well, that's something, I guess.'

'In the end, he did change his will. But he left the house to Flora and me, not Gran. He also gave Arabella a life estate. That meant we'd only inherit the house after she died. Gran was livid, but what could she do? She stayed on at Rosemont Hall because she insisted that it was her home. And now' – he pauses, choosing his words – 'let's just say, she's not very rational when it comes to Rosemont Hall.'

Ignoring the obvious understatement, I nod.

'My mom first spoke to Ian Kendall when Henry Windham died. He told her about the inheritance, the life estate, and about Gran "applying some pressure" to get Henry to change his will. Mom was disgusted with the whole thing, and still is. She told me that when she was growing up, Gran would rave sometimes about Rosemont Hall, and how Arabella had stolen the life she should have had.

'Mom didn't want anything to do with the place or the Windham family. To her, Tim was her dad. He'd worked his way up from nothing, and it was ingrained in her to do the same. She was no gold digger, and she certainly didn't need or want anything from the likes of Henry Windham.' He shrugs disdainfully. 'Flora and I felt the same. It was family history best forgotten. Plus, at the time Henry died, I'd just finished my engineering degree. Flora was married and had started a small fashion boutique. We had our lives in America. What were we going to do with a crumbling old pile in England?'

What indeed?

'Anyway, Arabella was alive for some years. Gran worked as her housekeeper and companion until she died.' He shakes his head. 'They probably made each other miserable, for all I know.'

'Remarkable. I thought Mrs Bradford was devoted to Arabella.'

'Anyway, that's it.' Jack runs his finger along the line of my jaw. 'The whole story.'

'It's all so terrible, yet fascinating at the same time.'

He nods. 'Though, as far as I know, Henry Windham and Arabella were content in their marriage. At least until Gran tried to make things difficult. And I guess she had her reasons – a ruined life and a broken heart.'

'It's hard to know who to feel sorriest for,' I say. 'And there's one other thing too – the fire.' I tell him what I learned from Mr Wakefield. 'Sir George tried to blame a servant, but nothing was ever proven. Do you think she had anything to do with it?'

Jack frowns. 'Gran is strong-willed, that's for sure. But I find it hard to believe she'd do something like that.'

'Me too. I can't see her wanting to harm Rosemont Hall.'

'But if she was accused, it might explain why she left England. I guess the only person who knows for sure is her.'

'Yes,' I say. 'You're probably right.'

Jack rolls onto his back. 'So now, the house will be sold. Flora doesn't want it. I didn't either...'

He stops talking and seems to be debating with himself. For a dreadful moment, I worry that he's about to get out of bed and go on his way. 'The sale should complete in a few weeks,' he says. 'Then the debts of the estate can be paid.'

'But surely you know that your grandmother wants you to keep the house?' I recall Mrs Bradford's past ravings about the house being torn apart brick by brick, and about how the heirs were 'peasants' not to be more appreciative.

He gives me a sideways glance. 'She's tried the "you should appreciate where you came from" lecture a few times. Then she tried the "I worked so hard to get this for you and you're just throwing it away" card.' He shakes his head. 'I'm afraid those don't work very well with me. I guess Gran and I aren't on the same wavelength. Maybe we never will be.'

'Maybe not.'

'I'm meeting with Mr Kendall tomorrow,' he says. 'I'll drop off the letters to Gran on my way. Henry must have wedged them behind the painting. Unless Gran put them there herself.'

'Sounds reasonable.'

'And then I'm flying home to America. I'm a non-exec director of my former company, and we have an important board meeting coming up. This was just a whirlwind visit.'

'Yes, Jack.' I turn away.

'Hey,' he says, cupping my chin with his hand. 'Don't look so glum. This could be the first of many whirlwind visits.'

'OK.' I cocoon into his arms.

'But you didn't answer my question. Do you want to go to Rosemont Hall and take a look at that painting?'

'Right now?'

'Well, maybe not *just* now...'

My answer dies on my lips as he covers them with his.

# 44

*27 June 1952*
*Rosemont Hall*

*My darling,*

*My hand is shaking as I write these words. You were right all along – my father guessed our secret plans and set out to ruin them. I should have known from the moment that SHE arrived – some simpering little girl with a rich daddy and dreams of being lady of the manor. I'm ashamed to say that I was still labouring under the delusion that Father meant to honour me, not marry me off. Why did I not suspect that he was capable of such cruelty? Why did I think I was a match for his cunning and ruthlessness?*

*This morning, I went to tell him once and for all that you and I will marry. He laughed in my face. He told me that he burnt the note I sent you – telling you that at the ball I was planning to play along with my father for the sake of appearances and then renounce everything in the light of day. My heart aches thinking of the torment that last night must have caused you!*

*But I told him that none of that mattered, and there is nothing he can do to keep us apart. And then he dropped his bombshell – his 'belief' that you started the fire. My father said that he found the lighter you gave me for my birthday in the wreckage. Such tosh! But the constable was all too happy to believe him.*

*I know you've done nothing wrong. You would never lift a finger to harm your beloved Rosemont Hall. I understand that you've fled to safety. My darling, I will try to clear your name and find out who really set the fire. And then you can return. I want you with me forever, as we have planned all along. Write and let me know that you are safe. Write that you love me still.*

*—H*

## 45

I return to Rosemont Hall, no longer a burglar and, in fact, a different person in so many ways. I have to pinch myself as Jack and I approach the house in his hire car because it feels like I'm with the right person coming home to the place where I belong. I glance over at him, trying to burn his profile into my mind for when he leaves – tomorrow. In an instant, the fantasy shatters, leaving a dark, empty hole inside.

'You ready?' Jack glances over at me.

'Yes, let's do it.'

Though I'm still dressed in my burglar black, this time I enter much more respectably through the front door and we go upstairs to the landing. Jack seems to have caught my enthusiasm for the mystery; he stands back from the painting of the girl in the pink dress and studies it thoughtfully.

'She was so beautiful,' I say.

'And you're sure it's Gran?' He cocks his head.

'That's what she told me.'

'I guess she does look a little bit like Flora.'

I laugh, remembering how Flora saw no resemblance to herself.

'It all fits, Jack,' I say. 'Everything points in one direction.'

'Yeah, you keep saying.' He gives me a sideways glance. 'But now that we're here, before we go lifting paintings and removing heavy frames, can you just run me through it again?'

'Of course.' I explain how Sir George met the artist Francisco Walredo in Spain during the Civil War. The two of them became friends. The names in Walredo's sketchbook – Feldmann, Stein, Rabinowicz, etc. – were most probably Jewish clients who, prior to WWII, had commissioned him to 'hide' their precious artwork from the Nazis. But a decade later, the time for heroism had passed. Sir George was forced to sell his beloved paintings, and Tio Francisco went back to smuggling and petty art crime. But when it came time to part with his most beloved painting, Sir George wrote to his friend for help in his 'hour of need'. The Rembrandt was withdrawn from the auction, and the original frame was removed from the John Singer Sargent and replaced with a new one. Walredo came to Rosemont Hall, ostensibly to paint Henry's portrait to put over the Rembrandt. But instead, he painted a young beauty who had caught his eye – Maryanne Reilly. He painted her in a style that he'd used for his other over paintings – the same as the one on the *Antiques Roadshow* that hid the Cassatt.

Jack frowns and hangs on my every word. 'And Sir George went to all that trouble so he could keep the painting and also collect the insurance money?'

'Which was never paid out.'

Jack stares at the painting in silence. 'Well,' he says finally, 'although I haven't actually seen the infamous knicker drawer evidence, it all sounds pretty convincing.'

Blushing, I cross my fingers behind my back. We just *have* to find something.

Jack's hand brushes mine. 'OK, let's see if you're right.'

We each grab a side of the ornate gold frame. I stand on tiptoes to steady my side while he lifts the painting off the wall. There's a sharp cracking noise and a rain of white plaster as together we stagger forward under the unexpected weight and ease the bottom edge to the floor.

I keep the frame upright while Jack kneels down and studies the back of the painting. A heavy piece of board is bolted to the back along with wire used for hanging. No marks of identification or provenance are visible.

Jack pulls out a Swiss Army knife. 'Good thing I was a Boy Scout.' He finds the right tool, a tiny adjustable wrench, and starts loosening the bolts.

'Be careful.' My stomach feels suddenly queasy. Are we about to find an important 'lost' Rembrandt? Or just a pretty picture of a girl in a pink dress? 'Do you think we should leave it to an expert?'

Jack laughs softly. 'I think you qualify.'

When the bolts are off, he attempts to remove the board, but it's wedged too tightly into the edges of the frame. I watch as Jack the Engineer analyses the situation and finds a weak spot in one of the mitred corners.

'We may have to do this the hard way.' He inserts the tiny screwdriver to pry the frame apart. The wood and nails give way with a loud crack and a cloud of dust. The long side of the frame comes loose, hanging onto the bottom by a few nails. He wrenches it all the way off. I move around the painting to his side.

'Look!' I say, fizzing with excitement. 'There are two canvases – one behind the other.' In fact, there's a sandwich of various layers of thin plywood, cloth, scrim and wadding behind the top canvas. It was clearly done by an expert framer – or art smuggler.

'I'll be damned.' Jack runs his fingers reverently over the layers. 'Quite a clever feat of engineering. It's like one painting has been hermetically sealed behind another. You'd never have any idea it was there.'

He puts his Swiss army knife back in his pocket. 'I think we'd better leave it for now. What do you think?'

'I completely agree.' As much as I'd like to see the unveiling of the second canvas, it needs to be done with proper tools by proper art restorers. I'm suddenly conscious of the cold and damp. The paintings need to be moved to safety as soon as possible.

'OK. Grab your end.'

Together, we lift the heavy frame and double canvases and lean them against the wall. The girl in the pink dress stares back at us, her smile as inscrutable as ever.

'I wonder if *she* knew what she was hiding,' I say softly.

'Grandma Maryanne?' Jack says. 'It's hard to say. But if she'd tell anyone, it would be you.'

I laugh, assuming he's joking. But he shakes his head.

'I'm serious,' he says. 'Before I came to the house that night and found you "burgling" it' – he teases my hair playfully – 'I stopped by the cottage and saw Gran. I was worried about what you said – that she was struggling with the idea of moving out of Rosemont Hall.'

'Is she OK?'

'I think she's accepted the situation, though she's not happy about it. She wouldn't say very much. As I said, we aren't that close.'

'That's too bad.'

'But she did tell me that she'd met "a lovely girl who really seems to care about the things that matter". I'll spare you the "...and why can't you be more like her?" part of the conversation.'

'Thanks.' Secretly, I'm pleased that Mrs Bradford and I are finally on the same side.

'And who knows? Maybe Henry guessed the truth. After all, he left the painting to her.' He reaches over and laces his fingers with mine.

My chest wells up. 'It's so sad. I mean, all that time she was the housekeeper here, looking up at her own portrait. And Arabella – how much did she know? I will ask your grandma. I'd love to know more...'

'That's my Amy.' Jack laughs and squeezes my hand.

*My Amy.*

I lean in and kiss his cheek.

'Anyway,' he says, kissing me back, 'the past is the past, and we may never know the whole story. But whatever it is, I'd say you've helped write an important new chapter of it.'

* * *

Racing too fast, the clock winds down, and suddenly, my time with Jack is over. We leave the house together and he drives me back to the hotel to get my car. He gives me one last, searching kiss in the car park. 'I'll call you before I head off to the airport,' he says as our lips reluctantly part.

My heart torn in two, I just smile and nod.

'And I'll let you know what Sotheby's says about the painting. But in the meantime, let's not tell Gran about your "hunch", OK? Let's get the results first.'

'Of course, Jack.' My voice quavers.

He touches my chin. 'Come on, Amy, let's see a smile. Everything's going to be fine – you'll see.'

'Yes, Jack.' I swallow hard. 'But I really don't see how...'

He stops me with another kiss.

'I *will* see you soon.' His breath in my ear makes me quiver all over. But I must stop it. Jack is off to see the solicitor and then back to America. He says I need to trust him. That he'll come back soon, and we'll keep in touch... and after that, who knows what might happen?

But I know what will happen. He'll go. I'll stay. It was nice – lovely, actually – while it lasted, like the proverbial candle burning at both ends. The end of 'Jack and me' is bittersweet. Just like real life.

'Goodbye,' he whispers.

I reverse out of the car park, my hands trembling on the steering wheel. Finding what might be a lost Rembrandt has left me drained and exhausted (not to mention late for work). When I reach the village, I pull over and shove all my copies of the Rosemont Hall particulars into an overflowing rubbish bin. The house itself is forever etched in my mind, along with my vision of what it could be if someone took on the labour of love. *If.*

But that someone won't be Jack.

And it won't be me.

* * *

When I return to the office, my colleagues greet me with pained indifference. Jonathan checks his watch when I enter and gives a little smirk. Patricia fakes a concerned look when I plunk down at my desk.

'I hope whatever you had isn't catching, Amy,' she says.

'Me too.' I'm aware that my eyes are red and I look rubbish. 'But with a bad case of flu, you never know.' I blow my nose loudly for effect.

I ignore her horrified look. Claire comes in from the back, breathless and smiling.

'Oh, Amy,' she says, 'did they tell you my news?'

'No,' I say. 'But I'm sure Patricia was just about to.'

'I've got a pupillage in Birmingham with a really top chambers! I gave notice this morning – I'll be leaving here in two weeks.'

'That's great!' I go around to her desk and give her a hug. 'Fantastic!'

She tells me all about her new job, and I'm overjoyed for her. But secretly I wonder when this painful spate of goodbyes is going to end. I look around at the others, wishing it was one of them leaving rather than Claire.

All morning, I go through my tasks by rote. But inside my chest, there's a gnawing hollowness that won't go away. My skin still tingles with the ghost of Jack Faraday's touch. The phone rings and I forget to answer it. Emails come in and I just stare at the names on the computer screen. Mr Bowen-Knowles comes out, starts speaking to me in his usual nasal drone, leaves me a pile of papers, and I've no idea what he's said.

Late in the day, a large brown envelope is delivered by courier. It's from Mr Kendall, addressed to me, with a compliments slip attached to the top: *Mrs Bradford didn't want these, so Mr Jack said to give them to you. Yours, Ian Kendall, Esq.*

I shove the envelope in my handbag. I don't want any questions – I can't answer them.

Just before I head home, Jack phones from the airport. Our conversation is brief, and I feign cheerfulness and bubbly faith.

But hearing his voice so far away, the cracks in my heart grow a little wider.

'Gran was in one of her moods,' he says when I tell him about the envelope from the solicitor. 'I got another earful about not respecting the family history and Rosemont Hall.' He laughs uncomfortably. 'You probably agree with her.'

'Maybe a little bit.'

'She took some convincing even to let me get the painting looked at by an expert in London. She thought I was trying to sell it out from under her. I tried to make her see sense.' He sighs. 'I guess Flora and I haven't been the best grandchildren in the world.'

'She's a one-off, your grandmother.'

'That's putting it nicely. Anyway, I'd better go.'

'OK.' I can't bring myself to say goodbye so I quickly hang up the phone.

I sit at my desk in the empty office staring at the four beige walls. Focus on the present, breath by breath. Focus on the positives: the painting will be delivered to Sotheby's in London for examination by an expert. As for what that expert will find, I have a pretty good idea. As for what my future holds...

I shudder to think.

# 46

*Rosemont Hall*
*30 August 1952*

*Darling, I married her. Last weekend, in a ceremony in the village church before my father, a hundred well-wishers, and a God that doesn't exist. There really was no choice. Please let me explain…*

*A fire investigator came from Lloyds – a local man called Wakefield. He immediately questioned my father's well-rehearsed charade. He found the gold lighter you had given me in the wreckage. But he also found traces of accelerant that he believes started the fire. 'How could a servant do this without being seen?' he asked. Clearly, he was not a man to let the matter lie.*

*My father instantly confronted me – nearly begged me. Such a pathetic thing. He needed the protection of HER father, who is a Lord. The family association would place him above suspicion. And he showed me the true state of the finances, which was much worse than I'd imagined. If I didn't marry, I would have to sell Rosemont Hall. And how could I do that? I may never see you again – I must try to accept that – but it's still your home. You are the mistress here; your presence haunts every corner of the house.*

*My father says you've gone to America, the land of opportunity. He says that if I marry without a fuss, he will give me your address. If only my letters can reach you, then perhaps there is still hope. I believe the insurance man will declare an open verdict. He won't implicate my father directly, but he won't pay out either. When that happens, you can return and I will have this sham of a marriage annulled. In the meantime, there will be no children – I will make certain of that.*

*You trusted me once and I betrayed you. I dare not ask again. But you have only to say the word and once again I shall be yours.*

## 47

At home, Mum and Dad are in the lounge watching *Midsomer Murders*. I slip past them into my room and take the brown envelope out of my handbag. Slitting it open, I remove the bundle of letters addressed to 'A Reilly'. All the envelopes have an American address and a stamp, but no postmark – they were never sent. Nonetheless, each one has been slit open along the top. Someone has read them.

I suddenly feel like I'm rifling through someone else's dirty laundry: truly 'poking my nose where it doesn't belong'. When I read the original letters between 'H' and 'A', I assumed that both correspondents were deceased. But now that I know the truth, I feel uncomfortable reading through letters addressed to Mrs Bradford, even if she doesn't want them.

I retie the bundle and set it on top of the bureau. When I get into bed, I pick up a book from the bedside table and stare at the page for several minutes before realising I'm holding it upside down. How can I concentrate on reading fiction when a real-life love story is waiting just across the room for me to discover it?

Maybe I'll just read one or two of the letters. After all, someone's opened them already. They might contain something important. If I don't look, I'll never know – and neither will Mrs Bradford. I retrieve the stack from the bureau and sit on the bed.

It isn't until five in the morning that I finally turn off the light.

# 48

*Rosemont Hall*
*1 April 1953*

*My darling,*

*I know that I may never see you again. I curse the long years ahead. My marriage is a life sentence, the house a prison. Without you, I hope it crumbles to the ground.*

*Overnight, my father has turned old. He walks through the wreckage, tapping his stick like a blind man, cursing to himself. Sometimes, he talks to his last beloved painting – the Rembrandt – as if it's still hanging there on the empty wall. The insurance man refuses to settle the claim. He thinks that my father has spirited the painting away. He can't prove anything, but too many questions remain unanswered.*

*Cleverer still is my wife's father. He carefully hid the fact that Arabella's fortune was nowhere near as much as promised. We've put every penny into fixing the roof – there's nothing left to restore the east wing.*

*In spite of everything, one comfort remains for me. The*

*painter left behind an unexpected and precious gift. A framed canvas, discarded in his attic studio. A picture of a girl in a pink dress, the silk clinging to her body in a way that makes me ache for her. She's clutching a bundle of letters, and love shines from her eyes. I had no idea that you'd sat for him! Perhaps that was the surprise you were so eager to tell me. In any case, the painting is so lovely and lifelike – my fondest salvation and greatest torment.*

*I took it from the attic and hung it on the landing. My father saw it and began to cackle like a madman. I've seen him stop in front of it, staring like he's trying to see through the pigment and canvas. Like it somehow holds the key to his own fate.*

*Perhaps you think it cruel of me to have hung your portrait where it taunts my wife every time she sees it. But if she minds, she has never said. Every night I give her a sisterly kiss on the forehead, and we go off to our separate bedrooms. Poor Arabella. None of this is her doing.*

*Be that as it may, I would gladly trade her life for a single moment with you, my love. I suppose that makes me as much of a demon as my father.*

# 49

As the sky lightens through the net curtains, I carefully refold each of the letters, a knot of sorrow in my chest. After Henry's marriage to Arabella, the letters reduced in frequency as Henry's despair and resignation came home to roost. He never 'made anything of himself' without Maryanne at his side. Eventually he got a job as a civil servant, which didn't provide enough money for the upkeep of a house like Rosemont Hall. His life settled into a muted rhythm, though he continued to keep an account of certain key events – the death of his father, a near-miss for Arabella when she cut herself on a rusty blade and got blood poisoning. This event isn't explained, but it makes me wonder about her own despair at the state of her marriage. She too was a victim of circumstance, and I feel desperately sorry for her.

Some of the later letters went on to speculate about what Miss Reilly's life might have been like after she fled, and why she never answered any of Henry's love letters. Henry concluded that her silence was down to her own superior internal strength, and the supposition that her life had in fact turned out well. I sigh. Did he ever suspect that his letters went unreceived?

Over the forty long years of his marriage to Arabella, the house gradually fell into a worse and worse state. He speaks of the cracks in the plaster, the leaks in the roof, the woodworm, and the gathering layers of dust as if they were a comfort to him. Perhaps the crumbling walls of Rosemont Hall absorbed the pain of a broken heart.

My eyes are red and puffy from lack of sleep and deciphering Henry's tiny, deliberate handwriting. His words of love echo in my head – sometimes poetic, but ultimately futile.

And I even spare a thought for Sir George – a 'devil' by all accounts. I reread the letter he sent to Henry, noticing his sense of loss as he speaks of selling off his art and his grand plan for Henry to 'restore the family fortunes'. In the end, Sir George's schemes failed miserably and ruined many lives, including his own. And if I'm right about the painting we found, then I agree with Henry's assessment that his father was a little mad. I suppose that by entombing his beloved Rembrandt, Sir George thought that he could keep it for himself out of reach of the world. Perhaps simply having it in the house was enough for him. Even hidden, it still belonged to him.

And what if Jack and I hadn't found the painting? Would another treasure have been lost forever? Because even if I do end up saving the Rembrandt, I still haven't saved Rosemont Hall.

I put the letters back in the envelope along with the lighter, the sketchbook, and the original bundle of letters from my knicker drawer. I get dressed and slip out the back door before Mum can ply me with a breakfast I couldn't possibly stomach. Half-dazed, I drive into Bath, but I don't go to the office.

Instead, I go to the mellow stone Georgian terrace that houses the offices of Ian Kendall, Esq.

Mr Kendall's office has the warm, comforting look of a gentleman country solicitor's. There's a spacious waiting area with bookshelves on one wall, filled with neat, leather-bound law books in tan, burgundy, and green. His assistant is a middle-aged woman with glasses, who greets me when I enter. 'Mr Kendall is on the phone,' she says when I tell her my name. 'But he might be able to fit you in before his next client arrives. Would you like some coffee?'

'Yes, thank you.' I sit down on one of the leather chesterfield sofas and thumb through the latest *Country Life*.

I wait for twenty minutes until he's free. We exchange friendly greetings as he ushers me into his office and I sit down in a comfy leather chair across from his antique banker's desk. We make a bit of small talk about his office, the weather, and the local property market.

'I came to see you about the letters.' I cut to the chase.

'What about them?'

'Has Mrs Bradford read them? Did she hide them in the hollow behind the painting?'

'No.' Mr Kendall sits back in his chair. 'She denied knowing anything about them. And I believe her.'

'So who put them there? Henry Windham?'

'Or Arabella.'

My hunch confirmed, I let out a long sigh. 'Are you certain?'

He steeples his fingers like a wise sage. 'I was the family solicitor. To many people that means more than just a lawyer. Confidante, therapist – confessor. Arabella and I had tea together once or twice a year.'

'So she knew? That all those years her husband was in love with someone else? Henry continued to write love letters to

Maryanne Reilly even after they were married, but Arabella made sure that they were never sent?'

'That's the gist of it.' Mr Kendall does his best to sound lawyerly and indifferent, but the sad look in his eyes tells the truth.

'So Maryanne Reilly – Mrs Bradford – never knew that Henry had tried to find her?'

'Maybe not.'

'That poor woman!' I blurt out. 'And poor Arabella and Henry—'

I stop. The past is the past. Henry and Arabella are dead. Mrs Bradford is bitter and unstable. Rosemont Hall will become a golf clubhouse and conference centre if it's lucky, and crumble to dust if it isn't. Either way, the walls will forget what they know, and the voices they once heard will fade away.

Mr Kendall steeples his fingers. 'Strange, isn't it, Ms Wood? But also, in a way, fitting. All along, you've been the one who's shown the most interest in Rosemont Hall. You're the best person to preserve what we know of its history. At least, that's what Jack said when I told him his grandmother didn't want the letters. He's entrusted them to you.'

'I'm sure that's very noble,' I say. 'But I can't take them. You once told me that the house was less important than the people who live in it. The others are dead, but Mrs Bradford is still alive. After all, if I was her…' It strikes me then how alike we are – both loving men who were unattainable to us, and both loving Rosemont Hall – 'I'd want to know the truth.'

Mr Kendall shrugs. 'As far as the estate is concerned, the letters passed to Jack when Mrs Bradford didn't want them, and he said to give them to you. What you do next is up to you.'

I stand up. 'Thank you for clarifying that, Mr Kendall. You've been very helpful.'

'It's been a pleasure.' He stands up, and we shake hands.

As I'm about to go out the door, he stops me. 'One more thing, Ms Wood – since you're here. The final probate decree is supposed to come in this week. Please can you let Mr Bowen-Knowles know that the sale of Rosemont Hall should be able to complete immediately after?'

'Of course. We'll have our paperwork ready.' The words catch in my throat.

As I leave Mr Kendall's office, I have a strange sense of anticipation and foreboding, like somewhere, a wave is building up and about to crash over my head. I text Jack saying that I've read the letters, and can he please ring me. At the very least, I want to keep him informed (and remind him that I haven't stopped thinking about him). I get an almost immediate reply:

Will phone later. Love, Jack.

I reread the last two words about ten times. Then I do a quick directory search on my phone. For the Cup o' Comfort tearoom in the village.

# 50

The little bell on the door jingles as I enter. The tea shop has a cosy glow about it; the gas fire is lit, and the heady scent of baking and coffee wafts from the counter where a fresh lemon cake is cooling. I choose a table by the fire and when Gwen comes over to take my order, I ask for a pot of tea for two and a plate of cake and salted-caramel flapjacks. I remove the bundle of letters from my handbag, sit back, and wait. After a few minutes, the bell tinkles again.

Maryanne Bradford enters the café. Her back is hunched, her hair grey and unruly, and her ankles swollen, but her eyes are piercing as she looks at me. Despite her advanced years, she is a strong and indomitable force. The girl in the pink dress – paramour of the late Henry Windham – grandmother to Jack and Flora – the housekeeper with an axe to grind.

She hobbles towards me, her cane thumping across the floor. Captain, her faithful, blind Saint Bernard, pads behind her; his nose quivers and he growls in my direction. If my heart wasn't already thundering, it is now.

'Down, Captain,' she rasps.

The huge dog slinks on his belly under the table and lies down on my feet, his pink tongue lolling out. Unable to stand up for fear of losing a leg, I stay seated, the bundle of letters in my lap. Mrs Bradford's eyes remain fixed on my face as she scrapes a chair across the floor and lowers herself into it.

'It's good to see you,' I say. 'Are you well?'

'As can be expected at my age.' She chuckles.

I smile back. We aren't exactly friends, nor exactly allies, and yet, who knows? Maybe one day, we could end up being both.

I put the letters between us on the table. 'These belong to you,' I say. My hands fumble to untie the pink ribbon.

The lines on her face deepen, all companionability gone. 'I told Jack I didn't want them.'

'Just hear me out – please. They were written after you left. But they were never posted.'

She presses her mouth into a line.

'You were upset because Henry never wrote to you,' I say. 'When actually, he did.'

She clenches her gnarled hands into fists. 'Don't mention Henry,' she snaps. 'He was just as bad as his father. Worse – because he was weak, and stupid too. He thought he could outplay his father at a game of human chess. But the winner was never in doubt.'

'Maybe so. But the letters confirm that his feelings for you were real.'

'What use are Henry's feelings?' She tsks angrily. 'When I was a girl, I loved staying awake late at night reading silly books. Some people call them classics – *Jane Eyre*, *Pride and Prejudice*, *Wuthering Heights*. But I call them dangerous. They gave girls like me the wrong impression. That life was some kind of grand "rags-to-riches" romance, and if we looked pretty and acted sweetly, then we'd have the world at our feet.'

'I guess you could see it that way.' I gulp.

'I had a pretty face, so I felt entitled to something better than my lot. Rosemont Hall was my Pemberley, my Thornfield, my fairy tale castle. You know?'

I nod, knowing all too well.

'Back then, Henry was just another freckle-faced, snot-nosed boy. At age twelve, he went off to boarding school. When he came back for school holidays, I barely recognised him. He'd become a proper young man.

'When I was sixteen, Henry came upon me reading a book in the rose garden.' She wrinkles her nose. 'It was *Jane Eyre*, if you want to know. We got to talking about books, and then... other things. I remember every second of that summer.' She smiles dreamily, her mind far away. 'He would chase me through the gardens and steal a kiss under the weeping beech. I was "his Annie" – he's the only person who's ever called me that.'

'Annie,' I whisper. 'A'.

'But no matter what the books promised, there was never any hope for Henry and me.' She glares at me like it's all my fault.

'I know it's painful, Mrs Bradford, but please hear me out.'

She curves her lips over her dentures like she's tasted something sour. After a long moment, she sits back obediently in the chair.

'You thought that Henry never gave you another thought. But he did. I think that Arabella must have intercepted Henry's letters before they were sent.'

I summarise the salient points: Henry loved her. He wanted her to live at Rosemont Hall. He didn't throw her over willingly.

If she came back, then he planned to leave Arabella and have the marriage annulled. But none of it ever happened. I leave out how devastated Arabella must have been when she found out. In the end, it's her story that won't fully be told.

As I speak, Mrs Bradford's face, hard-set with years of resignation, begins to soften.

'All those years...' she says, 'I loved him. I never forgot him. Or forgave him.'

'I can understand that.' My throat wells up as I think about her tangled and tragic life. She may have been the villain when it came to blackmailing Henry, but she was a victim too – one of several, it seems.

She continues to stare at the bundle of letters without touching them.

'I'm sorry,' I whisper.

In a sudden movement, she sweeps the letters off the table. They flutter to the floor like wounded doves. Captain jumps up and barks, his hackles raised.

Mrs Bradford calmly leans back and pours herself a cup of tea.

'You were *his Annie*,' I say. 'He never stopped loving you.'

'What does it matter now?'

'It matters to me,' I say. 'Tell me your story.'

She analyses my face. For a second, I'm worried that I've spooked her. I want to look away, but I force myself not to.

'I suppose I should be glad you're interested.' She plops four sugars into her tea. 'None of the others were. You've earned the right to the whole story.'

I smile encouragingly. *Friends...?*

'Henry and I sent each other little notes.' She stirs the tea absently. 'It started as a silly game, using initials only in case they were ever intercepted. But as time went on, everything got more urgent. We just *had* to see each other, and when we couldn't, we just *had* to tell the other everything.' She smiles. 'I lived for those notes; for his words spoken from the heart. When he returned from university that last time, we met up in the attic of the house. It was our special place.' She pauses for a moment, lost in the memories. 'One thing led to another, and all of a sudden, I was pregnant.'

She plops an extra sugar cube into her tea and watches it dissolve. 'I was so besotted with Henry that I didn't consider it a bad thing. He'd promised me the world, you see. Or at least, Rosemont Hall. He was always writing how we belonged there together. I bought it, hook, line and sinker. But there was one tiny little detail that never seemed to get sorted.'

'His father?'

'His father.' She sniffs. 'Henry had been waffling for weeks. He'd promised to tell his father about us, but each letter held another excuse as to why he'd kept quiet. I suspected that he was losing his nerve. Until Henry came of age, Sir George could revoke his inheritance. But it was more than that. Henry adored that old devil. He was a lapdog – always there to lick his father's boots, no matter how often he got kicked.

'And then the preparations for the party began. I suspected Sir George was up to something – he wrote to Henry as much. Henry thought that the party was the surprise. And then, when the artist turned up, he thought the portrait was the surprise. But I knew, or should have known, otherwise. Because why on earth would Sir George spend every last penny on an extravagant party for a son who was a disappointment to him?'

She stares down at her cup. 'Henry said his father had "plans" for him, but he was too thick to guess what they might be. I guessed that someone was coming to the party that he wanted to impress. Sir George couldn't afford to have regular servants, but he hired some girls from the village to make it look like he did. I got myself taken on as a servant for the party.

'The other girls and I tried on the costumes we found upstairs. It was great fun pretending we were ladies, and I almost told them my secret. That soon I would be Mrs Henry Windham, the Lady of the Manor.

'When the others went back to work, I tiptoed up the back stairs to the attic. I was still wearing the pink dress – I wanted to surprise Henry. But Henry wasn't there. The entire attic had been taken over by an artist. A Spanish chap that Sir George knew from the war. As soon as he saw me, he asked if I would sit for him so he could sketch me. I said yes, though I had no idea he would end up painting my portrait. All I wanted was for Henry to come as promised. I sat in a chair and twisted his note in my hand until it was practically in shreds. But when someone did finally come up the stairs, I felt suddenly afraid. I jumped up and hid behind the door.'

'What did you see?'

'It was Sir George, not Henry,' she says. 'He looked at the door with his demon black eyes almost as if he could sense my presence. The artist took out a canvas and they stood and poured over it together. I remember thinking it odd – the canvas was white and blank – there was no painting on it.'

'A blank canvas?' I lean forward in my chair.

'Sir George examined it carefully like it was the Mona Lisa. They spoke in low voices, but I heard Sir George say: "It does look good – I'd never even know it was there."

'"That's because I am the best," the Spanish chap said.'

'What do you think they were they talking about?'

'I've no idea. But I sensed he was up to no good. And all of a sudden, he was onto Henry and me. I'd turn around and find Sir George watching me with those cold black eyes. I couldn't see Henry alone – his father kept him busy, running errands and entertaining guests.

'I knew the game was up the minute Arabella arrived, looking like some kind of pale, fragile, porcelain doll. I served tea to her and her father while Henry and Sir George were closeted up in the study together. She was so frail and simpering – all huge eyes and sharp cheekbones.' She snorts in disgust. 'Her father was singing Henry's praises and talking about how he'd pay for a lavish wedding. But the look on her face...' She chuckles. 'I think the news shocked her as well.

'Anyway, I went back downstairs and told the cook that I was ill. I went home to think. I suspected that if Sir George wanted Henry to go from lapdog to pedigree stud, he'd do it. I was devastated and angry. I wanted Henry to look me in the eye, and I wanted to hurt him.'

'It sounds awful,' I whisper.

'That night, I dressed up in a maid's costume and blended into the background, bringing up serving trays and filling glasses of champagne. The party was in full swing – everyone was decked out to the nines in sparkling gowns and black tie. It was an occasion from another era – nothing seemed real.

'But in the middle of the dancing, Sir George silenced the musicians. Henry came forward, leading Arabella by the hand. She was a mousey little waif in a green silk dress. Sir George announced the engagement, and Henry smiled at his bride-to-be. He looked contented – even pleasantly surprised. I knew it was all over.' Her eyes flare. 'But I'd come prepared, you see. I'd brought with me every little simpering love note that Henry had ever written to me. I put them on the tray of drinks that I carried into the ballroom. When they made the announcement, I dropped the tray and the notes scattered everywhere like invasive dandelion seeds.' She chuckles softly. 'It was less than they deserved, but it disrupted the moment.

'A quarter of an hour later, Sir George came down to the kitchens. He grabbed me by the arm and pulled me into the pantry; I still remember the stink of his breath against my face.' She grimaces. 'He had a letter in his hands – the last one that Henry wrote to me. "Whatever you're playing at, it stops now," he said. He took out the gold cigarette lighter I'd given Henry and lit the edge of the paper. We stood there together watching it burn. Then he dropped it on the floor and snuffed out the flame underfoot.

'"It's rubbish," he said. "Just like you are." He thrust a purse into my hand. "You'll get the morning train to Portsmouth, and the boat leaving tomorrow afternoon. To New York."

'"No!" I screamed. "Henry loves me. He won't marry *her*."

'Sir George laughed in my face; then he pushed me hard to the floor. I knew that if I lost the baby, I'd lose everything. I lay still, fearing, praying.

'"You will be provided for if you leave now. And if you don't..." He didn't need to finish the threat. He slammed the door and left me crumpled in a ball. The last ember went out on the paper and everything was dark – so dark.'

'But that's terrible,' I blurt out.

'Terrible?' She takes a sip of her tea. 'So many things in life are terrible.'

'What happened next?'

'When I finally stopped shaking, I got up and went home. There was no sign of Henry – he didn't try and find me. The walk home is the thing I remember most clearly. The guests were leaving in their fancy cars. The lights passed over me, but no one stopped to offer me a ride.

'But by the time I got near to the village, there were lights and sirens going the other way – back towards the house. The sky turned an awful shade of deep red. I didn't know at the time, but the east wing was burning.'

'So you didn't start the fire?'

'Of course not.' She glares at me. 'I was still stupid enough to cling to the hope that I might live at Rosemont Hall. I loved that house. I'd never do anything to harm it.'

'Sorry.'

'I was up all night,' she continues. 'I didn't want to believe that it was all over, and if it was, I didn't want to let Henry off that easily. I wanted to confront him – make him tell me to my face that he no longer loved me and wanted me to go away. But just before dawn, someone knocked on our door. My sister answered. I heard the words "constable", "fire", and "a few questions". Sir George had implicated me.'

'It's criminal!' I say.

'It was convenient for him. Whereas I had a baby to think about. I couldn't go to jail for something I didn't do.'

'Of course not. And the gold lighter that the surveyor found was the one you gave Henry?'

'Yes.' She shrugs. 'All those years and suddenly it shows up. Along with you, Amy Wood.' She stops talking and stares into her empty teacup. 'Anyway – that's it. End of story.'

Tears of indignation well up in my eyes. She must have felt so lost in those terrible days after the fire. All alone on a slow boat to America, holed up in steerage with a fatherless baby in her belly and grief in her heart. 'I'm so sorry,' I say.

She looks up at me, the steel back in her face. 'It's ancient history...' She makes a sweeping gesture with her hand. 'And now, you know it.' She levers herself out of the chair. Captain – I'd almost forgotten he was there – jumps to his feet, growling in his throat.

'But that's not quite the end of the story, is it, Mrs Bradford?' I say. 'You came back to England, all those years later. Why did you do that?'

With a tetchy sigh, she sits back down. Captain lies at her feet, eyeing me like I might be lunch.

'I came back because this is where I belong. But I waited too long. Henry was an old man.'

'What happened between the two of you?'

'*She'd* had her claws into him for all those years. Arabella hated Rosemont Hall – thought it was too big, too draughty, too empty – the two of them knocking about like old bones. She didn't care if it fell to ruin. It's no wonder he suffered a stroke.'

'But when you saw him, didn't he mention the letters that he wrote? Did he ask you why you never responded?'

She shakes her head. 'It wasn't like that. By the time I returned, he barely even knew me. I guess' – her bold voice falters – 'that I must have changed too. I wasn't "Annie" any more. Not the one who lived in his memories.'

'You were apart for a long time.' I bow my head, thinking how empty and hollow those years must have been.

'Yes,' she muses. 'A lifetime.'

'But he left the house to Jack and Flora.'

'And do you think he did that out of the goodness of his heart?' She lets out a brittle laugh.

'No, but...'

'I know that Jack and his lot think I blackmailed Henry. But believe me, he extracted his price.'

'And what was that?'

'That Arabella never be told about my daughter, of course. And that I stick around until Arabella died and look after her.'

'So that's why you did it?'

'Can you think of any other reason?'

'Yes.' I smile wistfully. 'Because Rosemont Hall is your home.'

She raises a bristly eyebrow but says nothing.

'You had to come back, didn't you? Despite the terrible thing that happened to you, you braved the humiliation and the upheaval. The thousands of miles and all the years. You did what you had to do in order to come back to Rosemont Hall. It's your home; its heart resonates with yours. You can't just let it go.'

'It's not my choice, is it?' Her tone is sarcastic, but her eyes are shiny and moist.

'You need to tell your story,' I say. 'To Jack, Flora, and your daughter. The truth deserves to be told and they deserve to know. Yours was the great love story of Rosemont Hall.'

'They're not interested,' she says. 'It's ancient history.'

'It's *their* history! The house is part of you, and it's part of them too. Like it or not.'

She stands up, leaning against her cane, her hand quivering with the strain of her years. Captain gets to his shaggy feet, standing loyally by her side.

'You're a dark horse, Amy Wood, that's for sure. You clearly read too many novels, but your heart is in the right place. But for me, it was never about the house. It was Henry that I loved – I was no gold digger, or home wrecker. And in the end, it was no great love story. Henry made his choice, and all I did was make sure that he left the house to his true heirs – his flesh and blood.'

'I understand.'

'And in return, I respected his last wish. I stayed on to take care of Arabella. By then, we were just two old ladies. We drank sherry, played backgammon, watched *Countdown*, and did the crossword together. What came before hardly mattered. We were content enough together.' A tear dribbles down her cheek. 'I miss her.'

I reach out and give her gnarled hand a squeeze.

Smiling sadly, she withdraws her hand. 'I said much the same to Jack when he came to give me the letters. He spouted some drivel about how he was finally starting to understand how I felt about Rosemont Hall.'

'Jack said that?'

'He never would have realised it on his own. I think someone opened his eyes. Now, I wonder who that could have been?'

Her blue eyes meet mine. She knows about Jack and me.

'Um, right,' I mutter, my cheeks glowing pink.

'I told him that I'm settling into the cottage, thank you very much. I have a comfortable chair in front of a cosy fireplace, a reading lamp with a green glass shade, a brass bed with a handmade quilt, and an Aga that actually works.'

'It sounds lovely.'

'And Gwen has a TV with Sky,' she adds proudly.

'Great.' I smile.

'Though... I can hear her snoring through the wall...'

'Oh – well, here... I've got extras.' I dig into my handbag and find a packet of unused ear plugs. She takes them warily, putting them in the pocket of her bulky cardigan.

'Thanks,' she says. 'Why don't you stop by for a cuppa sometime?' The words surprise us both.

'OK,' I say. 'I'd like that.'

'I can always use someone handy with a dust rag to help reach the high shelves.'

'Sure!'

She turns to leave, manoeuvring herself around the papers scattered on the floor.

'What about the letters?' I say.

'Keep them.' She waves offhandedly. 'Shove them in an attic, burn them, or read them out at my funeral. Or use them to write your history book. Send me a copy when it's done – if I'm still alive.'

'But don't you want to know how Henry felt about you in his own words?'

Her toothless laugh seems almost sad. 'Henry Windham is dead and gone. And the house, well...' She shrugs. The huge dog slinks behind her as she clomps across the room and out the door. Her words hang in the air like restless spirits.

*And the house, well...*

# PART V

There is a spot, 'mid barren hills,
Where winter howls, and driving rain;
But, if the dreary tempest chills,
There is a light that warms again.
The house is old, the trees are bare,
Moonless above bends twilight's dome;
But what on earth is half so dear—
So longed for—as the hearth of home?

*— EMILY BRONTË – 'A LITTLE WHILE, A LITTLE WHILE'*

# 51

I pick up the scattered letters and put them back in the bag. Mrs Bradford's story has shaken me to the core. It's tragic that 'the girl in the pink dress' lived her whole life regretting a failed romance. Will my fate be the same?

Over the next few days, I go to work as normal, but I feel like I'm holding my breath. I can't sleep, I can't focus. My nerves are frazzled from waiting, from uncertainty. I long for a resolution, but fear what it might be.

A few days after my chat with Mrs Bradford, I'm putting concealer under my eyes in the disabled loo when my phone rings. It's Jack – calling me for the first time since he returned to the States. Just hearing his 'Hi, Amy, is that you?' turns my knees to jelly. But the connection is bad; he sounds as far away as he actually is.

'Sorry I didn't call you sooner,' he says. 'I wanted to have some news first.'

'And...?'

'You won't believe this. Or actually... what am I saying? You of all people *will* believe it.'

'Can you speak a bit louder?' I cup my hand around the earpiece.

'You were right! Damn it, Amy, it's a Rembrandt. An honest-to-God real Rembrandt. Called *Orientale*.' Jack pronounces it 'Ori-ENT-al'. 'The expert has done all kinds of tests and research on its provenance. There's absolutely no doubt.'

I hold the phone away from my ear, waiting for a flood of happy vindication to sweep over me. But all I feel is an intense regret, like Rosemont Hall has finally given up its last secret. The final thread in the tapestry is in place, but the ends are already starting to unravel.

'It's amazing, Amy...' Jack is saying. 'You found buried treasure – a lost Rembrandt! And to think I doubted you. We haven't known each other long, but already I've learned that when you say something—'

*I love you!* The words scream out inside my head, but I can't say them. If I've learned one thing from Mrs Bradford, it's that words, whether written on paper or said over a telephone line, don't make a difference when it truly matters. 'Anyway,' he continues, 'I need to talk to Gran and see what she wants to do with it. It's worth a lot of money.'

'That's wonderful, Jack,' I hear myself saying. 'I'm so pleased.'

*Tell him! You have to tell him.*

'She'll probably want to donate it to a museum,' Jack says. 'Maybe the Tate Britain or the National Gallery. It should be given back to the public. Don't you agree?'

'Absolutely. It's best if everyone can enjoy it.' My voice catches.

There's a pause. 'Amy? Are you all right? You sound a bit strange.'

'I'm fine, Jack – just a bit overwhelmed.'

'Sure, I get that. Anyway, I wanted you to be the first to know. You're incorrigible, Amy Wood. Incorrigible, and amazing.'

'So are you, Jack,' I manage. 'And thanks for telling me.'

'Amy?'

I end the call as the tears begin to roll fast and furiously down my face. 'I love you,' I whisper into the dead line.

## 52

I half expect a miracle – like a curse has been lifted from Rosemont Hall. Mrs Bradford now knows the truth about her lost love, and a valuable painting has been recovered. After our conversation, Jack emailed me with the name of the expert so I can speak to him myself. I make a note of the number but don't call. Even days later, I can't make sense of everything that's happened – or, not happened.

Because Rosemont Hall is still going to be sold to Hexagon. Jack still lives in America. I haven't told him how I feel, because what's the point? I'm still living in my parents' bungalow, still working at Tetherington Bowen-Knowles. I'm no closer to getting my own flat or going back to teaching. All I have to show for my experience is the memories – and the story I've uncovered.

Which is why one evening after work, I begin writing everything down. I start with my strange premonition on that very first phone call with Mr Kendall. That somehow, my life would never be the same.

I describe my first impressions of Rosemont Hall: its beauty and grandeur, my sadness that it's become a white (well, grey and decaying) elephant, and most of all, the strong connection I've felt with the house and its history.

I also write down Maryanne Bradford's story, transcribing the letters and ordering them so that the story they tell – the schemes, the deceptions and misconceptions, and ultimately the unrealised hopes – are preserved. Surely Mrs Bradford and the other unsung, undocumented women of Rosemont Hall deserve no less.

Mum brings me tea and biscuits, and I sense she's happy to see me in my element – writing – rather than working at a stodgy old estate agency. By the time my head starts to droop, I've got thousands of words. I'm tired and far from happy, but at least I'm moving forward.

Days pass. I keep waiting. Something is going to happen – something...

Things do happen, but not what I was expecting.

First, I get a new instruction to sell another Bristol Docks flat. It's a quarter of the size of the penthouse, but there's a nice feeling of light and space and a great view of the SS *Great Britain*. I return to the office feeling upbeat. The flat will surely sell itself, and maybe even prompt a bidding war.

Next, I get a call from Mary Blundell. I learn that Fred has been released (apparently, the Picasso was a forgery, so his sentence was reduced from art smuggling to failure to declare an item at customs). They're ready to buy a property with a modest budget of £850,000 (the Picasso forgery was clearly worth *something*), which is close to the asking price of the new Bristol flat. Within two hours, they've 'found' some extra cash, made an offer, and the vendor has accepted. I'm proud to have helped them find their perfect home.

With the commission I earn from the sale, I calculate that

I'll have enough for a down payment on a flat. A modest flat, small and quaint, maybe with a few original features like a ceiling rose and a fireplace. As I'm checking through our files to see if there's anything suitable on the market, I get another call – from the headmaster of the school in Edinburgh.

'Your former advisor says you'd be a great fit,' the man says. 'That you're bright, and funny, and you live every moment of the books you teach.'

'Thanks,' I say. 'I didn't want to leave teaching, but unfortunately, there was a "situation".'

'You mean getting sacked?' He gives a hearty laugh. 'I like a lass who stands up for her principles. Not that I approve of revenge via mobile phone.'

'It was more like a bad aim.' After all these months, I manage a chuckle.

'We like strong women here. You'll make a good role model. Shall I set up an interview?'

When the call ends, my mind is awash with possibilities. I could have another new start, this time in cold, grey, historic Edinburgh. I could rent a flat in an elegant terraced house made of soot-stained stone, sew tartan curtains for the windows, buy some antique furniture off eBay and take a course in restoration. Leave behind the world of 'flexible accommodation', 'prime development opportunities' and 'exclusive recreational facilities' and return to my true calling. I'll surround myself with like-minded colleagues with lilting accents and go back to reading, teaching, and *living* the books I love. I'll work hard at being a positive role model, ensuring that each 'lass' knows how to stand up for her principles. In my spare time, I'll hold little soirées on Burns Night and Hogmanay. Eventually, maybe I'll meet someone.

*Meet someone.* That prospect makes me feel like I've severed a limb and am slowly bleeding to death.

I scroll through my junk email folder, only to find a message I've missed – a chill wind from the past. The subject is 'Hey Stranger' and it's from Simon. As I hover the cursor between 'open' and 'delete', I catalogue my emotions and discover that I feel nothing. Simon no longer figures in my woes. I open the message.

> Hey Amy, how are things? I hope you're well. I just wanted to say I'm sorry about what happened. You'll be interested to know that we didn't buy that flat – it was outrageously small for the price, don't you think? In fact, Ashley's gone back to America to marry some Ivy boy and become the next Mrs Bigwig. Made me realise how much I miss you, babe. You were a bit mad – but in a good way. We had some good times, didn't we? Anyway, maybe we can have dinner or a drink – and then see what happens?
>
> Luv and kisses,
>
> Simon

Instead of totting up the things that infuriate me, I calmly hit delete. Simon's an arse, and I'm well shot of him. Strangely, I understand why Mrs Bradford didn't want to read the letters from Henry. As they say, you can't step twice into the same river. Some things are well and truly in the past.

And as for things slipping away into the past, a reminder pops up on screen. Tomorrow morning Hexagon is signing the paperwork to purchase Rosemont Hall. Despite my best efforts, there's been no miracle, no fairy tale ending.

This, after all, is real life.

## 53

I arrive at Mr Kendall's office for the completion meeting. Colleen, his assistant, gives me a kindly smile. 'He'll be with you shortly,' she says. 'He's just on a call.'

I perch on the edge of a sofa idly flipping through *Country Life*, but I'm not in the mood for rich people and posh houses. Where are Mr Netelbaum and his henchmen? They're late.

I drum my fingers on my knee, then take out my mobile and check for messages. There are none. While I'm waiting, I take out a notebook – now that I'm back to square one, I need a life plan. The blank page stares back at me. I try to jot down a few bullet points:

- *finish book on Rosemont Hall*
- *nail Edinburgh interview*
- *look for flat*
- *join internet dating site*

One by one, I cross out the bullets. Right now, I just can't face another 'new future'.

The door opens; I tense up as a small army of men in suits enters the office. Nigel Netelbaum runs a hand through his greased-back ginger hair. 'Nice to see you, Amy,' he says. 'Let me introduce you to my colleagues.'

But I'm already staring at one of his cohort. The sandy hair and boyish grin that once seemed endearing, but now remind me of a scary clown.

David Waters.

'Amy.' He has the nerve to wink – at me, but also towards the group. He's obviously told all of his new buddies about our past 'association'.

'Mr Waters,' I say through my teeth. 'You've got a new job.'

'Yeah, I'm working full time for Hexagon now. The design for the new golf course and clubhouse at Rosemont Hall is almost done. All glass and mod cons – with a touch of Georgian style. Everything else goes.' He smiles smugly. 'I was going to ring you,' he adds, 'but somehow, it didn't "come up".'

I give him a pained smile and focus on the others – a CFO, a COO, and a couple of directors. Two of them have golf club ties. After the round of handshakes, I have the overwhelming urge to douse my hands with sanitiser.

'Hello, everyone. Sorry to keep you waiting.' Mr Kendall appears in the doorway looking flustered. I know he'll be sad to see the last of Rosemont Hall, though he'll feel better when Hexagon completes and he gets paid. 'Please help yourselves to coffee and biscuits.'

The others help themselves to the food and drink on the conference table, and we take our seats. Mr Kendall hovers by the door, clearly nervous, and that makes me nervous too.

He clears his throat and adjusts his glasses. 'Thanks for coming, gentlemen – and Ms Wood.'

'Sure,' Mr Netelbaum interrupts. 'We're all very excited

about this project. Thanks to David here, the planners are more or less on board, and we should be up and running in a few months.'

'And if the whole building falls down first, we won't have to bother,' David adds.

I glare at him.

'Yes, well...' Mr Kendall says, 'I'm afraid there's been a slight last-minute hiccup.'

'What do you mean?' Mr Netelbaum says.

'One of the heirs has got cold feet.'

'Cold feet? What's that supposed to mean?' Mr Netelbaum suddenly morphs into the wolf at the door.

'About selling. To you – Hexagon – that is.'

I grip the edge of the table.

'What?' Mr Netelbaum slams his coffee cup on the table. 'What do you mean – *to us*? Where the hell is Jack Faraday? Get him on the horn.'

'Mr Jack is sorry he can't attend today,' Mr Kendall says. 'He wanted to. But the truth is, we've received a higher offer. A better offer.'

I stifle a gasp.

'That's outrageous,' Mr Netelbaum yells. 'We're signing the paperwork now. The funds are ready to be wired. They can't just back out.'

'Actually, they can,' I cut in. 'No contracts have been exchanged, so technically, the heirs can sell to whomever they like. I'd say you were gazumped.'

Mr Kendall nods sheepishly.

'You!' Nigel Netelbaum turns the force of his anger at me. 'You've been playing us all along. Don't think I don't know it. David here has told us all about you. That you were opposed to us from the start, and even willing to take off your clothes to get him onside. You're nothing but a backstabbing little tart.'

'How dare you—'

'Gentlemen, please,' Mr Kendall intervenes. 'I agree it's unfortunate, but in the end, they didn't feel that your plans were right for Rosemont Hall. The house has been part of their family history for two hundred years. They've decided that they *do* care what happens to it.'

I feel like I'm floating above the table.

'So we're done here,' Mr Kendall says. 'My assistant will be happy to validate your parking on the way out.'

'Take that house and shove it up your ass,' Mr Netelbaum spits. 'Come on,' he says, gesturing to his colleagues. 'We've wasted enough time here.'

The army of suits rises and storms out. David Waters's face is red; he doesn't look at me.

'Have a nice day,' I say brightly. 'Good to see you again, David.'

When the men are gone, Mr Kendall sits down opposite me, takes out a handkerchief, and wipes his brow.

'Sorry about that,' he says. 'It really was a last-minute thing.'

'But Mr Kendall, is it true? Has there really been a higher offer?' My elation turns to silent panic. What will the house become now? Flats? A conference centre? Nothing?

He sits back and steeples his fingers. 'It's all true. The offer was confirmed yesterday. It's one of your clients, as it turns out.'

'One of *my* clients?' I lean forward.

'Well, maybe not a client exactly, but the buyer is insisting that you get a commission.'

'Me?'

'It was you who convinced them to make the purchase. Here, have a look.'

He takes a stack of papers from the credenza and hands them to me. 'This is the charter of the new Rosemont Hall Charitable Trust,' he says. 'Not all the paperwork has been filed, of course, but once the financing is confirmed, we only need to dot the i's and cross the t's.'

'But... I don't understand.'

'You sure you don't want something to drink?' He opens the credenza again and takes out a decanter of brandy, pouring two glasses and handing one to me. I knock it back in one.

'Now, I'll explain...'

My eyes widen as he tells me about the new buyer – a charitable trust. 'The benefactor decided that the house should be saved,' he says. 'It will be restored and opened to the public. The venture will need to be self-supporting: tearooms, adventure playgrounds, wedding and film bookings... That's where you come in.'

'Me?'

'Of course.' He looks surprised that I'm so dim. 'Didn't Jack mention any of this?'

The truth dawns like a desert morning.

He continues. 'Well, of course, Maryanne Bradford is the principal benefactor. She'll be funding the purchase of Flora's share of the house with the proceeds from the Rembrandt when it's sold at auction. Jack will be keeping his share.'

'Keeping his share?' My heart jolts like a catapult. Jack Faraday is keeping Rosemont Hall. Jack Faraday and Mrs Bradford – who can buy Flora's share because of the 'buried treasure' I found. Jack Faraday wants me involved with the plans. Jack Faraday wants *me*.

'Amy?' he says. 'Would you like another brandy?'

'Yes please – I think I need it.'

# 54

I leave Mr Kendall's office in a minicab. I'm tipsy, overwhelmed, and still trying to make sense of the emotions swirling in my head. The world looks different: bright and clear, full of life and colour. Full of potential for a future I couldn't have dreamed of. Enthusiasm fizzes in my veins as I ponder the things Mr Kendall told me.

Apparently, Jack and his grandmother envision me taking charge of the trust and house renovations, after which it will open to the public. I'll be a paid employee – if I choose to accept the job. I have questions, of course, but ones I can't ask: does Jack intend to live here? Does he want something more than the few nights we've had together? And why the hell didn't Jack tell me all this himself? (I try to summon the appropriate level of indignation on this point, but frankly, I'm way too happy to do so.) There's a lot to think about and a lot of details to be sorted, but for now, none of that matters. The pieces are falling into place...

*I've saved Rosemont Hall.*

As the taxi arrives at the bungalow, my mobile rings. It's

him. My hand trembles as I hit the button. 'Hello!' I say breathlessly.

'Amy,' he says in his lovely deep voice, 'how are you? I hear my little surprise caused quite the bust up at the lawyer's office.'

'Yes, it did.' I beam. 'Everyone was certainly surprised. But how? Why?'

'I'll fill you in on everything when I see you next. I'll arrange a trip and we can go on that road trip we talked about. But for now, let's just say, Gran and I had a long heart to heart. She told me her story – fascinating stuff, and heartbreaking too – just like something from one of your books. But ancient grudges and broken hearts aside, the place will always be her home. She asked me not to sell up.'

'Good for her!'

'Yeah. She's happy living in the cottage with Gwen but wants to be able to visit the house. Talk to it, clean it, wander the halls – whatever the heck she does.'

'I can understand that.'

'I'm sure you can.' He chuckles. 'Anyway, for the first time we had a conversation about what she thought and felt, not what *I* should feel or do. It worked wonders. And it's all down to you, Amy.'

'I'm just so shocked. In a good way.'

'She wanted me to give you a message. Something about how "maybe the great love story of Rosemont Hall is yet to come". Does that mean anything to you?'

'Umm, yes. Thanks.' I shiver inside with delight.

'Good. I guess it's one more anecdote to add to your book. How's that going, by the way?'

I step out of the cab, grinning from ear to ear. 'Great,' I say. 'It's going great. Writing it is a lot easier now that I've stopped worrying about the ending.'

# EPILOGUE

## ONE YEAR LATER…

The grand opening of Rosemont Hall is held on a Saturday in late May. The day before, the last of the scaffolding comes down, the caterers set up in the new kitchen, and a huge marquee is erected on the south lawn to house refreshments for the hundreds of people – locals, press, bloggers, and lovers of old houses from all over the country – that are expected to be there.

I spend the day in a flurry of activity: chasing florists, confirming directions, stapling books of tickets, putting up signs to loos and overflow parking, dusting for the tenth time the portrait of the girl in a pink dress. She's been cleaned and restored and still hangs in pride of place above the staircase landing. But she's alone now. The Rembrandt she hid for so many years has been auctioned and bought by the Tate Britain. Now it too will be on view in London for the whole world to appreciate.

I work late into the night to make everything perfect – just the way the fated ancestors would have wanted. By the time I return to my parents' bungalow (I've been far too busy to look for my own flat), I'm tired and elated, nervous and happy, all at once. The past year has flown by as I've learned to manage builders, restorers, craftspeople, painters, plasterers, gardeners, English Heritage, the local council – not to mention, handling a number of *very* distracting visits from Jack.

The house has been restored top to bottom, inside and out. It will take a few more seasons for the garden to return to its best, and my grander ideas like the adventure playground, the organic tearoom, and the farm shop haven't been realised yet. And while the east wing has been shored up and stabilised, the restoration of the ballroom has yet to begin.

I'm proud of what I've achieved so far. Restoring Rosemont Hall has been the most exciting adventure of my life so far, and I've thrown myself into all aspects of managing the place. I'm looking forward to the next phase – running tours, writing leaflets, teaching people about the house and its history, and helping to create *new* memories and history. While at times amid the dust and chaos of construction I've missed the well-trodden path of teaching literature, now, when I walk through the beautifully proportioned rooms of Rosemont Hall, I know I've chosen the right vocation.

And when Jack phones me from the airport asking if everything is ready for the grand opening, I'm proud to say that, barring any surprises, it is.

The morning of the grand opening dawns bright and crisp. Dad's wisteria casts a purple glow outside my bedroom window and birds are chirping in the garden. I dress in old clothes in case I encounter any last-minute jobs, but I have a new dress (red silk sheath with matching heels and fancy hat) for later. I give Mum and Dad a kiss and I'm off.

As I drive through the freshly painted iron gates and glimpse Rosemont Hall from a distance, I get the same electric thrill as if I'm seeing it for the first time. But instead of a sad and forbidding edifice riddled with dry rot and unhappy secrets, it appears transformed – just as I am. The brickwork on the outside has been cleaned and repointed, nymphs frolic in a playful spray of water in the fountain, the hedges have been trimmed, and the beds replanted with roses and bee-friendly flowers. I park the car and get out, savouring the silence, the sunlight, and the *knowing* that this is where I belong.

I spend the next few hours handling some mini disasters: scones from the Cup o' Comfort that didn't rise, two waitresses who haven't turned up, a power failure in the posh Portaloos, a loose paving stone by the door. By the time I manage to sneak off and change into my dress, a camera crew for George Clarke's latest renovation show has arrived. I leave them to set up, brief the volunteer guides, and polish the glass cases where the Windham letters and the artist's sketchbook are preserved. Finally, I relax and sample the food in the marquee.

The office staff of Tetherington Bowen-Knowles arrives (minus Claire, but including Mrs Harvey's niece, Sally, with a rosy-faced toddler tucked in a pram). Alistair Bowen-Knowles greets me with a handshake and a brief glance at my chest. Jonathan sniffs and commandeers a roving waitress with a tray of champagne flutes. I feel oddly grateful to my former colleagues: without their indifference to that long-ago telephone call from Mr Kendall, I wouldn't be here today. I raise my glass and propose a toast. 'Here's to estate agents,' I say, 'and to finding our clients the perfect homes.'

We clink glasses, and then my colleagues are off to schmooze some of my former clients here for the occasion: Ronan and Crystal (the latter resplendent in a hot-pink minidress and matching fishnets), Mr Patel, and Mary and Fred Blundell. As the band plays, more and more people arrive: the

Wakefields (who have found a lovely little cottage only about a mile away), and my parents. Mum gushes to anyone who will listen about how the restoration of Rosemont Hall is all down to me.

'Thanks, Mum,' I say. 'But lots of people helped out.'

'Nonsense,' she says. 'Credit where credit is due. And make sure that boyfriend of yours takes you out for a nice dinner later.' She winks at Dad. 'We were hoping to have the bungalow to ourselves for tonight.'

'Oh, I'll definitely be *very* late.' I shudder. Now that the renovations are over, I really need to find a flat...

A while later, Claire arrives with Raj and her son in tow. 'Well, well...' She gives me a hug. 'I see why you fell for this place. It's really quite something.'

'It is.' I hand her a glass of champagne.

'And how's the book going?' During the last year, Claire has indulged me by reading some of my draft chapters. Her honest, no-holds-barred, Earth-to-Amy comments have sometimes stung a little, but I've come to accept that – just occasionally – I need help getting my head out of the clouds.

'It's good, I think. I sent it off to three agents. Fingers crossed and all that.'

Rolling her eyes, she gives me a quick hug. 'I'm sure it's better than good, Amy. Remember, you just have to believe it here.' She taps her chest.

'Thanks, but there's one important thing missing.' I check my watch, secretly worried. Jack's flight landed early this morning, and yet, he's not here.

'You mean the dashing hero?' Claire shrugs. 'I wouldn't worry. It's his house – he's sure to be here.'

I don't bother to correct her – the house belongs to the trust and to all the people of this fine land. Jack Faraday has been granted the right to live in a suite of rooms on the first floor. Mrs Bradford also has the right to a room in the house, but so far, she's decided to stay on with Gwen. I visit her at least once a week for a 'cuppa' (and to dust the high shelves). She's been teaching me how to bake scones and sew cushions and curtains, and is an invaluable source of information about how the house looked back in the day. Sure, she talks to herself and has two-sided arguments with Arabella, and she's tried to run the workmen off the project. Captain, her humongous St Bernard, still adores sleeping in the canopy bed on the first floor, rumpling the blankets and chewing old books (in fact, he was the culprit all along). All that aside, I consider her a friend. And who knows... fingers crossed that someday we might even be *family*.

Now, I spot her hovering around the bar with Captain slobbering at her feet. She's cackling to the bartender, who keeps refilling her glass with what I'm pretty sure is whisky. She catches my eye and waves her cane at me. 'Amy Wood,' she half-shrieks. 'Poking your nose into anything and everything, as usual.' Her smile is crooked but warm. 'Sit down, have a drink. Enjoy yourself!'

I take the glass she hands me and we clink glasses. But in truth, I'm too on edge to enjoy myself. Jack still hasn't arrived. It's increasingly difficult to keep smiling and make small talk. The band is playing swing tunes and people are dancing. One or two guests begin to leave.

'Keep your chin up,' she says. 'If a thing is meant to be, then it will be.' She gives my hand a squeeze and turns back to the bartender. I weave my way through the crowd, hoping, by some miracle, what's 'meant to be' is that I'll spot Jack. I don't. Instead, I see Mr Kendall, who waves me over.

'It's amazing what you've done, Amy.' He beams. 'You've

saved the place single-handedly. It's going to be a real success now, I can tell.'

'Not single-handedly.' I blush. 'Jack and Mrs Bradford's money helped a lot.'

'Yes, but it took more than money. It took the right person who could perform a genuine labour of love. You belong here, just as much as any marble floor or fancy fireplace. You're a proud feature of the house. And certainly... *original*.'

'Thanks. I just wish—'

Maybe the bubbly has gone to my head, or maybe the emotions of the day have finally taken their toll. But suddenly, I'm fighting back tears.

'What?' Mr Kendall looks concerned.

'I just wish Jack was here. I don't know what happened.'

'Ah – Jack,' Mr Kendall says. 'He's always full of surprises.'

A cascade of panic tumbles in my chest. 'You mean he's not coming? All this – and he's not coming?'

'I believe he was detained,' Mr Kendall says. 'That's all I know.' He points to the programme of events. 'But you'd best be getting on. According to this, it's time for your speech.'

He steers me towards the podium. He's right – I need to get on stage and thank everyone for coming. The band stops playing; the dance floor clears. They're waiting for me.

'No,' I whisper to Mr Kendall, 'I need a minute.'

'Come on, Amy, this is your moment.'

I know he's right. Stepping forward, I tap the microphone.

'Ladies and gentlemen,' I say. As everyone turns to look at me, my nerves vanish. I belong up here. *I can do this.*

'Welcome to the grand opening of Rosemont Hall. Thank you so much for coming.' I can't keep from smiling. 'For those of you who don't know the whole story, let's just say that a little over a year ago, Rosemont Hall was a house in peril – no offence to any golfers in the room.'

I enjoy the laughter that filters through the crowd.

'But after a lot of hard work by dedicated people, we've achieved the best possible result for this national treasure.'

My estate agent friends give a little cheer. And then suddenly, my mind goes blank. Jack should be here. The next part of my prepared speech is about him.

'And, umm... anyway, if I tried to thank everyone, we wouldn't have time for drinking or dancing,' I say. 'But rest assured, each and every one of you is playing a part in the ongoing story of Rosemont Hall. Especially...'

At that moment, the door to the marquee flaps and Jack steps through. His smile is devastating as Mr Kendall gestures him to the front.

And then he's there at my side. My knees go weak with joy.

'I don't want to steal your thunder,' he whispers in my ear, 'but I'd like to say a few words. Is that OK?'

My hand trembles as I pass him the microphone.

'For those of you who don't know me,' he says, 'I'm Jack Faraday. While some people may say I've got no right to be here' – he winks at his grandmother, who downs a shot of whisky and clacks her dentures in response – 'sometimes things turn out differently than you expect.'

There's a smattering of laughter and murmuring in the crowd.

'A year ago, I would have done anything to get rid of this place. To me, it was a decaying white elephant on the wrong side of the Atlantic. Whether it became a golf course or crumbled to dust was all the same to me. But then, like Saul on the road to Damascus, someone opened my eyes. Someone with a passion for history and heritage, someone willing to fight for the things that matter. Someone who cares not just about houses, but about people too. Someone who is the heart and vision behind the new Rosemont Hall. Ladies and gentlemen, please raise your glasses to Amy Wood.'

'Hear hear!' The air rings with the clinking of glasses. Jack takes my hand, smiling. I feel warm and cosy all over, like my heart has curled up in front of a fireplace.

But Jack lets go of my hand and speaks into the microphone again. 'There's one additional piece of business that I'd like to settle while Amy's up here,' he says.

I look at him quizzically. We've both said our pieces, and I'm anxious to leave the stage.

'When I first met Amy, she thought I was going to tear Rosemont Hall apart brick by brick – and she hated me for it. In fact, ever since then, I've given her many reasons to be annoyed, infuriated, and generally pissed off.' He grins. 'Including the fact that I was late arriving today.'

I nod my head; the crowd chuckles.

'But I'd like to assure her that I was delayed due to some preparations of my own.'

Someone (Dad!) whistles.

'Because apparently, some jewellers in London don't open until eleven o'clock.'

Everyone including me gasps as he takes out a small velvet box. 'So, in spite of all the water under the bridge, Amy, I hope you can find it in your heart to love me even half as much as I love you.'

He opens the box – nestled inside is a ring of pink and blue sapphires surrounded by diamonds and seed pearls. Removing it, he slips it on my finger. 'It's not a family heirloom,' he says. 'But I hope that someday it will be. Amy Wood – will you marry me?'

Right there, in front of my guests, the staff, my parents, my former co-workers, Mrs Bradford, the TV cameras, God and everyone, I grab him by the collar and kiss him silly.

He's laughing as we finally come up for air. 'So, what do you say? Has Rosemont Hall got its love story? And have *you* got your happy ending?'

'Yes!' My heart is bursting with joy. 'Oh, yes.'

The crowd cheers as Jack leads me off stage and out of the marquee. The band plays again and I can't feel the ground beneath my feet as we walk hand in hand across the lawn to the front of the house, and he leads me inside. We go through a door marked 'Private' and up the back stairs, laughing and stealing kisses. And in that moment, overwhelmed by love and desire, I know that I've been given an incredible gift.

I'll be coming here again. I'll be coming... *home.*

# A LETTER FROM LAUREN

Thank you for reading *The House of Second Chances.* If you enjoyed this book, please can I ask you to leave a review. It really helps other readers find my books and might help someone discover their perfect next read. If you want to keep up-to-date on my new releases, or are interested in becoming a beta reader for my books, please sign up at the following link. Your email address will never be shared and you can unsubscribe at any time.

https://www.laurenwestwoodwriter.com

Old houses live many lives, and so, too, do authors. Since this book was first published in 2016 as *Finding Home*, I have had many ups and downs in my writing career. But like the most stalwart pile of bricks and mortar, I'm still standing. I have my readers to thank for that, as you make the journey fulfilling and worthwhile.

Rosemont Hall is a fictional house, but there are thousands of historic houses that have been lost or are in peril in the UK. For more information about country houses at risk and an archive of these lost treasures, please see Matthew Beckett's excellent blog and website: https://thecountryseat.org.uk/. Other resources include the National Trust, the Landmark Trust, and English Heritage, whose many employees and volunteers work tirelessly to preserve our heritage and make it part of our future.

Thanks so much to Francesca Best and the team at Boldwood Books for giving this book a new life. I'd also like to thank Kiya Evans, Ronan Winters, Francisco Gochez, Chris King, and Alison Smith for your ongoing support. Most of all, thank you to my family for your love and patience. You mean everything to me.

L—

Surrey, 2024

# ABOUT THE AUTHOR

**Lauren Westwood** writes about old houses and quirky historical mysteries. She is also an award-winning children's author (Laurel Remington), a mother of three, and works as a lawyer in renewable energy. Lauren is originally from California, and now lives in the UK, in an old house built in 1604.

Sign up to Lauren Westwood's mailing list for news, competitions and updates on future books.

Visit Lauren's website: www.laurenwestwoodwriter.com

Follow Lauren on social media here:

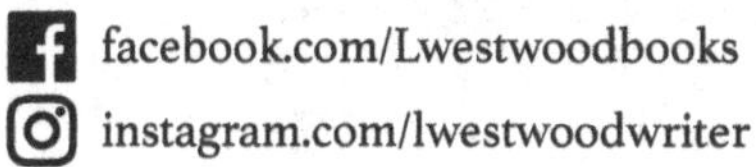

facebook.com/Lwestwoodbooks

instagram.com/lwestwoodwriter

# ABOUT THE AUTHOR

# ALSO BY LAUREN WESTWOOD

**Secrets and Love Series**

The House of Second Chances

The House of Hidden Secrets

The House of Love and Dreams

www.ingramcontent.com/pod-product-compliance
Lightning Source LLC
La Vergne TN
LVHW030916080826
845145LV00013B/2919

*9781836569985*